REDEMPTION & REPERCUSSIONS

Inspired By True Events

A Novel By

SHALONDA "SJ" JOHNSON

THE TMG FIRM

New York

The TMG Firm, LLC
112 W. 34th Street
17th and 18th Floors
New York, NY 10120
www.thetmgfirm.com

ISBN: 978-0-99835-655-6
Library of Congress Control Number: 2016963020
All rights reserved

First The TMG Firm Trade Paperback Edition April 2017
Printed in the United States of America

Cover created and designed by Brittani Williams for TSPub Creative, LLC.

Inspired By True Events

CHAPTER ONE

"Yes he wants me back girl," Nina spoke into her phone. "What do you mean is he for real? He better be for all the shit I did for him!" Despite herself, Nina let out a small laugh. "No, No; I'm serious. I'm just laughing because you got me cracking up thinking this is a joke and I'ma dead ass," Nina laughed into the phone.

"Nina, I'm just saying be careful girl," GeGe said solemnly.

"Yeah, yeah aight hold up; this my other line." Nina took a breath and switched to her professional speaking voice. "Nina Jones speaking. Uh huh. Yes. Oh, no problem. I will get that paperwork sent out immediately. I apologize for the delay. Thank you so much for your patience." Just like that, Nina knew that it was time to wrap up her conversation and prepare to get back in work mode.

"GeGe girl you still there?" she asked. "Yeah, that was my client worrying me to death. "Anyway girl," she sighed. "Yes, he wants me back and I'ma make his ass work for it!"

Nina pulled into her driveway and thought to herself how great it felt to have worked hard and earned all that she now had. It was an amazing feeling to own her plush condo and Maserati. *Not bad for a girl from the projects of Brooklyn, right? My family didn't believe it could happen; a young black girl with a dream of managing successful artists and getting mad money. Yup, I guess I proved their asses wrong,* she thought with a proud smile on her face. Nina then remembered that she was still on the phone.

"GeGe, girl, I am so sorry. I zoned out for a minute," she laughed. "I just got to the house; let me call you back so I can get ready. My boo, says he wants me to be at the restaurant by eight," she said as she glanced down at her watch out of habit and hung up the phone.

"I. Do. Not.Want. To. Be. Late." Nina stressed each word to herself as she thought about her day. Just thinking about it pissed her off all over again. *I was held up at the office because of my assistant. That girl drives me crazy.* Nina took in a deep breath before continuing her thought. Her assistant was on the brink of getting fired today. She made just too many mistakes, but Nina kept her around because her assistant had proven to be loyal. That meant the world to her. Nina was just glad to have ironed out all of the mess her assistant created in time to make it to her boo, Samir.

Nina and Samir had been together for nine years off and on. Technically this was one of their off times, but tonight they were about to be back on. Nina entered her condo and went through her regular routine. She said hi to the doorman Henry and then asked Pat the desk clerk if she had any messages or mail. As always, Nina immediately hit the elevator button to avoid everyone else in the lobby. She hated when anyone who wasn't her people berated her with questions or tried to be all up in her business. In the elevator, many thoughts went through her mind while she waited to arrive at the penthouse floor.

Did he really change? Does he still love me? Is he sincere? Does he want to work it out or does he just need me for something? These thoughts and more ran through Nina's mind putting her in a daze before she realized it. The soft ding from the elevator door as it arrived at her penthouse snapped Nina to attention. As soon as the doors opened, she sensed that something in her home was different from the way she left it this morning. Although she didn't always like to admit it, Nina had a slight case of OCD; so when something was moved, she knew. When Nina looked around the room, she noticed the throw rug that was usually directly in the middle of her living room was out of place, and her kitchen faucet was dripping water.

What the fuck is going on? Nina thought to herself, as she walked into the kitchen to turn off the running water. Then she headed towards the living room to straighten the rug. There is where she noticed one of the largest and prettiest flower arrangements she'd ever seen. It was on her mantle with a silver gift box, tied with a white satin bow, sitting on her loveseat.

Who the hell has been up in my spot? Henry's ass is... Nina's thoughts were cut short when she remembered her spare key. "But, I took it back when we broke up. He must've made a copy," Nina said aloud to the empty room. "Peach roses; my favorite," she said with a slight smile on her face as she brought one of the flowers to her nose. "Yup, it's him."

Now curious, Nina eyed the box still sitting on the loveseat. Before she has the box open, Nina smelled the familiar scent of Victoria Secret's Sheer Love, which was a favorite scent of both her and Samir. Inside the box were a black wrap around dress that would hug Nina in all the right places, a pair of sexy ass black stiletto red bottoms, and a familiar Tiffany's blue box containing a diamond pendant. Underneath it all laid a note reminding Nina to arrive at Mr. Chows at eight. "Damn, he always knows how to get to me," she said.

"Oh shit," Nina yelled after catching a glimpse of the clock. "Damn, let me hurry up it's 6:30."

Nina's iPhone began ringing off the hook. As much as she wanted to ignore it, Nina had to answer. She knew exactly who was calling before she even looked at the caller ID. *I know this is my bitch GeGe and I gotta tell her about this shit.*

"GeGe, girl, why did my boo sneak into my spot while I was at work today?"

There was a laugh and pause on the other end, until GeGe said, "Sneak? What exactly do you mean sneak? How in the hell did he get past security's ass?"

"Damn if I know. That's another story for another day. All I know is that he did it," Nina said, "and I'm glad he did because let me tell you girl, he left me mad peach roses." Nina didn't mention the other presents yet.

"Those your favorite?"

"Hell yeah they are" Nina said. "He also bought me a wrap dress and a pair of bomb ass red bottoms. And might I add a diamond pendant." Just thinking about how well Samir knew what she liked made Nina smile. "Girl, I almost pissed on myself. My boo is doing it up tonight." Nina waited for GeGe to respond. "Ge you still there?" she asked.

"Yeah, I'm here girl," GeGe replied. "Well, it sure seems like you finally got your man back, so I'ma let you go and get ready. I'ma holla later."

"Aight, GeGe call me... Well damn, she just hung up!" Nina was in too good of a mood to let GeGe's mess get to her. *I don't have time for her attitude right now. I would think that she would be happy for me. Oh well, she's probably stressing over her baby daddy that always seems to be missing in action, especially when I come around.* Nina thought to herself.

As Nina put her phone down, she noticed the time again and raced to the shower. While the warm water ran over her, Nina thought about how fine Samir is. His beard was always nicely shaped, and he was fit, but not overly muscular. Nina couldn't stand that muscular shit. To make matters better, he always smelled nice, and his dick game was proper. *Shit, if he just gets his mind right he would definitely be the one.* After showering, Nina had just thirty minutes to get dressed and make it to the restaurant. "Fuck it, I'm just going to retouch my makeup in the car and restyle my hair at every traffic light," Nina declared. This was a good call as Nina arrived at the restaurant just in time. *I hope I don't look rushed,* Nina thought. *Okay, time to do this.* Nina exhaled softly and stepped out of her car.

All eyes were on her. The split in the wrap dress showed just the right amount of Nina's long, toned legs. The parking valet's gaze traveled up her and took all of Nina in. *Damn, my shit is really on point tonight.* Nina smirked as she read the parking attendant's thoughts. He looked as if he wanted to lay Nina across the hood of her Maserati and do some things to her. *Hopefully, Samir will have the same reaction*, Nina thought as she tossed the valet her keys and walked inside.

"Hello. Welcome to Mr. Chows. Do you have a reservation?"

"Yes. I believe it should be under the name Jones, Nina Jones."

"Let me see. Oh yes, Nina Jones, you will be at table 6. Your guest is waiting."

"Thank you."

Nina's mind began to race just thinking about the man who was waiting for her at the table. *I'm gonna tear his ass up tonight for giving me the royal treatment*, she thought. Nina stopped mid-thought when she noticed that no one was sitting at table 6. Assuming that he stepped away to the restroom, Nina decided to sit down anyway. Suddenly someone slams their hand on the table so loudly, that Nina instinctively jumps back.

"Oh, so you the bitch that's been sleeping with my man?!" says the angry stranger, "Yeah well that shit stops today!"

CHAPTER TWO

"No, I don't want my shit shaped up like that! I want a full beard, not a damn goatee," Samir said with a laugh to his barber, Rah. Every time he came for a cut, he and Rah had a light-hearted argument on exactly how Samir's facial hair should look.

"Yeah, aight I know what you want. How long I been your barber; you been coming to this shop for how long?" Rah said. "Exactly, so let me do what I do."

Samir knew Rah had him. He threw his hands up to surrender, "Aight I'm just saying, you fuck me up that's your ass."

Rah turned his clippers back on. "Yeah, whatever. Deez nuts."

"Oh you got jokes, huh? Real dammit funny. Anyway man," Samir said changing the subject. "You still got that connect?"

Confused, Rah turned his clippers off. "Connect, connect for what?"

Samir almost couldn't believe Rah couldn't or wouldn't read between the lines. "Come on man, do I really gotta say that shit out loud and make shit hot."

Finally catching on Rah nodded. "Ohhhh! Yeah I'm still fucking with ole boy with the connect. But I ain't giving it to your ass. You out the game remember? You gave up the life." Rah was suddenly serious. "I ain't being responsible for getting you back in the game, so I can get blamed if something goes wrong. Hell nah, I can't have that on my conscious."

Samir understood, but his current needs outweighed Rah's warning. "Nah for real bro, shit's getting tight. A flicker of his old life flashed across Samir's mind. "You know I use to be the man out here," Samir said with a slight hint of nostalgia before reality snapped him back into the present. "Promoting these parties ain't getting me the paper I'm used too. I need to do my one-two real quick to get back on top." Samir shifted in his chair to look directly at Rah. "You know Traci's crazy ass said she gonna take me to court if I don't keep up with Layla tuition payments. You know she got lil shorty in private school. On top of that, my mortgage is sky high. And for what it's worth yo, I still gotta be shining out here in these streets."

Rah's eyes shifted to Samir's wrist. Although money was currently tight, Samir held onto some goods from his previous lifestyle.

"Yeah, I see you looking. Get up under that light so you can see it better," Samir joked. "Yup, that's a Rolex with the diamonds dancing. You know it's Chris Browning baby."

"Yo, you a wild boy," Rah said laughing. "Let me see that watch. Damn son, you right that shit dancing in the lights for real."

Satisfied with Rah's reaction, Samir leaned back into his chair. "Damn right you already know how I do. So back to the business. You gonna link me with the connect or what?" Still not convinced if he should give Samir what he wanted, Rah sighed and said, "Let me see what I can do."

That was good enough for Samir for now. "Aight, bet. Just holla at me." With that settled, Samir sat back and let Rah finish his cut. Samir left the barbershop feeling good and looking good. The fresh cut and the possibility of Rah introducing him to his connect had Samir thinking that the pieces may finally fall back into place. He was about to be back on top again and reclaim his position as the man out in these streets. With the money to treat Layla like the princess she is, Samir would be whole. Not to mention, he would be able to keep her mother off his back. Samir smiled at the possibilities, but his smile quickly faded when he saw the bright orange envelope sticking out from under his windshield wiper. He was all too familiar with the envelope and didn't even have to look inside to know that there was a parking ticket waiting for him. "Fuck! Another fucking ticket," Samir yelled. "I swear these cops love my Benz."

Samir yanked the envelope from under his wiper when his phone rang.

"Hello, who this?" the voice on the other end asked.

After the ticket, Samir was in no mood for games. "What you mean who is this? Nigga you called my phone! Like I said, who is this?" *If niggas don't stop fucking playing with me,* Samir thought as he checked the caller ID to make sure it wasn't one of his homies playing around. He didn't recognize the number.

Unfazed, the voice on the phone coolly and calmly replied, "I'ma say this one time and one time only. If you get back in the streets I'ma kill you this time." Then the phone went silent. Samir checked his phone screen, and just as he had thought, the caller had hung up. The threat momentarily put a knot in Samir's stomach, but he checked himself. Samir was far from being a punk. No threat, especially across the phone could shake him and stop any of the plans he had for these streets.

With a smirk, Samir said to himself, "Yeah whatever nigga. Ole bitch ass ain't ready for the king." The phone call lit an angry spark in Samir and was the motivation he needed to put his plan into action sooner than later. *Let me hit my barber and tell him to hurry up and put me on. I'm about to crush the game and that bitch nigga that had enough balls to threaten me,* Samir thought.

"Yo, Rah you got the info I need?"

"Yeah, something like that. I'm still working on it."

"Oh aight cool. Well just...," Samir stopped mid-sentence to check his phone to see who was beeping in. "Oh, this Nina's fine ass. Let me hit you back." Samir switched over to Nina's call. "Well, well, well, Ms. Nina."

"Cut the shit Samir. You left a message for me at the office asking me to call. I'm calling. So what's up?

"Damn Nina why you so cold baby?"

"I'm hanging up."

"Nina!" Samir yelled a little more loudly than he intended, "don't hang up. Please just listen."

"I'm listening."

Fuck it. I'ma shoot my shot, Samir thought. "Meet me at Mr. Chows tonight, so we can talk. I need you back for real, Samir said sincerely. "I'll text you all the info. All I need you to do is just show up and listen. Okay?" The silence was a little too much for Samir. "You still there?"

"Aight Samir, see you later, and you better not be late!"

"Okay, baby I won't. I love you." Silence again. Samir instinctively looked at his phone screen. He couldn't believe she just hung up on him. "Did she just hang up on me? If one more person bangs on me today, I'm kicking somebody's ass," Samir joked to himself. "That's just like Nina though; she is such a bad ass. Real spicy, I like that shit." His mind drifted further onto Nina. He loved her body. She has a small waist, big cakes, and a pretty ass face. Not to mention the sex! They would go at it all night long. Just like he liked it and the pussy stay wet! Plus, she made her own money. Just thinking about Nina's pussy made him hard. *Let me text her pretty ass the info for tonight,* he thought. *I'ma fuck the shit outta her after dinner, and she don't even know it.* Samir's ringing phone pulled him from his thoughts. "Damn, my phone stay ringing when I'm doing something."

"Hello." Samir couldn't hide that he was pissed off, but that all changed when he heard who it was on the other end. "Oh shit. What up B?" Samir whispered a silent thank you to Rah for keeping his word. "Yeah, I asked Rah to link us up so we can make some moves together."

"Oh aight cool," B replied. "We 'bout to do it big! I'm glad I got somebody on my team I can trust." B paused for a second before continuing. "Listen, I know you use to be the man out here and everything, but now I am. I don't tolerate no funny business and no fuck boy shit. That gets dealt with immediately. Understand?"

"B come on man, you know me. I don't play those types of games. I'm the most solid brotha you'll ever meet, but don't treat me like no fucking worker. That's how it gotta be, or me and you can just save ourselves some time and part ways now. Feel me?"

"Okay, settle down young man," B laughed. He had much respect for Samir. "You always did have balls. I'ma let you get away with that one cause you my ninja."

"Ninja? What?" Samir asked.

"Yeah, I'm trying to stop using the N-word. Black people need to rise above all of this oppression."

9

Samir could only laugh. "You over here selling poison and you talking about not using the N-word?"

"Fuck outta here! I ain't explaining myself to you," B chuckled. "Anyway meet me in Brownsville at the old spot. You ready to work?"

"You already know," Samir bluntly answered.

CHAPTER THREE

"Bitch what are you talking about?" Nina said through her gritted teeth. There was no way that this hoodrat was going to make her yell and scream in public. She had a reputation to uphold and beating this whore's ass in the middle of Mr. Chow's would not help her image. Besides, they had already attracted too much attention after this nutcase banged on the table.

"Like I said, fuckin with my man is gonna stop today if I got anything to do with it."

Nina composed herself before she responded. "Listen, I don't know if you're psycho or delusional, but I don't know what the hell you're talking about."

"Oh okay I see what you doing, he already prepped you for this." Nina let the stranger continue with the hopes of figuring out what was going on. "Let me guess; he told you if any bitches ever come up to you, play dumb and leave that bitch talking to herself. Then you're supposed to call him immediately because bitches be on his dick and they will say anything to get him. Right? So you expect me to believe he's never mentioned Traci?"

Nina maintained her straight face, but inside she felt her stomach drop and her heart begin to break. That's exactly what she had been told, several times. Nina was conflicted. Should she listen to Samir and do as she was told or should she pick this crazy bitch's brain to see what's really up? She decided on the latter. "Like I said, I don't know what you are talking about, and I hope you find the chick that's fucking your man." *Your point,* she thought to herself as she saw a hint of doubt in the stranger's eyes.

Just then the waiter arrived. "Good evening, ladies. Can I start you all off with one of our exquisite house wines or perhaps another wine from our exclusive wine collection?"

Neither woman immediately answered. Nina stared at the stranger with her try me face before turning politely to the waiter. "Oh no, I'm sorry I won't be staying. Here's a little something for your trouble." Nina handed the waiter a fifty dollar bill and walked out of the restaurant with her head held high like the queen she was.

After exiting the restaurant, Nina was able to let her true feelings show. She was so pissed that she shook uncontrollably and must have dropped her phone a dozen times trying to dial Samir's number. "Shit, I can't hold onto my phone! How in the hell am I supposed to drive without killing myself?" Nina yelled. "I won't be able to go anywhere until I speak to Samir's ass and get this shit straight." Nina pulled over and dialed Samir's number once more.

Samir picked up on the first ring. "Hey babe, I know you're pissed that I'm late, but I'm stuck in traffic. Let me call you right back."

Samir could barely finish his sentence before Nina screamed, "No fuck that, you talking to me now! Who the fuck is Traci, Samir?"

"Traci?"

"Look don't play dumb with me. The bitch just came up to me in the restaurant and told me she's gonna put an end to me fucking her man. Let me guess; you started messing with this skeezer during our off time. Samir didn't have a chance to answer before Nina began again. "Now the chick can't get enough of the dick?" The more Nina talked, the angrier she got. That wasn't a rhetorical question. Answer me dammit!" At this point, Nina was hysterical. She couldn't believe he was cheating again.

"Nina, I'm sorry this happened, but..."

"But, what?" Nina said cutting him off.

Samir collected himself. "Nina that's my baby momma. I have a five-year-old daughter."

Nina was speechless. She was devastated and suddenly felt nauseous. He had taken her voice with his response. Nina was no longer able to yell, and almost inaudibly she asked "You had a baby on me Samir? And with a freaking random ass psycho bitch?!" Nina closed her eyes and waited for the answer, silently praying that this was all a dream.

Samir took a deep breath. "No, I had a baby on you with my wife."

Nina dropped her phone as tears streamed down her face. She stared off into the traffic that passed her parked car. *This cannot be happening to me, not me. Not Nina Jones who can get any man she wants, but instead I fall in love with a married man who has a child,* she thought. But she knew it was true. This wasn't a dream. It wasn't even a nightmare. This was her life. *Damn.* This realization made the tears fall even harder.

"Nina, Nina, Nina!" Samir's screaming brought Nina's attention back to her phone. Nina picked it up off of the floor, wiped her face and hung up the phone.

Nina drove home in a daze. "How could I be so stupid and fall for his lies," she whispered. In her mind she replayed all of the times Samir's behavior seemed suspicious and all the lies she told herself to make excuses for him. It all made sense now. Before she knew it, Nina had pulled into her parking garage. Nina pulled down the visor and checked her reflection. Her face was a mess, and anyone who looked at her would be able to tell she had been crying. "Shit!" She violently flipped the visor up. Upon entering her building, Nina skipped her usual routine. She rushed past everyone, including Henry and Pat. She even took the stairs to avoid the elevator attendant. The penthouse was a long way up by stairs, but it was worth it to Nina to avoid the curious stares of her neighbors. After climbing what seemed like a million flights of stairs, Nina arrived at the penthouse floor. She pulled out the key card that gave her sole access to her floor and entered her home from the stairwell. The door closed behind her with a faint click. As soon as it closed, Nina fell to the floor. Tears, once again, welled in her eyes. She hugged herself into the fetal position and quietly sobbed. Nina was lost. "What do I do now?" she asked herself in between sobs. "I'm not promiscuous out in these streets. I don't have men on speed dial," Nina reasoned. "Samir was my life, my world, my everything. It didn't matter if we were having one of our off times; I never slept with another man. I never even called another man." Nina felt stupid for her loyalty. She pulled herself from the floor. "I can't stay down here forever." Nina winced. All of the crying had given her a headache. Her first stop would be to get an aspirin. Before she made it to her bathroom, she heard her front door swing open. It was Samir.

Nina walked over to him and slapped the shit out of him! His feelings were hurt because she had never hit him before, but he understood. He grabbed Nina's hands, but she was able to pull away and slap him again. Samir could see the pain in her eyes and if slapping him made her feel any better, then he would man up and take it.

"How could you do this to me?" Nina yelled. Samir responded by pulling her close and whispering in her ear, "I'm sorry Nina. I'm sorry baby; I love you."

Nina melted. She was prepared for an excuse, but she could not handle his apology right now. She wanted to be mad, mad enough to let him go. His apology broke down all of her defenses, and she began sobbing in his arms. Nina didn't want to be the cliché girlfriend by forgiving him so easily. It's just that she loved him so much. She was conflicted. Samir pulled Nina's face into his and kissed her. Nina wasn't gullible enough to believe that his kiss would solve all their problems or erase all of the lies. She did know that right then, at that moment, his kiss felt right. She allowed Samir to undress her, one piece of clothing at a time. Nina closed her eyes and let it happen. She needed him, and she could tell that he needed her too.

Samir took his time. He gently turned Nina around and lightly kissed her on her back. His hands found her waist. Nina intuitively knew what Samir wanted. He applied slight pressure to her waist, confirming her thoughts, and she slowly dropped to her knees. Nina looked over her shoulder at Samir as he undressed. *Damn, he's sexy.* As Samir, met Nina on the floor, she felt his breath against the back of her neck, as his hands gripped her hair. Samir hesitated. Nina could tell he wanted to say something. He thought differently of it and held his tongue. They both knew that now wasn't the time for apologies. His hard dick grazed her ass, and Nina became instantly soaking wet. Samir drove himself into Nina, and a moan escaped her lips.

"Fuck me," Nina said breathlessly. Samir tightened his grip on her hair and positioned Nina so that she had more of an arch in her back. He then did exactly as she asked; he fucked her. After both climaxing, Samir and Nina laid in silence with their eyes closed, breathing heavily. When Nina opened her eyes, Samir was staring deeply at her. Once again, she could tell he wanted to say something. This time Nina willed him to say it. *Come on, say it. You owe me that much,* she pleaded internally. Instead, he shook his head, as if he were trying to rattle the thought away.

Samir stood and slowly dressed. He stood silently over Nina for a moment before he leaned down and then kissed her on the forehead. Nina closed her eyes and accepted the sweet gesture because she wanted to remember what may have been the last intimate moment they would share. She opened her eyes just in time to see Samir reaching for her front door.

"What do I do now?" Nina softly said.

With his back still facing her, Samir replied, "Keep loving me," and walked out the door.

CHAPTER FOUR

Samir sat in his car staring out of the window. He couldn't stop everything that just went down with Nina from running through his mind. *I really fucked this up. I should've left Traci's trifling ass a long time ago.* Samir banged his fists against the steering wheel. "Shit!" he yelled. *I should've told Nina myself instead of letting her find out the way she did. I can't stand Traci's ass for this one,* he thought. Samir closed his eyes and laid his head against his headrest. "Just sitting here ain't helping nothing," he said to himself. Samir figured it was still early and the only way to get Nina off of his mind was to get some work done.

He hated what he was about to do. Logically he knew there were other ways, more legal ways to get money, but he needed money now. It wasn't his ego or the need to be the man in the streets. He had to provide for his baby girl Layla, who had immediate and expensive needs. Samir pulled his phone out of his pocket and dialed. "Yo, B what up? I need to come through and check you. That's cool?" Samir was careful with his language over the phone because he never knew who was listening. Some people called it being paranoid, Samir called it being careful.

"Yeah, come through ninja, I got you."

"Bet. On my way my ninja." Samir said with a laugh remembering his earlier conversation with B.

The game was a lot different now than it used to be. Hell, Samir himself was a different man. He used to be mercilessly ruthless to the game and anyone crazy enough to cross him. Samir wasn't cruel; he just did what he had to do while still respecting the unspoken code of the street. He knew a lot of niggas weren't going to be happy that he was back; but that was their problem, not his.

When Samir rolled up to the Brownsville Houses, a lot of memories from his old life came back to him. Some were good, some were bad, but none were forgettable. It was good to know that unlike last time, his reputation was out there. No more having to prove himself like he had to back then. Too many people thought because he was what the ladies called a pretty-boy, he was one to be fucked with. Once he kicked enough ass, the streets knew that he wasn't the one. *Aight, here we go,* Samir thought as he hopped out of his car. He immediately saw a few of his old workers, mixed in with some dudes he had never seen before. They were all posted up in front of the building where he was meeting B. Samir noticed that the new kids looked like straight up stick up kids. *I know what they 'bout,* Samir thought. He decided to go around to the back entrance. He wasn't scared in the least, but he knew the new kids didn't know him, so he was being extra precautious. *In due time*, he thought, but today just wasn't the day. Samir had no interest in fucking these kids up. Besides, as bad as his day was, once he started putting his foot to their asses; nothing would be able to stop him.

Samir entered through the back entrance making sure to check his surroundings thoroughly. He hadn't been in the game in a while, so he wanted to make sure he didn't overlook anything that could get him locked up, robbed or killed. He stopped for a second to determine whether he should take the elevator or the stairs. He already knew that the elevator smelled like piss. There was also a chance that the elevator would stop on another floor and it was possible for a stick-up kid to be waiting when the doors opened. On the other hand, if he took the stairs he could get blindsided and cornered at any turn. *Fuck it;* he said to himself, "I'ma hop on the elevator." He reasoned that there he could be more prepared for drama on the elevator than in the stairway. Samir was shocked when the elevator didn't smell as bad as he anticipated. *Wow! I guess ain't nobody have a drunk night,* he thought. He hit the button for the fifth floor, making sure to keep his hand on his gun. He was thankful when the elevator only stopped on the floor he chose. "Straight up, no stops? Word," Samir said as he walked to B's apartment door and then knocked.

Samir heard steps approaching from behind the other side of the door. After several locks had turned, an entirely naked woman yanked the door open and said, "yeah, you Samir, right? We been waiting for you. We been watching you the whole time, B waiting for you in the other room."

"Oh aight," Samir responded and headed towards the other room. When he walked through the living room, Samir saw two girls bottling up coke and to their left sat racks on racks of money. Just looking at the money made Samir's dick hard.

Samir entered B's room and said, "What up B?!" B was sitting calmly at his desk. Behind him was a wall of surveillance screens that showed everything in and around his spot.

B looked up from his work and greeted Samir. "What up Samir?! Here, this all you." B slid three keys of coke across his desk towards Samir. Samir began to salivate; he was ready to get money.

"Yo, just like that? Good looking out B. You know I got you, I owe you big time."

"Yeah aight, we'll see. Just bring me back my bread in five days. You already know; don't make me come look for you about my paper."

Samir quickly did the math in his head. He knew he could move enough product to have B's money back faster than five days. "Damn boy, you ain't even gotta come at me like that. I got one better; I'll bring it back to you in three." Samir put the keys away and nonchalantly left B and his apartment behind. Samir had work to do, the three days that he promised B would come quickly. He began to formulate his plan in his head. As soon as he was behind the wheel of his car, Samir pulled his phone out and made a call to his man Rog.

"Yo my dude, I'm straight. You got me on that paper?"

"Hell yeah, "Rog replied, "it's been light out here for months, glad you back in the game. Yo, who put you on? I hope it wasn't grimy-ass B?"

"Huh? I don't know what you're talking about. I'ma talk to you when I see you." *Rog is bugging*, Samir thought. *He knows*

*better than to ask me some shit like that on the phone. Fucks
wrong with him.*

"Oh aight, we'll talk when we link.

Same spot, right?"

"Yeah, slide through."

Samir sat there for a second, thinking about what Rog said
before he pulled off. *I knew I shouldn't have fucked with B. He
still on that bullshit,* he thought. Once he slightly cleared his
mind, he headed to Rog's, while blasting 2Pac. Even though he
loved Biggie and related to his lyrics; Pac's music made him
extremely focused. When Samir stopped at the next stoplight, he
was closer to his own spot than he realized. He decided to make
a run home before he continued to Rog's. When Samir opened
his front door, Traci rushed him yelling and throwing wild
punches. "Where the fuck you been? You ain't been home in
days! Who the fuck is this bitch Nina?"

Samir pushed Traci off of him. "Don't you ever and I mean
ever run up on me like that! Why the fuck are you talking to
Nina? Stay the fuck in your lane! I'm tired of this shit. Since you
got amnesia and don't know how to play your position anymore;
get your shit and get the fuck out! I'm divorcing your dumb ass!
Take all of your shit and leave Layla at my mother's house."

Traci heard something in Samir's voice she never heard
before. She knew this time he was serious. He was such an
asshole. She should be mad at him for cheating, but she was a
sucker for love. An even bigger one for not working, which she
hadn't done since marrying him. She knew they both did their
thing, so she didn't know why she let finding out about Nina
make her so mad. Traci grabbed onto Samir and begged him to
reconsider. He was done. He broke away from Traci and walked
out of the house not caring to remember why he initially stopped
there. Traci had ruined his mood. The way she was acting was
precisely why Samir always put his money over any relationship
other than the one with his daughter. "Let me keep my head and
get this money. I'm not letting Traci get to me," Samir said to
himself as he hopped back into his car and sped off.

Moments later, he rolled up on Rog's block, and it looked
like a scene straight out of a movie. Everything seemed to move
in slow motion. There were at least twelve cop cars. All of them

sat empty, except one, with the lights still glaring. As the light reflected against the house, Samir saw the cops leading people out onto the street. He recognized one of them as his man Dino. Samir's eyes followed the scene back out to the one non-empty car. *This could not be happening.* In the front seat sat an officer. Another officer stood just outside of the car speaking into his walkie-talkie. Against the hood of the car was Rog with his hands cuffed behind his back. Samir and Rog locked eyes. *That could've been me if I hadn't stopped by the house and argued with Traci.* Rog looked away; he knew there was no helping him now. Samir knew it too. So as not to draw any attention to himself, Samir ducked slightly lower in his seat and slowly continued down the street. "Fuck! How in the hell am I gonna get this money back to B?"

All of the day's drama weighed down on Samir, so he did the only thing he could do. He drove back home to find Traci and Layla gone. He got into his bed and went to sleep with the hope that tomorrow would be better. The next morning Samir got a call from B.

"Yo, how is it looking out there? You getting my money together? Days ain't long."

"Oh yeah B. I got everything under control, everything looking good," Samir lied.

Good, good. Look we having a party at Griffin in a couple of days. It's gonna be lit. Come through and just bring the money then. Cool?"

"Aight, I got you," Samir said willing his words to be true. Samir hung up the phone. He had to think of something and time was running out. He couldn't wait for Rog to get released from jail. He hadn't heard anything from his crew, and he wasn't even sure if Rog would get bail. One thing Samir knew for sure was that he wasn't posting up on any corner trying to make sells. That just wasn't him anymore. He'd passed that stage of the game a long time ago. The only thing he could do was reach out to some of the people he used to run with. Samir called his man Rock who linked him with an old Dominican cat from Washington Heights named Demario.

Samir heard good things about Demario. The word was he was the man, and he had a direct connect in Columbia.

20

Fortunately for Samir, his timing couldn't be better. Demario's connect had a delay with his shipment, so he needed work, and he needed it fast. The meeting between the two went smoothly. Demario had the money, Samir had the work and just like that he was back in the game. He didn't care that he didn't maximize his profits on that deal. His biggest concern was paying B what he was owed. *Fuck giving it to him in a couple of days. I'm going to Brownsville right now, to give this fucker all his money,* Samir thought. He jumped into his car, headed back to the FDR, crossed the Manhattan Bridge and hopped onto the BQE. Samir made it to Brownsville in no time. Since the last two days had been hectic, he figured now was the moment to slow down and relax a little bit. While riding through the streets, Samir saw one of his boys he hadn't seen in years posted outside of the bodega. "Yo, Tee! What up boy?" Samir called out of the passenger side window.

Tee stood up straight and shielded his eyes to get a better view of who was speaking to him. "Oh shit! No, it ain't my nigga Samir? What up?! You still ridin clean in these streets I see."

"Yeah you know me, you know how I get down," Samir said, secretly glad that Tee had noticed his whip.

"Word on the street is that you back my dude. Put a nigga on."

Samir chuckled. "Damn, I see these streets still be talking too much." It suddenly occurred to Samir that there were too many people on the street to have this conversation out in the open. "Nah, I'm cooling, doing my little one two. Get in the car and take this quick ride with me, so we can finish talking," Samir said. Tee walked to the car and hopped in the passenger seat. With the windows rolled up and the door closed, Samir felt it was safe to talk business as he drove down Mother Gatson Boulevard. "Yeah, I got that work. I'm back in the game."

Tee nodded his head. "You still working with the same team?"

Samir usually wouldn't discuss these things, but he wanted to see if the word on B was true. "Yeah, I'm working with B. You know him?" Samir waited for a response hoping Tee's response would be different from Rog's.

"Yeah, yeah that nigga. I've heard of him."

Not getting the information he wanted, Samir continued the conversation. "Yo, I'm just going to get my connects through his work, then I'm bouncing."

Again, Tee nodded. "Oh, aight. I'm trying to link up with you asap then. I'm wit whatever, so we can start gettin this money again. We was stacking that bread."

"No doubt." Samir smiled. "Yeah, we was getting paper. Shit, I might just shut it down and make these niggas wish I never considered this occupation. Cause I'ma stop up all they money."

"Yo Samir, you always got me cracking the fuck up. Only your ass would call the game an occupation. I swear you always stay with a business mentality."

"Damn right, I got to! I'ma take this street mindset to the boardroom and chop corporate America's ass one day," Samir said. "I ain't gon' let this knowledge go to waste. I'ma be somebody. You know I'm one of the greatest?! I just gotta get back up real quick; then I'm going legit again." Samir had to calm himself. When he talked about his dreams, he got a little too excited. He knew his capabilities; he just needed a chance and the money to make it all happen. Samir exhaled and looked out the window. He saw a gas station and decided to pull over.

Samir threw the car into park. "Let me hop out and pump this gas real quick. Yo, I'm glad we met up. You might be the missing piece I need to take over the game again and exit quietly." As Samir exited the car, he noticed that Tee pulled out his phone. He figured Tee was hype about an opportunity to get back to the top of the game. When he passed the front window of the car, the two men locked eyes. Samir gave Tee a friendly head nod. Tee, on the other hand, looked away as if to say, "nigga get out of my business." That didn't sit right with Samir. Something felt funny to him, but he couldn't put his finger on it. *Maybe I'm overthinking this*, he thought and walked inside. "Thirty on pump seven," he politely said to the gentleman behind the glass. He was very conflicted as he paid the cashier. Sure, he had this funny feeling, but Tee had always been solid in the past. He was always straight-up and never made any snake moves. Still, his gut was telling him to get the hell away from Tee and fast. Samir finished pumping his gas and got back into the car.

"So yeah, like I said, I'm definitely giving taking over this game some thought," Samir said. He had more to say and would have continued, but Tee had a look on his face that made Samir stop short.

Tee's expression relaxed. "I feel you son. Yo, just drop me off down the street a couple of blocks from here."

"Oh okay, cool," Samir said betraying what he was actually thinking. Samir was no fool; he knew what was going on. He gripped the steering wheel with his left hand, removed his right and positioned it to be ready to knock the shit out of Tee if he made a move. *Fuck me for not having my grip*, Samir thought. *This nigga changed.*

"Yo right here is good. I'ma check you later, but before I dip…" Tee said with a snarl in his voice and a chrome .45 in his hand. "Run that work you got and whatever little bit of chump change you got too!" Tee had a look on his face that Samir knew all too well, but this was the first time he was on the receiving end. "Yeah, I been dreaming about this day to get at you for fucking my ex, Traci," Tee said with fire in his eyes, "and I heard B got a bag on your head, you dumb muthafucka. He ain't letting you take his spot, but I'm sure about to take your's."

Before Tee could finish his sentence, Samir heard tires squeal as a car stopped diagonally in front of his, blocking him in. Tee jumped out of Samir's car just as the doors of the other car flung open. Out jumped two shooters with their guns blazing. Samir grabbed his door handle with the plan to run but was too late as the first bullet burst through the front windshield. Shattered glass flew into his face, and he instinctively raised his hands to shield it. Time seem to stand still until his arm was hit with what felt like a blazing hot hammer. He had no time to react to the pain if he was going to get himself out of this alive. He threw the gearshift into reverse and hit the gas. The engine revved, but the car didn't budge. *Don't panic, keep your head, think*, Samir thought to himself while bullets flew all around him. The warm stickiness on his thigh let him know that he had been hit a second time.

In the background he heard Tee, who now stood outside of the car with a smirk, say, "I just hit his ass!"

Samir pressed the gas again and again, but the car still didn't move. "What the fuck?!" In Samir's hurry, he failed to notice that the car was in neutral. After a third bullet had ripped through his stomach, he knew he had to take a chance and run. He was a sitting target in the car. Samir jumped out of the car and was shot two more times in the back as he ran back towards the gas station. He was running on pure adrenaline. With almost each step Samir looked over his shoulder to make sure he wasn't being chased. When he felt sure enough that no one was behind him, Samir slowed his pace eventually to a walk. He knew too much movement would cause the bullets to travel. He had kept himself alive this long and didn't want to make any mistakes now. He started to become tired and lightheaded. *Don't fall asleep. Keep your eyes open,* he repeated to himself. He didn't want to fall asleep, but he couldn't continue to stand. He slumped against the newspaper box in front of the convenience store. The world around him blurred, but he was still able to recognize a guy, who rode up on his bicycle. Samir didn't have much energy, but he used all he had to beg the man to call 911. "Please," he gasped and against everything he knew was right, Samir closed his eyes.

"Sir, sir, can you hear me? Are you okay? Sir. What's your name?" The sound of voices broke through the darkness surrounding him. "Sir, can you hear me? Can you open your eyes?" He attempted to will his eyes to open, but they remained closed. "We have a gunshot victim here with multiple gunshot wounds. Looks like four or five, but there could be more. There's too much blood. We gotta go!" The calm voice was reassuring to Samir. He felt himself being strapped down. "Okay, we have to move, now! Ready? 1, 2, 3, lift." Samir felt himself rise and pushed forward. "Sir, we have you now, and we're going to do everything we can for you. But you have to do your part. You fight. Okay?" Samir thought he felt himself nod as the oxygen mask slipped over his nose and mouth. "Stay with me, sir. Stay with me." Samir's world went black.

CHAPTER FIVE

Since the moment Samir left her apartment, Nina was in no mood to interact with anyone, especially her assistant. She forwarded all of her office calls to her cell phone and worked from home. Nina just couldn't deal with the office or anyone taking a look at her and asking what was wrong. She knew as soon as she tried to brush them off, she would burst into tears. She didn't want or need anyone's sympathy right now. What she needed was to figure out her life and what she was going to do after everything Samir dropped on her. Her mind wondered to him throughout the day, but thankfully her constantly ringing phone kept her well distracted. Nina's phone rang once again. She checked the caller ID. It was GeGe.

"What up Nina? You doing okay girl?"

"I guess. I mean, he was my world. Would I be stupid to stay with him?" Nina bit her bottom lip and waited for an answer.

"Uhh, yes girl! He played the fuck outta you. You deserve better and he ain't it."

"But Ge, I was with him for nine years. Nine years! Come on; you don't just throw something like that away." Nina shifted in her seat uncomfortably.

"Girl you stupid if you stay, cause I know I wouldn't."

"Aight Ge, I'ma talk to you later. A client is beeping in." Nina was lying; there wasn't a beep. She got off the phone to avoid cursing at GeGe. She was seconds away from saying some foul things that friends just shouldn't say to one another. Nina loved GeGe, but lately, she seemed like such a hater. It wasn't just because she and GeGe didn't always agree, it was more because of the nasty ass way she expressed her opinion. "And I was going to ask her hating ass to come with me this weekend," Nina said as she put her phone down. "Forget that; I don't have time for her. One of my most prestigious clients is performing in the city in a couple of days. I need to focus on prepping her and making her look like a star, instead of wasting time going back and forth with GeGe." Nina pulled out her laptop, determined not to let GeGe further ruin her mood. She stared at her computer for a few minutes before she was able to focus enough to work. "Okay, get it together girl. The bank does not accept broken hearts as a form of payment on a mortgage," Nina laughed to herself. Just as she began to type, her buzzer broke the relative silence.

"If it ain't one thing, it's another." Nina put her laptop down a little annoyed with the new distraction and waited for the intercom to stop ringing. "Ugh, really. Right when I'm ready to work." Nina took a deep breath and begrudgingly got off her bed to answer the intercom.

"Hello, Miss. Sorry to disturb you; however, I'm afraid that your car alarm seems to be going off," Pat the desk clerk said. There was a brief pause before she continued. "It also appears that someone has vandalized it. In fact, I think that it's more accurate to say that someone is vandalizing your car. I know how you feel about your privacy. I remember you told me to contact you before calling the authorities in non-emergency situations. How would you like me to proceed?"

I. Cannot. Fuckin. Win! Nina thought. "Thank you, Pat. I'll handle it. If I need you to call the cops, I'll let you know," Nina said and hung up. "I'm going to kick someone's ass today! People wanna play with me, well let's see how they like it when I take all my shit out on them." Nina hurriedly slipped on some sweats and her sneakers. She was almost out of the door when she remembered to grab her phone. *Just in case I need to tell Pat to the call the cops or even the paramedics for this asshole,* Nina thought sliding the phone into her sweatpants pocket. As the elevator descended to the lobby, Nina felt herself growing angrier and angrier with each floor she passed. By the time she arrived, she was fuming. She nodded at Pat as she passed and headed to the parking garage with a mission. Nina pulled her

26

keys out and disarmed her alarm. "What the..." she was stopped in her tracks when she saw Traci standing beside her car.

"Yeah, bitch come the fuck on over here before I total your shit. And bring my man with you!"

"Traci get your crazy ass away from my car, and Samir's not here! I haven't even seen him!"

"Whatever," Traci snarled. "I told you to stop fucking with him. Now he's leaving me for you. Why couldn't you find your own man and leave mine alone?!" Traci swung the bat. Shards of glass flew through the air as Nina's passenger side mirror exploded. Traci lifted the bat again, placed it on her shoulder and smirked at Nina, daring her to try and stop her.

When Nina saw the smirk, she knew it had gone way beyond the talking stage. "I'm about to fuck you up," she shouted. She pulled her phone out of her pocket to call Pat because Nina knew once she started swinging it was going to take an army to pull her off of Traci. When she unlocked her phone, Nina noticed that she had three missed calls from Samir.

Amused Traci called out, "So what are you going to do bitch, talk on the phone?"

"Shut the fuck up! Your ass-kicking is coming soon enough, whore." Nina hit the missed call deciding it was best to call Samir. She wanted to beat the shit out of Traci not see another sister locked up. As soon as the call connected Nina screamed, "Come get your bitch ass wife from my house, I'm about to..."

"Miss. Miss. Please listen," an unfamiliar voice interrupted. "This is Nurse Lopez at Kings County Hospital. Mr. Wright has been involved in a very serious incident, and we need to get in contact with a family member. Are you the family of Mr. Samir Wright?"

"Hospital? What happened to Samir?" Nina yelled.

Overhearing the conversation Traci put the bat down and shifted her focus from the car to Nina. "Oh my goodness, what happened? Nina, what happened," Traci wailed.

Nina listened as Nurse Lopez continued on the phone. "I can't go into details over the phone, but it is imperative that we speak to a family member. Do you have any contact information for a family member?"

Although Traci stood just ten feet in front of her, Nina replied no to the nurse's inquiry.

"If you aren't familiar with a family member or are unable to pass the message along, I would also recommend that a friend comes to be here for him."

"I'm on my way," Nina said. She looked at her car, quickly realized it was in no condition to drive and ran to the front of her building to hail a cab.

"Nina, what the fuck happened to Samir!" Traci yelled behind her. "Nina!"

Nina ignored her cries and hopped in the first cab that she saw. "Kings County Hospital, please, and fast. She could feel the tears welling in her eyes as she tried not to imagine her life with Samir in it.

"You okay Ma?" the cabbie politely asked.

Nina shook her head no. "Please just get me to the hospital as quickly as possible, thank you."

The cab pulled away from the curb suddenly and smoothly merged into traffic. Nina leaned her head against the back seat. The tears finally broke, and Nina began to reminisce about the first time she met Samir.

March, Philadelphia, nine years ago:

"Excuse me Miss, um can you help me fill this slip out?" "Huh, you never been to FedEx Kinkos before?" Nina didn't mean to say this out loud. She knew if her boss overheard she would hear about it. She was glad when the handsome customer didn't seem to mind her slip of the tongue.

"Yeah I've been here before and even filled out lots of forms," he said with a smile. "I just never mailed anything internationally before, so I want to make sure that I fill out everything correctly."

Nina sighed to herself. "Aight give me a second to put these boxes down, and I'll be right over to help." Nina couldn't help but feel the stranger's eyes on her ass as she sat the boxes down in the corner. When she turned around Nina caught him trying to act as if he wasn't doing exactly what she thought he was doing, staring at her ass. "Let me see the slip," she said reaching out to him. "It looks like you have everything filled out and in the proper place, but you forgot to sign at the bottom."

"Thank you. Um, what's your name?"

Nina was used to guys hitting on her at work, but it didn't stop her from being slightly curious. "Why?"

"Cause I just want to know the name of the person that was nice enough to help me send this important package off," he said and smiled.

"Yeah right!" she said after laughing.

"No, for real. I think you're cute and I wanna get to know you. You could start by giving me your number after telling me your name."

"Nah I don't give my number to Philly guys."

"That's good to know because I'm not from Philly. I'm from New York."

Nina shifted her stance in surprise. "Oh okay, that's nice."

"So what's up, can I get your name and number? You know, since I'm not from Philly and all."

"Hmmm. I don't know. For now, how about I just start with my name. It's Nina", she said sliding her sweater out of the way so that her name tag showed.

"I'm Samir," he replied.

"Nice to meet you Samir. Is there anything else I can help you with?" Nina said before pulling her phone out to check it. "I'm not rushing you, but I have to finish up here. It's almost time for me get off."

"Yo, you are playing a dangerous game walking around without a case on your phone," Samir said with a laugh. "Why you ain't got a case on it?"

"I can't find one. All anyone ever has are the smaller ones, so I just have to be mad careful until I can get my hands on one."

Samir saw his opportunity to show Nina that he just wasn't some clown off of the streets. "Word. I got you! I got a case, I'ma be right back with it. When I bring it back, and it fits your phone, you gotta give me your number. Bet?"

"Yeah aight, bet. You probably don't have one, though; I told you they're out everywhere. But if you have one and it fits then I'll give you my number."

"Shake on it."

"Aight cool." Nina couldn't help but smile at Samir's confidence as he headed out of the door. Nina stayed busy and the day passed by quickly until it was closing time. "I knew he was full of shit," she mumbled before heading to the back of the store to get her things. Nina turned down the lights and walked towards the door. She smiled when she saw Samir standing on the other side.

She opened the door. "Oh wow you actually came back," Nina said not hiding her surprise.

"I told you I would. Here see if the case fits."

Nina took the case from Samir and popped it on her phone. "It's a perfect match."

"Yeah I know; a perfect match just like us."

Nina burst out laughing. "You are so corny, but I have to admit that it was cute. Plus you kept your word and found me a case, and now I'm keeping mine. Here's my number, call me."

Nina was jolted back to the present when the car next to hers loudly blew its horn. The smile she wore mere seconds ago vanished as she remembered where she was going and why. Nina knocked on the Plexiglas in front of her. "How much longer?" she asked.

"Not much longer. Traffic was backed up for a few, but we should be there in about five minutes," the cabbie said sympathetically. "I've been speeding the whole way." Nina slumped back into the seat and tried to prepare herself for all of the unknowns at the hospital. The cab stopped abruptly. Nina paid for her ride, tipped the cabbie an extra twenty dollars and bolted through the hospital's sliding glass doors. She stopped at the information desk and hoped the receptionist could help her find Nurse Lopez. Lopez was such a common last name, Nina could only hope that since this was a smaller hospital, she wouldn't have any problems tracking her down.

Hello, I'm looking for Nurse Lopez. I talked to her about twenty minutes; she told me a friend of mine had been admitted.

"Did you get Nurse Lopez's first name?"

"No, I'm sorry. I just know Nurse Lopez."

The receptionist looked through her computer. "You're in luck; it seems there's only one Nurse Lopez on call today. Take the elevator to the sixth floor and ask for her at the nurses' station."

"Thank you," Nina shouted over her shoulder and ran to the elevator. She pressed the button for the sixth floor and instantly felt her stomach turn. Each time the elevator passed a level, Nina grew more and more nauseous. Her stomach was in knots. When she arrived at her floor, she walked directly to the nurses' station.

Nina leaned against the large desk. "Hello, I need to speak to Nurse Lopez."

"She's busy at the moment, may I help you?"

"May I have Samir Wright's room."

"I'm sorry, there's no one by that name on this floor." Nina's heart dropped, and she momentarily lost her breath. "You're wrong; look again," Nina pleaded. "Please."

"Miss, there is no one on this floor by that name."

Nina tried to keep her cool, but her emotions were too raw. She was seconds away from jacking the nurse up by her scrubs. It must have shown all over her face because another nurse quickly approached Nina and asked if there was anything that she could do to help. Nina looked at her with tears of anger in her eyes and explained the situation to the second nurse.

"Follow me," the nurse said before leading Nina away from the nurse's station. "May I ask your name?" the nurse asked.

"Nina, and like I just said I'm looking for Samir Wright."

The nurse cut Nina off before she had a chance to repeat her explanation. "Just one second, please." The nurse walked away and returned a short time later.

Nina began speaking again. "Ma'am, do you know where Samir is? I spoke to a nurse earlier who said he was here and then another says he's not."

Again Nina was cut off. "Yes, Nina you spoke to me earlier. I'm Nurse Lopez. I apologize for being so short earlier, but I couldn't speak to you until I was able to approve your visit." The nurse gave a polite smile. "First let me put your mind at ease. Yes, Samir Wright is a patient at this hospital. Nurse Warren was unable to provide this information to you as Mr. Wright is currently what we call a secure patient. Due to the nature of his injuries and the circumstances surrounding them, Mr. Wright has been admitted under an undisclosed pseudonym. I can't provide you with an update on his condition as you are not his immediate family. However, I am able to share this information with you as Mr. Wright placed you on the approved visitor list during one of his more lucid moments."

"Is he?" Nina began.

"Nina I wish I could provide more information; however, my hands are tied. Let me escort you to his room. He was awake as of a moment ago, and you should be able to speak directly to him."

"Thank you, and I apologize for my behavior earlier."

"No worries," Nurse Lopez said with a smile. "This is his room here. Take care."

Nina slowly pushed the door open and quietly crept in. She was more nervous than she had ever been and closed her eyes to compose herself. The room was absolutely quiet except for the clicks and beeps of the machines. Nina felt her eyes begin to sting behind her closed lids. She slowly opened her eyes. Through the blur of tears, she saw Samir sitting up in his bed. She ran to him, afraid to touch him. Nina stood by his bedside and wept.

Samir couldn't stand that this was the second time in a few days that he had put tears in her eyes. *Damn, here I am shot up, and I'm worrying about her*. The thought made Samir grin. "What's with all the crying?" he asked Nina.

She looked up, slightly startled. "What's with all the crying? Really?" Nina asked as she wiped the tears from her face. "I was so scared that I would come here and they tell me you didn't make it. I don't know what I would have done."

"So I guess you not mad at me anymore, huh?"

"You got jokes now Samir?" Nina finally let herself smile. "Look, what you did wasn't cool; but now isn't the time to discuss it. So for now, no I'm not mad. But you ain't getting no ass for a while, not like you can do anything anyway in your condition."

"Girl please I will toss you across this bed and tear your ass up right now. Try me. You looking all good as shit too." Samir tried to lift himself off of the bed but was stopped by the sharp pain that ran through his side. He bit his bottom lip to try and stifle his moan.

"Samir stop let me help you. Don't try to get up; you need to lay back down. Nina helped Samir lower himself back onto the bed. "What does your doctor have to say about all of this," Nina said waving her hand above Samir's bandaged wounds.

"He said I was lucky to make it out of surgery, but now 90% of what happens next is in my hands. Doc says that I need my rest to heal, but you know damn well I can't just sit here. I don't want to lay in the bed helpless." Samir took in a deep breath and winced from the pain before continuing. "Getting shot wasn't the hard part, surviving these wounds is what matters. Doc knows his shit, but I gotta get outta here. I can't be in here taking all of these painkillers and shit. You know I ain't never been no drugy, so I ain't starting now."

"I know babe you will be fine, just lay back down. I will get you outta here soon enough," Nina said.

"Aight. Do me a favor, close the door. I got something serious to talk to you about."

Nina walked across the room and closed the door. As she walked back towards Samir, she could barely hide the fear in her eyes.

"I know who shot me."

"What! Are you serious?"

"Yeah. It was Tee, my mans or he used to be. He's Traci's ex from way back. That's why I think maybe her, B or both of them, set me up. Right before he shot me, Tee said something about Traci and that B had a hit out on me."

Nina saw red at the sound of Traci's name and her possible involvement in Samir's shooting. *This bitch*, she thought. *Traci wants to play, well now is the perfect time to show her who she's fucking with.* Without uttering a word, Nina continued to listen to Samir, all the while thinking about how she was going to get Traci back come hell or high water.

"Yo, you can't tell anyone. I don't trust anybody out here but you. I gotta get them back, and I'm gonna need your help."

Nina moved in close, looked him directly in his eyes and gave him a kiss. Before pulling back, she said softly... "I got you!"

33

CHAPTER SIX

Nina left the hospital days ago with the weight of the world off of her shoulders and a new purpose. Knowing that Samir was alive and going to be okay gave her the strength that she needed to make her move on B and Traci. In a strange way, Nina was honored that Samir asked her to help take them out. It actually turned her on. Samir hadn't shared the full plan yet, but Nina wanted to be ready for whatever he needed. She called the office, passed all of her clients to a capable co-worker and took a leave of absence. Nina then called GeGe and told her that she was going out of town for a while. The last thing she needed was GeGe calling her nonstop.

The next thing Nina had to handle was her car situation. Traci messed up her car to the point that it wasn't moving anytime soon and Nina would need a car when it was time to pick Samir up from the hospital. She called her insurance company to submit a claim and to arrange for a rental. *If she weren't about to get hers, that bitch Traci would be paying for this. I shouldn't even have to submit a claim*, Nina thought as she waited for the agent to make arrangements with the rental car company.

"Okay, Ms. Jones, everything for your rental is all set-up. Your reservation is confirmed, and you have until seven o'clock tonight to pick-up the vehicle. Is there anything else that I can do for you?"

"No, you've taken care of everything. Thank you," Nina replied hanging up the phone.

With work and her rental taken care of Nina planned to use the next few hours to get some much-needed rest and relaxation.

She pulled out her softest blanket, made herself a cup of tea and sat in her favorite chair taking in the view that her penthouse afforded her. Staring at the world beyond the window usually calmed her. Today it just wasn't happening. Thoughts of Samir ran through her mind. She wondered what her life would be like after he was released from the hospital tomorrow. The shooting put her feelings for him in perspective. Nina no doubt loved Samir, but was she willing to ignore that he was married? Her thoughts paused. She laughed to herself at the irony of worrying about his marriage, when she was actively involved in a revenge plot against his wife, Traci. "I guess his marriage isn't a problem," she whispered with a sly smile as she blew the mug of steaming tea. For the next few minutes, Nina's mind once again raced with thoughts of Samir. She realized that she had too much going on to sit idly. *Fuck it! Let me go and get this rental.* Nina threw the blanket to the side and ran downstairs to hail a cab.

Nina sat silently in the driver's seat of the rented convertible tapping her fingers on the steering wheel. "Okay Nina, what are you going to do with yourself now?" she asked herself. For the first time today her mind drew a blank. *Home it is,* Nina thought while starting the car and lowering the roof. *The fresh air will do me some good.* Nina pulled out of the parking space and merged into traffic with the plan to head home. The short ride home soon turned into hours of aimless driving through the city. The cool wind blowing through her hair helped her think. Eventually, she ended up in Brownsville. *This is the wrong part of town to be cruising with the top down* at night, Nina thought noticing where she was. At the next red light, she put the top back up planning to head back closer to her condo. While at the light, a group of guys crossed the street in front of Nina's car. There wasn't anything special about most of the guys except one of them. He was wearing something that stood out from the rest. The platinum and diamond looking chain around his neck sparkled in the streetlight. Nina immediately recognized the chain. She did a double take to make sure she wasn't seeing things.

Yoooo, that's my man's chain! That has to be the fuck boy Tee who shot Samir, Nina thought. Although in her gut Nina knew she was right about the chain, she didn't want to jump to conclusions without getting a closer look. She noticed the group of guys headed into the bodega on the corner. Nina quickly pulled the car onto a side block, parked and followed the guys into the store. The store was small, and it didn't take long for her to figure out which aisle the guys were on. She collected herself and walked towards the guys. When she neared the one she suspected was Tee she bumped into him as if by accident to get a closer look at him and the chain.

Nina turned on the false charm. "Oh, I'm so sorry. I didn't even see you. I apologize," she said all while keeping her eyes on the chain.

Tee looked at her with lust in his eyes. "No problem Ma. You fine as hell. You got a man?"

"Yeah, but I like your chain. It's original," Nina purred. She touched the chain and pretended to admire it. A chill ran up her spine when she saw the S&N engraved on the back of the cross. *Gotcha fucka*, Nina thought. Nina fought to keep her composure. She was angry enough to snatch the chain from his neck and smack him with it, but Nina was smarter than that. She had no problem with delayed gratification, and she knew payback would be greater if she just waited.

Nina smiled at Tee making sure her outward appearance gave no indication of what she was thinking. "So are you Catholic?" Tee gave her a slightly confused looked. "You know since your chain is a rosary and all."

Tee responded, but Nina didn't hear a word he said. She was mesmerized by the chain and couldn't pull her eyes away from it. She felt her anger growing again as she looked at the chain she bought Samir hang around Tee's neck. *Do not deviate from the plan*, the words Samir spoke to her earlier rang through Nina's mind. *Plan it out, do not deviate*. This time she heard the words in Samir's voice, and it flipped her focus like a switch. She looked at Tee's face intently. He probably assumed she was flirting, when in actuality she was burning his face into her memory, so she would never forget what he looked like. Tee continued with his flirting, but Nina cut him short, said goodbye then they parted ways. Nina ran back to the car and slumped down in the seat, making herself invisible. She waited for Tee and his boys to walk out of the store. As they passed, she followed far enough behind them to not be noticed but close enough to see which building they walked into. *Bingo*, she thought. Nina pulled out her iPhone, took a few pictures and pulled away. She smiled anticipating sharing all of the information that she collected with Samir. Nina caught a glimpse of her reflection in the driver's side window as she turned at the stop sign; her smile still plastered across her face. For a split second, the smile scared her. *Who am I turning into? Why am I smiling at the thought of getting these assholes back?* Then she remembered Samir and what they had done to him. *I'm that bitch that's gonna make them pay. On everything I love, I'm getting their bitch-asses back!*

CHAPTER SEVEN

The morning after Nina's reconnaissance, Samir sat in the passenger seat of the rental car fuming. "I can't believe that pussy Tee, got enough balls to walk around wearing my shit!" Samir grew angrier with every detail she shared.

Nina worried that she shouldn't have shared this information with Samir so soon after his discharge from the hospital. "Babe, I can't tell you anything else if this is how you're gonna handle it." She kicked herself for opening her mouth. Nina had the best intentions, but she forgot to consider that despite how strong he looked; Samir hadn't fully healed. Before she told him anything else, she wanted to make sure that he could keep calm. The last thing she needed was him becoming agitated, moving around and possibly reopening his wounds. "You have to calm down. I know you're pissed, but I got you, okay?"

Samir hated being in this position. He had always taken care of himself, but now that his mind was stronger than his body he would for the first time have to depend on someone else. He turned to look at Nina. He couldn't believe that this beautiful and intelligent woman loved him enough to risk it all to avenge him.

"For real, I'm handling this. Okay?" Nina couldn't read the look on his face. She questioned if he regretted asking her for help? Could he tell that she was a bit scared? "Samir?"

"Yeah?" All of the anger Samir felt just five minutes ago turned into doubt. He looked at Nina and hoped she didn't see his needing help as a weakness.

"I got you," she repeated.

Samir decided to believe her. "Aight. You really wanna do this? I mean I'ma get them regardless, but with your help, it will be a lot easier, you can pull out if you want."

"Samir hush. I told you, I'm down. This guy almost killed the only person that matters to me, so as far as I'm concerned, he can get it." Nina looked at Samir intently. Besides, the fact of the matter is these fuck boys are still out there. I'm also pretty sure that word has spread you didn't die, so we have no choice to get them before they try to get you again."

Samir's ringing phone interrupted their conversation. Nina hated that phone. It's cracked screen, which was the result of the attack on Samir, was a horrible reminder of what happened to him.

"Hold on babe. Hello, hello. Yo, who's dis?"

"It's B muthafucka! Where's my money?"

"First off calm the fuck down, you ain't gotta be talking to me like that! Anyway my bad on missing that deadline, B. Some fucker robbed and shot my ass. I just got outta the hospital."

"I don't wanna hear that shit," B replied. "I don't give a shit if you got shot up and robbed. You still living right? So give me my fucking money!"

"B I got you. I ain't gonna shit you. I just need a little time son, you know I wouldn't keep your money. We go too far back for that."

"Man fuck that way back shit. I don't know you no more like that so I don't know what the hell you would or wouldn't do," B snarled. "Like I said get my money to me. You got two days, and that's being nice cause you over there leaking." B hung up the phone.

"Fuck!! B still wants his damn money," Samir said to Nina. "What I'm trying to figure out is if that's his cover or if he ain't have nothing to do with me getting robbed. So for right now we just gonna focus on Tee."

"Cool," Nina said shaking her head in agreeance.

"So did you get a chance to give Tee your number yesterday?"

"No, I wanted to make sure it was him. Like I was saying before your call, I assume the dude wearing your chain was Tee, but I'm not totally sure. I wanna check out Facebook and some other social media pages to see if the dude with the chain is really Tee. That idiot has to be on at least one page showing off his guns and other stupid hood shit. By the way, what's his real name?"

"Terrance Berdly," Samir answered.

Nina pulled out her phone and went to the search option on Facebook. She waited patiently for the list of users with the name Terrance Berdly to return. Luckily the list was short and the second profile picture caught her attention. She clicked it to get a better view. "Yup, that's him. That's the dude I talked to yesterday in the bodega."

"Let me see." Samir took the phone from Nina's hand. "Wait, this bastard posted a picture wearing my chain. I'm gonna break his fucking neck!" Samir was so angry he was trembling trying to keep from breaking Nina's phone.

"Calm down Samir; I know what we can do. I'ma send him a message on Facebook to get his number and act like I'm interested in him. I'll arrange a meet up. We can get your chain back plus rob his dumb ass."

Samir hated to break it to Nina, but Tee would not just be getting robbed tonight or any other night for that matter. "Babe, we're gonna get my chain back, but we ain't robbin him. We gotta kill him. You understand that?" Samir paused for a second. "You still in?"

"Still in? Babe, I never left. Let's do this." Nina leaned over and kissed Samir. "And make this the last time you ask me if I'm in. Now hand me my phone." Nina sent a message to Tee's inbox. Within five minutes he responded. "Yo, he is mad thirsty," Nina laughed. The two exchanged numbers and planned to meet up later that night. "Step one complete." A satisfied grin came across Nina's face. "Now let's get you to my place, so you can safely rest up. No one's getting past Pat, she doesn't play any games."

Nina got Samir settled into her place and instructed Pat that no one, not even registered guests were allowed up to her floor. She gave him his medication and put him on her bed to rest. "I'll be right back, babe. If you need anything, anything at all, call me. And remember I have my key so just in case someone gets past Pat, do not answer the door!" Nina instructed and slid out the front door. She leaned against the wall in the hallway and closed her eyes for a second. Seeing Samir medicated and laid up in her bed reminded her once again how delicate his condition was. He was nowhere near healed. There was no way he would be able to take care of Tee, and if he were shot again, there was no way that he would survive. The thought made Nina shutter. She absolutely would not be able to live with herself if anything else happened to him. As she stood against the wall, it occurred to her that earlier while they were in the car talking, Samir mentioned exactly where he stashed his guns in his house. *I gotta do what I gotta do*, Nina thought as she headed downstairs to the car.

As Nina pulled out of Samir's driveway, she was grateful that Traci wasn't home. *Thank goodness, I don't even have time for her right now.* She took her phone, called Tee and asked him to meet her in 15 minutes. He agreed and suggested they meet at a studio right off of Atlantic Avenue.

Nina was a ball of nerves, but ready to handle business when she pulled up to the agreed upon location. *Okay, here we go*, she thought as she hit redial on her phone. She cleared her throat and spoke casually, "Tee what up, I'm outside."

"Aight, I'm coming out now," he said and hung up the phone. A few minutes later Tee lightly tapped on the passenger side window. Nina unlocked the door, and he slid into the car. "What up sexy? You don't mind driving do you because it ain't no point in taking two cars."

His broke ass probably doesn't even have a car. Who does he think he's fooling? Nina thought, but she replied "Nah that's perfect for me. So where are you taking me?"

"Don't worry about that, a nigga gotta few tricks up his sleeves. You just focus and worry about driving. Everybody knows women drivers in New York will crash a car quick, with y'all non-driving asses."

Nina couldn't help but burst out laughing. "Oh my God shut up! You literally made me laugh out loud. I like that, a sense of humor is always a plus." For a second Nina felt bad for what she was about to do. Tee seemed like a nice guy, but none of that mattered after he shot Samir. Tee had the bad luck of fucking with the wrong ones this time.

Unaware of Nina's true feelings, Tee laughed along with her. "Yeah you know it's true," he said with a smile. "Yo, go back out to the Ville where we first met. I gotta make a stop before we head out."

"Aight." As they drove, Nina could feel Tee staring at her. She tried to distract him with small talk, but every other sentence he was complimenting her looks. Guys commenting on her looks was nothing new to Nina. She was used to guys responding to her like this, but Tee had a very charming way about him that could be very distracting. In spite of it all, Nina stayed focused. Any momentary doubts she had disappeared when she envisioned Samir laid up in the hospital. She knew what she was here to do and regardless of how nice he seemed, Tee was a cold-blooded killer. Her palms grew sweaty with anticipation as she pulled up to the building Tee pointed out. "I'll wait in the car," Nina said motioning for Tee to get out of the car. He gave her a strange look. "Nah ma, it ain't happening. It gets crazy in the Ville, and you just can't be sitting in no car like a sitting duck. I don't want you waiting out here for me, and somebody come snatch that ass up."

"There you go with the jokes again," Nina quickly replied. She turned off the car and then popped the trunk. "Just let me get my purse real quick, and I'll be right there."

Tee nodded his head okay.

With her mind on the end goal, Nina wanted to make sure she was prepared to shoot Tee once she decided exactly where it was going down. She opened the trunk and slyly pulled out the baby 9 millimeter. Nina glanced back up to make sure Tee wasn't watching her as she slid the gun in the front of her jeans near her pelvic bone. "Shit!," she whispered to herself when she noticed that her shirt wasn't long enough to cover the gun. *Think fast, Nina.* She quickly pulled the gun from her waist and tossed it into her black clutch purse. *This will have to do,* she thought and closed the trunk. Nina plastered a smile on her face and joined Tee in the walk towards his building.

The small talk continued until they reached Tee's apartment. When he opened the door, Nina was pleasantly surprised. It was nothing like what she expected. It was spotless and decorated to perfection. Nina noticed the leather couches still had that new

42

smell and would have been impressed if they didn't reflect how messed up Tee's priorities were. *He would rather have all this new shit in the pj's than to put that money towards something he could own. My people,* Nina thought as she laughed to herself.

She was broken from her thoughts when Tee yelled from the back room. "Yo come back here real quick."

Nina wasn't fooled at all. Tee wasn't slick in the least. *He's calling me to his bedroom to try and get some ass. That ain't happening,* Nina thought. "Nah, I'm good. Just hurry up, so we can go."

Not taking no for an answer Tee responded, "It's gonna take one sec, just come here."

Nina reluctantly headed into his bedroom and was greeted by Tee sitting on his bed. *I knew it. His ass is so transparent. I just wanna get this fake ass date over with already. His ass went from charming to annoying in no time.* Nina tried to resist when he grabbed her hand and sat her beside him, but she felt torn. There was no way she was doing anything with him, but if she resisted too much, she might put her entire plan into jeopardy. In a matter of seconds, Tee was all over Nina trying to kiss her. She stood up and headed towards the bedroom door. "Tee, I didn't come here for this shit! I'm leaving." Nina turned her back on him to walk away; she shouldn't have. She was smarter than this but was blinded by a thirst for revenge. The gun in her purse had caused her to forget to use common sense. Under any other circumstance, she would have never followed a strange man into his house, let alone his bedroom. Before she could reach the door Tee grabbed Nina from behind and threw her onto the bed. He laid on top of her and stared at her while she fought to get away. The look in his eyes made Nina freeze, and her worst fears were confirmed. He was about to rape her.

Tee used one hand and the weight of his body to hold Nina down. With his free hand, he forcibly unbuckled her jeans and said, "you gonna give me this pussy or I'ma take it!"

Nina struggled to get free, but his weight was just too much. She felt like she couldn't breathe as he ripped her panties and jammed his finger inside of her. "Get the fuck off me!" She screamed. Nina twisted and turned praying for even the smallest opportunity to free herself from him. "You sick bastard, let me go. Please!" Nina's pleas fell on deaf ears. "Help! Someone, please! Help!"

"Bitch ain't nobody coming here to help you! You in the hood, they hear that shit every day. Ain't nothing but background noise to them. Now shut the fuck up! I'ma enjoy this shit." Tee reached for his zipper and in the process shifted his weight. Nina saw her opportunity. She took both of her legs and kicked him with everything she had. He flew back off of the bed. Nina rolled off of the other side where her clutch and the nine waited. They both stood at the same time, both staring at the other with pure hatred.

"You sick fuck, you tried to fucking rape me!" Nina pulled her pants up and lifted the gun into view. It meant absolutely nothing to Tee.

"Yo, I fuck when I wanna fuck, and if you not gonna give it to me I'm just gonna take that shit. So put that gun down, baby. You ain't gonna do shit with that anyway besides piss me the fuck off. Now lay down and make this easy or not. It don't matter to me either way. I'd rather you enjoy yourself, but I don't give a shit if I gotta be rough. A nut is a nut for me. Now get over here bitch!" Tee started walking towards Nina.

"Fuck you; this is for Samir muthafucka!" Tee stopped mid-step, and his eyes widened. Nina squeezed the trigger three times. He fell to the floor. The sounds of the last minutes of life escaped his lips. His once confident glare turned to one of pleading. He parted his lips to say something, but blood filled his mouth making it impossible to speak. Nina walked up to Tee and stood over him staring him directly into his eyes. While she was sure he hoped for peace, she wanted his last minutes to be filled with nothing but fear.

She bent down and whispered into his ear, "Good thing it's all background noise, huh? At least I don't have to worry about anyone busting up in here to save you. Oh yeah, and I'm taking my man's chain back." Nina roughly slid the necklace from around Tee's neck causing his head to bang on the floor. "Oops, my bad." She stood up and gave him one last shot to the head. Blood splattered, but luckily most of it missed Nina. She dropped the gun and reached for her phone. After three rings, Samir answered.

44

"Nina? Where you at? Why are you not answering me? Nina? What the fuck, say something!" He knew she was on the other end; he could hear her breathing.

"I'm at Tee's apartment. I did it; it's done." Nina pulled the phone away from her face and walked out of Tee's bedroom.

CHAPTER EIGHT

Nina stood outside of Tee's bedroom while time stood still around her. Despite all of her earlier bravado, the fact that she had just killed a man rocked her to her core. It was nothing like what they show on television. It wasn't as easy as all the movies and hood stories had led her to believe. For all of her self-determined good reasons, Nina was no more than a murderer. She begged her feet to move. They did, slowly and zombie-like, but she was thankful they moved at all. The thump of her racing heart rang in Nina's ears as she moved towards the bathroom. She flipped the light switch and stared at herself in the mirror. *Breathe.* Nina turned on the cold water with the plan to splash her face. *You did what you had to do.* Nina felt light-headed. *Your life will never be the same.* She moved away from the sink and braced herself against the wall. *Stand!* She felt herself sinking. The room went black, and Nina whispered "I did this for you Samir. I did this for you, baby."

Samir sat parked in a silver Jaguar outside of Nina's place. The passenger door swung open, and Nina hopped in giving him one of the most sincere smiles Samir had ever seen.

"Hello Miss, you look beautiful." Samir meant it. He wasn't just spitting game like he had with so many others. He leaned over and gave her a kiss.

"Thank you." Nina smiled. "I wasn't sure what to wear because you wouldn't tell me where we're going. I hope it's appropriate."

"You're fine, stop worrying. You worry too much," Samir said with a laugh, "I've been telling you that for months now. So just chill, recline your seat and relax."

"Well excuse me, Mr. Wright." Nina giggled and took Samir's free hand.

"Don't be saying my government like that," Samir stopped his sentence short. "You know what, you can call me whatever you want. Because believe it or not you're my future wife." Nina looked at him curiously. "Don't look at me like that. I'm for real. I can already tell. I'ma take care of you forever Nina. Nina! Nina! Can you hear me? Nina! Answer me dammit! What the fuck did you do?"

Nina snapped awake at the sound of Samir's screaming. She looked down at her hand. She had forgotten she was still holding her phone. Nina lifted the phone back to her ear. "Hello."

"Nina, what the hell did you do? You gotta get outta of there! Now!"

"Samir I had to, I couldn't wait."

"Shit! Okay, What's done is done? Did you get a chance to check for the money?"

"No, not yet, I'm about to. I got your chain, though."

"Nina you gotta get the money!" Samir yelled.

"Look Samir; I got it." Nina shook her head, "I mean I'm gonna get it, but don't fucking yell at me. I'm doing this shit for you!"

"My bad okay. You know I didn't mean to yell at you aight? Just go look for the money then get the fuck outta there. You got any blood on you?"

For the first time, Nina looked at herself. "Just a little on my face."

"Any on your clothes?"

"None on my pants or shoes, but there is some on my shirt."

"Aight, don't wash off in his sink. That shit is traceable. I know it's your skin, but use one of the disinfecting wipes you carry around in your purse. Use a fresh one to wipe down anything you touched. Don't throw them in the trash. Put them back in your purse, and we'll get rid of them when you get here.

Get outta that shirt. Don't throw that away either. Nina, are you listening?"

"Yes, I heard you."

"Good. Now when you leave out, leave calmly and don't rush. Look outta the peephole before leaving and watch your surroundings. Pay attention to who is watching you without being too obvious. Be careful babe.

"Okay, baby I love you. See you in a little bit.

Nina got off the phone and carefully went through Tee's things making sure not to obviously disturb anything. Nina ignored all of the jewelry and electronics. She wanted one thing, cold hard cash. She needed to get B off of Samir's back. Nina changed her approach and headed for Tee's closet. She ignored his bloodied, bullet-ridden body as his blank eyes followed her across the room. Nina came across a shoebox that looked slightly out of place. She opened it to find five thousand dollars in cash. "Dammit, that ain't enough!" Nina couldn't hide her disappointment, but she didn't have time to keep searching. She grabbed a nondescript white t-shirt from Tee's closet and tied it to fit her better. *This will have to do. Too much time went by, I gotta get outta here now.* Nina headed for the bedroom door, but not before grabbing her purse and stuffing it with the money and evidence of what she had done. She reached the door but turned around to look at Tee's body once more. She couldn't resist herself, she walked over to Tee and kicked his body as hard as she could. *That's exactly what you get.* Nina turned to leave again when something caught her eye. She bent down to get a better look and noticed it was the corner of a knot of bills. She grabbed them and walked out. Nina couldn't be sure how much money it was, but it felt close in weight to the marked stack she just found in the closet. *Another five g's.* There was also a business card for the studio she picked him up from. Nina didn't need it, but she threw it in her purse with the knot and did a visual check to make sure she hadn't left anything behind or out of place. Everything looked normal, with the exception of Tee's dead body.

Nina put her ear to the front door to see if she could hear anyone. She didn't. *Good.* She then looked out of the peephole; she saw no one. *It's now or never.* Nina turned the doorknob and cracked the door. *Still no one, good.* She stepped into the hallway. *Almost out of here.* Nina walked with a quick but normal pace down the back steps. At every step she felt like someone, one of Tee's boys or a cop, would grab her and make her pay for shooting him. She wanted to look over her shoulder, but she knew that would make her suspicious to anyone paying attention to her. Nina kept walking until she reached the outside door. *Almost there.* She finally made it to her car. Her clothes were soaked with sweat, and her nerves were shot, but she made it. Just as she had done everything else since she walked out of Tee's apartment, Nina calmly started the car and pulled away.

She drove home in a haze. Although there wasn't any doubt to anything she had done, it all felt surreal. Somehow, in spite of driving without any real focus, Nina pulled into her parking garage. She walked through her lobby and rode the elevator to the penthouse. The gravity of everything fell upon Nina as soon as she reached her floor. Her hand trembled as she desperately tried to unlock her front door. *Come on dammit! I can't take this.* As if the lock heard her pleas, the door opened. Nina ran into the house, fell into Samir's arms and cried.

Samir rocked Nina the best he could in his condition. "Shh, I got you. I'm here, just let it out."

Nina continued to sob. Samir rubbed her back.

"Samir?"

"Yeah."

"I took care of him for you."

"Yeah, I know, and I thank you, but why did you do it by yourself? I thought we were gonna do it together? Samir felt himself getting angry at the thought of anything happening to her. He had to calm himself. "Nina, baby, why did you take it upon yourself to do that? What were you thinking?" Samir took a deep breath. "I'm sorry. I don't mean to yell. I just don't know what..." Samir stopped short. "You had me mad shook, okay? You better never do that shit to me again. You hear me?" Nina nodded.

"You okay to talk about it?"

Again Nina nodded.

"What exactly happened?"

Nina sat up, pulled herself from Samir's arm and laid her head on his shoulder. "Long story short I picked him up from some studio, then we went to his crib to pick up something or at least that's what I thought, cause he had other plans." Nina shifted on Samir's shoulder a bit. "He tried to rape me," she whispered.

"What, are you fucking serious right now?! He raped you?!" Forgetting his injuries, Samir hopped up from where he was sitting. Tears welled in his eyes. "I did this to you. I'm so fucking sorry. I should never have asked you to help. Can you forgive me?"

"Samir, no. You misunderstood. I said he tried, but he didn't." Nina patted the bed beside her. "Sit down." Samir did as she asked. "He tried, but I was able to push him off and get my gun. I shot his bum ass right then and there. Before I pulled the trigger, I let him know that it was all for you. You should have seen his eyes when I said your name. They lit up like Christmas trees; it was priceless. I can't lie, though, I was scared shitless, but it feels good to know I got rid of that piece of shit! Impressed, Samir kissed Nina on her cheek. "Word? Yo, you my fucking G!" He hated to bring the money up again, but he had to. "Did you find the money?"

"I found some, but not what I hoped I would. I was only able to find five thousand in the house, but I did find a knot in his pocket. I'm not totally sure how much it is but seems like its five thousand or better. Oh yeah, I almost forgot..." Nina walked over to her purse and pulled out Samir's chain.

"Yoooo, Nina!"

It made Nina smile to see Samir so happy. "I yanked it right off his neck," she said proudly.

"I know this sound like the most hood shit ever, but you love me don't you?"

"Hell yeah, I do! Jay said it best, all I need in this life of sin."

"Just me and my girlfriend," they finished in unison. They both laughed.

"Pass me the money Nina, with your corny ass. I need to see how close we are to hitting B off." Samir smiled.

Nina laughed. "Hey you said it with me," she said while passing the money and the business card to Samir.

"Oh, this is the studio you picked him up from?"

Nina nodded. "Yup, that's it."

"Yo, we running up in there! If the rest of my money ain't in there, we gonna take whatever money is.

CHAPTER NINE

Nina laid in bed replaying everything that happened yesterday. She was on a high. She fell asleep last night thankful that Tee wouldn't come after Samir ever again. The one downside was that Nina worried that Samir would be unable to give B back his money and his life would be in danger again.

Nina's phone vibrated, but she was in no mood to talk, so she sent it to voicemail. Immediately afterward a text came through. *Ugh.* Nina rolled over and looked at her phone. She didn't recognize the number, but after she read the message she saw it was GeGe. She wanted Nina to call her right away at the strange number. Nina debated with herself whether or not she was in the mood for GeGe's mess. GeGe was sometimes a hater, but she was her girl; really more like a sister. Nina dialed the number that GeGe texted her from.

GeGe answered on the first ring. "Nina, you back in town right?"

"Yeah, I'm just getting back," Nina replied keeping with the lie she previously told to GeGe.

"Thank goodness! You home?"

"Yeah, I'm here. What's up?"

"I'll be by in five minutes. Meet me outside."

"Okay, I'll be out front."

"Good, because I won't be able to call you back. I have to leave my cousin's phone at her house.

Nina was standing in front of her building when GeGe pulled up. As soon as she got into the car, she knew something was very wrong with GeGe.

"What's wrong Ge?"

GeGe began crying hysterically.

"Ge what's wrong? What happened?!"

"Nina, it's so fucked up. The dude I was messing with got murdered. His name was Tee. I can't believe this shit?"

Nina's heart skipped a beat. *Stay calm; she knows nothing.*

"Damn girl, that's fucked up. How are you holding up?"

"Honestly, I don't even know how the hell I'm doing. I never messed with someone that was killed before; it feels strange." GeGe stopped talking and blew her nose. "I just wonder who would want to off this dude. He was sweet and so funny. You know how I feel about somebody that's able to make me laugh."

"Girl that is so crazy. I'm so sorry to hear all of this." Nina had to shift the conversation to see what GeGe knew about the murder, if anything. "You said his name was Tee?"

"Yeah, but a lot of people in the streets called him Tee Byrd. Yo Nina, I'm the one who found him. I had to call the cops."

"Shit, girl!" Nina felt terrible. She saved Samir's life, but she never thought she'd mess GeGe up in the process.

"Yeah, it was messed up. My mind was gone as soon as I saw his body. I don't even know how I held it together to call the cops." GeGe wiped away tears from her eyes. "I was so jacked up I lost my phone and still don't know where it is. Anyway girl, I didn't mean to come over here and dump all this shit on you. I'ma get ready to leave. Thanks so much for letting me vent."

"It's cool girl. I'm always here for you, and you know that."

"Yeah, I know. You mind if I use your phone? I gotta call my mom to check on my baby."

Nina handed her the phone. She turned and looked out of the window to give GeGe as much privacy as she could while sitting next to her in the car. "Okay Ma, thanks." Nina looked towards GeGe in time to see her face twisted in confusion.

"Yo Nina, you knew Tee?"

"Nah, and again I'm so sorry about your man."

"You sure?"

Nina grew uncomfortable with GeGe's line of questioning. "Ge, what's up with the questions? I already told you I didn't."

"Then, why in the hell is his number in your phone? In your recent call log to be more exact. Why are you calling somebody you supposedly don't know?"

"Ge, give me back my phone, and I'll call you later."

GeGe gave Nina back her phone but grabbed her by the arm preventing her from leaving. "Nah Nina, I think you need to answer my question right now. You talking about you didn't know Tee, but clearly you did. Right?"

"Ge, girl you know I love you. I understand you're going through some things right now, but get your hands off me. I said I'd call you later."

"Answer my fucking questions!" GeGe screamed. "Something ain't fucking right, and I want answers now. Were you fucking him too?" GeGe paused waiting for Nina to answer. "I ain't letting this shit go Nina!"

Nina snapped. She pulled out the gun she kept by her side since last night and sat it on her lap. She couldn't bring herself to point it at GeGe, but she wanted her to understand she didn't have time for her bullshit. Nina hardly recognized the voice that came from her. "Like I said, I don't know what the fuck you're talking about and don't ever in your life threaten me."

"Yo Nina, what the fuck is your problem? How the hell are you gon' pull a damn gun on me?" GeGe was genuinely hurt, and it showed in her voice. "I thought we were better than that. This shit is not like you. Lying, carrying guns, let alone pulling it out on me. Nah, this ain't like you at all."

Nina looked away from GeGe's stare. She knew she was wrong for pulling the gun out and felt like shit for doing it. "Ge, my bad about the gun. I'm sorry."

" Sorry? Nah, fuck that Nina, I don't want your apology! I want to know what's going on."

Nina searched for the words to tell GeGe that she's the one who killed Tee. She wrestled with whether or not she should trust her. If so, how would she handle knowing she was responsible for taking his life?

"Nina, answer me!"

"Ge." *Oh shit, what am I about to do?* Nina questioned herself. "Where do I begin? Okay look, Tee was the fuck boy that tried to kill Samir."

"Wait, what the fuck?! Samir got shot? When? Where?" GeGe was shocked.

"It's a lot of shit you don't know, and that's my fault. Yes, he was shot, and Tee did it. After Samir got outta the hospital, I linked with Tee to pump him for information about the shooting and the money he stole."

"Money?" GeGe interrupted.

"Yeah, I wanted the info, so I could set his ass up to get back the money he stole from Samir. All of that changed when he tried to rape me, so I shot him. Although Nina decided to trust GeGe, she wasn't willing to share that she intended to kill Tee the entire time.

"What?! Tee tried to rape you, and he tried to kill Samir? What the fuck?" GeGe sat in shock. "Nina, please don't take this the wrong way because this a lot to take in. Are you sure it was Tee?"

"GeGe I wish it wasn't, just because I would never do anything to hurt you. Yeah, I'm sure, it was definitely Tee. He shot Samir and stole his money. He didn't use a mask or nothing, so Samir was looking him in the face when it all went down. And him trying to rape me, that goes without question how I know it was him. Ge, please know that I would never intentionally hurt you."

GeGe was stunned into silence. She took a moment to gather her thoughts and began to speak. "Nina, let me put your mind at ease. I was just fucking Tee; he wasn't my man. I know I was really upset when I first pulled up, but it's more because I've never seen a dead body outside of a funeral. That and the fact that I thought that my girl was lying to me had me tripping."

"Ge, I'm so fucking sorry for the gun. I can't begin to apologize enough."

"Look I forgive you, but don't ever let that shit happen again." GeGe looked Nina in her eyes. "I'm serious Nina, that will never fly again. I don't care what you are feeling. You pull a gun out again for any reason; it's fucking over."

"Understood. I hear you."

"Good!"

"Ge, since we're straight now, can I ask you something?"

"Sure. Knock yourself out."

"During any of your visits to Tee's did you see where he stashed his money by any chance?"

"Nah. I didn't. I never saw anything like that, but one time when we were at this studio he passed a paper bag to one of his boys. And don't quote me on this, but I swear I overheard him saying that it was all of the money. It didn't mean anything to me at the time, but maybe it had something to do with Samir's money. I don't know."

"If you never saw money before and he popped up with a bag full, I'm going to bet that was Samir's money. Yo, you seen or heard anything else?"

"Look Nina; I love you like a sister and all that. That's why I told you what I did, but I'm not getting in the middle of this shit. I have a child to think about. It's been too many bullets flying and even a dead body."

"Ge, you're already in the middle of it. You know too much. So, I'm asking you to please come upstairs with me and tell Samir everything you know."

"Nina."

"Ge, I swear you'll make it back to your baby and you know I'll never let anything happen to her. Plus, just think of all the good you can do for her with this money we're about to get our hands on." GeGe looked surprised.

"You thought I would ask you for help and not plan on cutting you in on any money we get after Samir get his back? Nah, negative. I wouldn't play you like that."

"Aight girl, I'm in. You just better make sure that no matter what happens, I make it back to my baby."

"Of course," Nina replied with a smile from ear to ear.

Samir was shocked when the two women walked into Nina's place. Last he knew GeGe thought Nina was out of town.

"Samir babe, GeGe knows. I told her everything."

"What the fuck Nina?! Are you trying to get us killed or locked up?!"

"Nah Samir, it ain't like that," GeGe said in defense of herself.

Samir heard none of it. He angrily stared at Nina. He couldn't believe she could be so reckless.

"Listen Samir. If you trust me, trust that GeGe has our backs. She's not telling anyone. In fact, she's down. She said she saw Tee give his man a bag full of money at the studio."

Samir still wasn't one hundred percent sure, but it was too late now. Nina had spilled it all. "Word, you saw this go down?"

Confident that Samir had cooled down a bit GeGe began speaking to him. "Yeah the dude was mad hype about it too, so it must've been a lot of money. Like I told Nina, I'm not sure it was yours, but I guess that it was."

"GeGe, you really down?" Samir asked tentatively.

"Shit yeah," she replied.

"Aight cool. So this is what you're gonna do. *Lord forgive me for involving Nina and her friend in my shit.* Y'all roll up to the studio saying that you paid Tee for some studio time. You know what; take some cash with you just in case they make you pay again. When you get safely inside, pull them things out and get my money."

Both women nodded indicating they understood the plan fully.

Nina grabbed a couple of guns and passed one to GeGe. For a split second, GeGe looked afraid but quickly recovered. She took a deep breath, exhaled and gripped the gun like it belonged in her hands. Nina knew that look. It was the look that meant everything she taught her was coming back. Nina proudly smiled.

"Let's get Samir's money back and how about we take this shit over while we at?!"

CHAPTER TEN

Seven Years Ago/Two Years Into Nina and Samir's Relationship

"Here put these on, so you don't fuck up your eardrums."

Nina looked at the clunky hearing protectors with mild disgust. "C'mon Samir, these things gon' mess up my hair," Nina said mockingly. "You know you're paying to get my hair done just because you think I'ma lose my hearing? Right?"

"Don't I pay for everything anyway? Just put on these ugly ass goggles and headphones, with your pretty ass."

"Aight, you win," Nina said with a laugh.

"Do you remember what I taught you when we practiced shooting on the rooftop?

Nina nodded.

"Okay, get ready for the kickback. You gotta be prepared for it, so it won't catch you off guard. Always keep your eye on the target and be confident in your shot. Never second guess yourself. You ready?"

Nina straightened her posture and raised the gun. "Yeah."

"Aight. Shoot!"

Samir leaned forward to get a better look at the target. "Perfect shot babe."

Nina curtsied and laughed. "Why thank you, kind sir," she said in her best fake southern belle accent.

"Seriously, I created a fucking monster, and I'm happy as hell! I want you always to be able to take care of yourself and anyone else. It's getting wild out here, you know?" Samir looked at Nina solemnly. "You never know when I might need you one day. You just never know.

"What do you mean you may need me one day? One day to do what?" Nina put her gun down and walked closer to Samir.

"I'm just saying you down for whatever right? Cause I ain't got time for no scared chic. My life is crazy. Can you handle that?"

Nina grabbed Samir's hand and looked him squarely in his eyes. "I told you when I met you I'm down for whatever as long as you got my back."

"Word?!"

Samir leaned in and kissed Nina. Her hand glided down his stomach to his crotch. Samir felt the familiar push against his jeans. He grabbed Nina and propped her against the shooting range table continuing to kiss her all over. Nina's breath got caught in her throat when he pushed her panties aside and slipped his finger inside of her. "I will never leave you," Nina moaned.

"I know. Remember that. You hear me?" Samir softly replied.

"Nina, you ready?" GeGe said loudly, snapping Nina back into reality. GeGe looked stunning, as did Nina. There was no way that any man would be able to resist either of them the way they looked. Getting into the studio wouldn't be a problem for them at all.

"Ge, I'm definitely ready. Ever since Tee tried to kill Samir, I'm on one. I don't care who I gotta go through; I'm getting Samir that money so he can pay B back." Nina bit her lip to get control of herself. "If we don't get B's money, he's gonna kill everybody down with Samir. For all of our sakes Ge, I can't let that happen."

"Me the fuck either, so let's get it! We gonna get B his money and me some real coins so I can finally spoil my daughter."

"She deserves it." Nina inhaled deeply, "Ge..." she opened her mouth to continue, but the words just wouldn't come. She reached over and patted GeGe's shoulder. GeGe fully understood her without words and nodded. "You're welcome."

The women exited the car. Nina pulled one of the two guns out of her purse. "Let's leave this one here, just in case something goes down," she said popping the trunk and placing the nine inside.

They gave each other one last look of confidence and then headed for the studio. Nina made the decision to let GeGe lead the way since there was more of a chance she might know one of the dudes posted in there. After the fifth knock, a large bouncer looking guy opened the door with a snarl.

"What the fuck you bitches want?" He said with an attitude.

"Who the fuck are you talking to fat boy? First off, I ain't no damn bitch! Second off, I paid mad money for a session, so you need to move your big ass and let us in." GeGe put her hand on her chin like she had a thought. "Matter of fact, give me back my fucking money! We ain't come here to be disrespected. I'ma go drop my stack somewhere else."

Nina was impressed with GeGe. She was good as hell. If she didn't know any better, she would have sworn that GeGe really paid for a session.

"My bad ma. We get a lot of groupie bitches that be coming up here causing trouble, trying to trap niggas before they blow up. Anyway, what's your name?"

"Kiana."

My girl is on it, Nina thought.

The guy pulled out his iPhone and scrolled through a few things. "Kiana, I don't see no Kiana on the schedule? When did you pay, better yet who did you pay? This here is my studio, and I don't see nothin about a Kiana or Kiana's payment."

"We paid Tee the other day. He told me to come in today, so I know my name is on that schedule. Look again."

"Damn girl, you ain't hear?"

"Hear what? You better not be trying to tell me his ass ran off with my money?"

"Nah, Tee's dead. Somebody ran up on him in his crib and popped his ass."

"Oh shit, for real?" This was the first time Nina spoke.

"Yeah man, it's true. He must have pissed the wrong person off."

"That's fucked up," GeGe began, "and I'm sorry about your man, but check it. I don't mean to be heartless, but I paid my money for this time, and I really need to lay my vocals. I'm trying to submit a demo and time is limited."

"I understand, business is business."

Both GeGe and Nina nodded.

"This right here is my business; I can't just be letting you come up in here, and I ain't get no money from you."

"But..." GeGe began.

"Okay look, you said you paid Tee, but you can't prove you did and I can't prove you didn't. So, if you ready to get to it, I'll let you pay half price for half the session time. That's the best I can do."

"Damn, I gotta pay again," GeGe said putting on her best disappointed voice. "What you think I should do girl?" she said looking at Nina.

"Just pay it. We gonna be in and out anyway. Plus, he is doing us a favor since Tee didn't give him the money," Nina said pretending to be the reasonable one.

"Aight, I guess that's true," GeGe said reaching into her purse for the money."

With his money in hand, the guy stepped aside to let GeGe and Nina in. "Pleasure doing business with you, the name is Black. Follow me; I'll show you to your booth."

The ladies fell in line behind Black making sure to observe their surroundings. Nina noticed there was only one accessible exit, which was the door they just walked through. The smell of weed was heavy in the air, and Effen and Henny bottles were lying around everywhere. Nina hoped that meant anyone in the studio was in no condition to try and stop what was about to go down.

"Here we are. This is the studio Tee usually books." Black said opening the door.

GeGe stepped into the recording booth. *Her ass is definitely fully committed*, Nina thought.

"You made arrangements with Tee for a particular producer or was Tee going to work on your tracks?" Black asked GeGe.

"Nah, we hadn't made it that far yet, we were going to discuss all of that today," Nina gave GeGe a look that said distract him, keep him occupied for a minute. "You got an office? We can go there and discuss all of the B I. Hell, if

61

everything works out I could be booking all kinds of studio time." GeGe turned to Nina, "Draya, I'll be back. I'ma go into Black's office to handle some business real quick."

"Cool," Nina responded.

"Yo, Draya make yourself at home. This shouldn't take too long."

Nina got to work as soon as Black and GeGe left the room. She felt around in the couch, but nothing was there. Nina knew this was a long shot, but had too much to lose not to check everywhere for the money. *Where could it be?* She ran up to the cabinet across the room and opened the double doors. The shelves were lined with a plethora of liquors. She pulled out the drawers one by one; each was filled with a different type of drug. *Fucking druggies*, she thought in disgust. The last drawer was about twice the size of the others with a lock. *It's gotta be in here*, she reasoned. Nina took her chances and tugged on the drawer. To her surprise, it wasn't locked. *Jackpot!* Nina was let down when she discovered the last drawer was filled with blunts and empty baggies. She was starting to feel like she was wasting her time. *Shit!* She closed the drawer with a little more force than she intended and noticed the back panel of the cabinet had shifted. Nina excitedly reached back into the cabinet to completely pull back the panel when someone walked into the room.

"Yo ma. What the fuck you doing?" a voice said from behind her.

Nina turned to face the voice, "I'm here with my girl that's about to lay down some vocals. She stepped out the room to handle something with Black."

"Well, it looks like you all up in some business that's not your's. So I'ma ask again. What the fuck are you doing?"

"Look brotha; it's not like that. Black told me to make myself comfortable. I was about to get a glass of something, but you came before I could make up my mind. That's all, my man. Now if you don't mind, I'd like to get back to getting my drink."

"Oh aight, cool. I got you ma. What you want dark or light? We got it all, but I guess you've already seen that."

"Yeah I did," Nina giggled seductively. "I'll take light. What's your name anyway?"

"Ladies first. What's your's?"

"Draya."

"I'm James. Nice to meet you ma. Now for that drink." Nina stepped to the side as James headed towards the cabinet. "You care which brand, Ms. Draya?" James asked playfully.

"Nah, not really. Just none of that cheap stuff."

"Yeah, I feel you." James grabbed a glass and poured a shot for Nina. "Here you go ma."

"Thanks." Nina had no intentions of drinking; she needed to be on point. As soon as he turned towards the cabinet, she poured the shot on the floor behind her.

"Damn, this piece of shit cabinet is falling apart."

Nina knew that meant the loose panel had fallen and tried to peek over his shoulder to get a better look. *Fuck!* James was too quick. Nina's gut told her that Samir's money or at least someone's money was stashed behind that panel in the cabinet. "You aight?"

"Yeah I'm cool, this raggedy ass cabinet getting on my nerves."

"Maybe it's too full. Too much weed and shit," Nina said playfully. "Maybe even some money, you look like you balling," she laughed. Nina waited to read James' reaction. He flinched slightly, almost unnoticeably. *I knew it!*

"Girl, what the hell you talkin 'bout? Ain't no bread in here."

"I was just messing with you and shit." Nina tried to erase any suspicion. "I know ain't no money in there."

"Boy, you in here running your mouth?" Black asked as he walked into the room.

"Nah, Draya in here making jokes," James responded nervously.

"Good, make sure you not. Close them lips about money in my spot unless you on the phone collecting that shit from people that owe me."

James walked out of the room embarrassed.

Black sat down next to the mixing board. "So Kiana, you ready to do this? You ain't got long, remember?"

"Yeah, sure just let me use the bathroom real quick. It's down here right? GeGe said pointing down the hallway.

"The second door." Black was clearly annoyed. "I might as well get comfortable on this couch. Women can't ever come straight back from the bathroom."

"Nah, I'll be right back. You good, Draya?"

"Yeah, I'm good. I don't have to go." Nina subtly nodded her head in the direction of the cabinet. GeGe winked and walked out of the room.

GeGe was gone for a few minutes before James walked back in. "Yo Black, you ain't gonna believe the shit I just heard..."

Before he could finish his sentence, GeGe came around the corner with her gun drawn and stuck it against the back of James' head. "No, you ain't gonna believe this. Get yo ass over there and sit on the couch!"

That's all Nina needed to set it off. She reached for her gun, but Black grabbed her wrist before she could get it out her bag.

Without warning, GeGe shot him in his hand. "Wrong move, bitch!"

Black let out a scream. "Fuck you, you crazy bitch! When I get my hands on you I'ma..."

GeGe interrupted him with a laugh. "Don't you mean hand, you fat bastard?! Now, no more funny business. Next time you get any bright ideas, I won't be aiming for your hands. Understood?"

Neither James nor Black answered, but that didn't stop GeGe from responding, "Good."

With gun in hand, Nina joined GeGe on the other side of the room.

"What the fuck you bitches want?"

"Shut your ass up," Nina responded. "Fuck you and your dumbass question. Don't ask another one or your hand will be the least of your worries." Nina turned to GeGe. "The back panel on that cabinet over there is loose. I think Samir's money is hidden behind it."

"Who the fuck is Samir?" Black yelled.

Nina couldn't help but notice the shift in James at the mention of Samir's name. That was all the confirmation she needed to know James was in on it. "Didn't I tell your ass to shut the fuck up?" Nina screamed. "Doesn't matter if you know who Samir is or not, his money is here and we are taking it back!"

Nina looked at the confusion on Black's face. "You know Black I feel bad you got caught up in all of this shit, but you really should watch the company you keep. Tee robbed Samir and left him for dead." Nina turned her attention to James. "That's right, he survived. Now back to the money. I know Tee stashed it in here and as you might've already noticed I figured out exactly where it is. So, if you gentlemen don't mind, me and my homegirl are taking back what belongs to him."

"And whatever else that's in there that I want," GeGe added.

"You and Tee bought this shit to my doorstep, James?"

"Yo Black, I ain't do shit, it was all Tee. He said..."

"Shut your lying ass up James! You keep talking and I'ma button your fucking lips with a bullet!" Nina wasn't bluffing.

"I bet you bitches the one who murked Tee, ain't you?" James growled through gritted teeth.

"You really testing my patience. One more comment or question, hell you breathe too hard in my direction and I'ma blow the back of your head off," Nina said in a serious tone.

The noise in the far corner drew her attention. GeGe was in the cabinet pulling on the back panel. When it finally gave way money flowed from the opening. GeGe's mouth fell open. Neither one of them expected there to be much more than Samir's money stashed, but this looked like Tee and James had been hitting people for a while.

Still careful not to reveal either one of their real names, Nina looked at GeGe and said, "Yo Kiana, dump that trash can and use that bag to load the money."

James couldn't stand the idea of them taking all of the money. "Yo, take the money Tee stole from Samir and get the fuck out! The rest of that ain't your's."

Nina pointed her gun at James' head.

"Fuck that, you said, you came for Samir's money! There's his money, so take it and get the fuck out!"

Nina smirked at his misguided confidence. "Yeah well James, I lied. Fuck you and your whole team. Samir's taking over, and we can't have you out here plotting the get back, now can we? Nina was about to shoot but had second thoughts. She trusted GeGe, but she still wanted an insurance policy. Instead of shooting James herself, she gave GeGe the go ahead. GeGe lifted her gun and shot James once in the head. His lifeless body slumped over onto the couch.

"Just leave..." Black began.

"You still running your mouth. You know James didn't know when to shut-up. You niggas never learn." Nina pointed her gun at Black and shot him right between the eyes. He fell onto James. Nina walked over to the couch and shot them both two more times in the head to make sure they were dead. She couldn't take the chance they would pull through like Samir had. "Ge, grab the bag and let's go!"

With the money in hand, Nina and GeGe walked out of the studio like nothing happened. Back in the safety of the car, Nina released the tension she felt the entire time she was in the studio with a long sigh. Without looking at her, Nina asked GeGe, "Are you down with everything that's about to go down?"

GeGe sat up and looked at Nina. "I don't know what's gonna happen from this point, but what I do know is that I love you like a sister and I'm riding 'til the muthafuckin wheels fall off!"

CHAPTER ELEVEN

Nina and GeGe walked through the front door of her condo silently. The gravity of the night's earlier events weighed upon them. They were momentarily mentally drained. Deep down Nina knew what they had done was wrong, but with every thought of the money in the bag, the regret was pushed further and further away from her mind. The reality of the situation was Samir's ability to pay B back was Nina's only concern. She wasn't one hundred percent sure what GeGe's mindset was, but the one thing she did know was whatever GeGe was thinking, the money would make it better. Nina dropped the suitcase that GeGe transferred the money into beside the front the door.

"Ge, for real, we came up," she softly said with a smile.

"Hell yeah! I always wanted to send my baby to a private school in the city. Now for the first time ever I can see it happening."

The two women stared at each other with knowing smiles for what seemed like forever and didn't break until they heard Samir come up behind them.

"Yo where the hell you been, what took you so damn long?" Samir walked up and hugged Nina. He would never admit it to either of them, but he was on the verge of tears when they were taking too long. For days now, he questioned if he had done the right thing by asking Nina for her help. Now, he had to worry about GeGe too. "Next time I'm going with y'all. I don't care if I'm healed or not. Yo, waiting for y'all to get back was stressing me the fuck out." Samir kissed Nina on the forehead and winked at GeGe. In the past twenty-four hours, he'd spent more time with GeGe than he'd ever had. In that short amount of time, he had bonded with her. He was glad she had Nina's back when he was unable to be there.

"Babe chill, you're no good to anyone if you're not one hundred. Me and Ge took care of it all, and we got it until you're ready. Aight?"

"Cool," Samir begrudgingly agreed.

"Oh, and by the way, I'm almost positive the whole stick-up murder plan was Tee's idea. I really don't think B had nothing to do with it."

Nina sparked Samir's interest. He looked back and forth between Nina and GeGe. "What make you say that?"

"This dude named James, who was at the studio, all but admitted it. At least his name was James until he tried to be a tough guy and he caught one of them bullets" Nina said with a laugh.

GeGe's mouth dropped. "Nina that ain't funny! We killed that nigga."

"Ge we can't bring that muthafucka back! I don't mean to make light of the situation, but it was funny when his face changed after you shot him. That tough guy shit went right out the door."

"Yeah it did, right?" GeGe confirmed.

"I think he thought we weren't gonna do nothing. Well, we surprised his ass."

"Girl you a trip."

Nina laughed again, and this time GeGe joined in.

"Aight. Enough of the dumb shit with y'all silly asses." Although Samir's words were serious, his tone was far less harsh. "What about the bread Nina?" He asked with hopeful anticipation. "Please tell me you got the cash. I really don't wanna go to war with B; at least not right now."

"Babe, we got your money and then some. We got the $50,000 plus $40,000 more!"

"Word? That's what the fuck I'm talking 'bout!" Samir pulled Nina close. "Give me a kiss girl."

"They thought they were just gonna give up the money they stole from you, but we weren't having that. We were like, nah, we taking all that." Nina winked, and GeGe reciprocated with a nod. "I think they been sticking people for a minute, 'cause there's no way all that money came from studio sessions. Trust me; no one is going to that studio like that. If you saw it, you would definitely agree."

Samir took Nina's words into serious consideration. "That might be something we can work with. Check this out, though. I spoke to B while y'all were gone and he said to meet him around the way tonight to drop that off. I told him I ain't have no problem giving him his money tonight, but I would have to send somebody 'cause I'm still healing and shit." Samir paused to choose his next words carefully. "So, since I can't make it and I don't trust nobody else out here, you gotta go for me," he quickly continued before Nina or GeGe had the chance to respond. "But I'ma be in the car waiting just in case this nigga tries some slick shit. Plus, I can't stay back here stressing while I wait for you to let me know wassup."

"Aight cool babe, I'm ready."

Samir hadn't expected Nina's answer to come so quickly. He was both surprised and thankful. He turned to GeGe for her response. "What about you GeGe? You cool with that?" "Just let me call my mom real quick and make sure she can watch my baby girl for a little longer. I'll tell her I'm going out of town with Nina on business and she'll be okay with it. Then I'll be ready no questions asked."

Again Samir was shocked. He'd been in the game for years before and never had a team as loyal and down as these two. *Damn, I'm lucky as hell to have Nina and grateful that GeGe's her homegirl.* He smiled. "Okay, so this is what you gonna do. I don't want B laying eyes on you, but since you doing the handoff, you gonna need to disguise yourself without being too obvious. Get some wigs, not none of those cheap ass Flatbush Avenue Chinese store shits in a wild ass color that looks all fake either. You gotta get the ones that look like real hair. It just gotta be a different color than your real hair and has to look like something you would wear every day. You gotta get makeup and sunglasses too. Same rules apply. They have to make you look different but normal. If B suspects for one second that you're trying to hide something or disguise yourself all hell will break loose! I don't want him or no one else recognizing you on the street after this drop." Samir felt like shit for sending Nina and

GeGe into the lion's den, but right now he had no other choice. "Aight, so you got two hours to get the stuff and meet me back here."

"No problem, see you in a few." Nina and GeGe replied as they headed towards the door.

"Yo Nina!"

"Yes, Samir," Nina said with mock irritation.

"I said it before and I'ma say again, you my fucking rider. You know that?"

"Damn right!" The door softly closed behind the two ladies as they left.

CHAPTER TWELVE

Nina and GeGe returned with several wigs in a little less than an hour. "Nina do you think any of these are gonna work cause this is different than last time. This time we can't just take care of the witnesses. B and his boys will still be moving around Brooklyn."

"Yeah, I think so. We should be good. We just need to look different than we usually do, so we can walk around afterward without any issues."

"You right. Hand me that bag. I wanna see which wig looks better." GeGe stuck her hand out to Nina. "Nina hand me the bag please."

Nina sat on the bed staring out into space, oblivious to GeGe's question. Her mind began to wander to another time as GeGe's voice faded.

"I'm coming, chill!" Nina yelled as she walked to her front door. Pat buzzed her letting her know Samir headed upstairs and now here he was ringing her doorbell like a madman. "Damn Samir, why the hell are you ringing my bell like you're..." Nina stopped mid sentence when she noticed how hard he was breathing. "Baby, what's wrong?"

Samir quickly walked past Nina and closed the door behind him. "You gotta hide this for me." Samir reached into the back of his waistband and handed Nina his .45.

Nina took the gun and just stared at it.

"Nina! Hurry up and stash it!"

Without another thought, she took the gun and ran into her room. *Think Nina!* She took the gun over to her panty drawer and hid it underneath all of her lingerie. *This gonna have to do for now.* With very little confidence in her mediocre choice of hiding place, she ran back to Samir. "Now tell me what the hell is going on!"

Samir held up his finger and took a moment to catch his breath.

"Samir!"

"Remember the dudes I had beef with?

Nina shook her head no.

"Yes, you do. You know the dudes?! The ones that talked mad shit every time they came to one of the parties I promoted. I pointed them out to you at the last party."

"Yeah, yeah, I remember now. So what happened?"

"Well, a little while back we got into it. One of them niggas tried to snuff me and then ran. That punk muthafucka missed, but I been looking for that nigga ever since. So, this morning I got word they were out on Broadway. Yo Nina, I had to go to Bushwick and get at least one of them. I rolled up on them and shouted, "pussies," begging for one of them to move! When they just stood there, it pissed me the fuck off. Nina I swear, I ain't mean to lose it, but I pulled out my four pound and started letting off. They scattered like roaches! A few of them hopped into a car and sped off. At that point, I was all in and started chasing them. After a few quick turns, they lost me. I was fucking pissed, so I kept looking for them. When I finally tracked them down, they were talking to the cops. The snitches pointed me out as soon as they saw me. I busted a U-turn, but I could see in the rearview that the cops weren't far behind. After a good minute, I lost them and then drove straight home to switch v's. I'm not sure if they were still following me or what." Samir paced the floor. "Shit! Nina, I fucked up! If they were still behind me, that means I brought them straight to your spot."

The buzz of Nina's intercom startled them both.

"Yes. Damn! Good looking Pat, thanks for letting me know." Nina hung up the intercom phone. Her face was like stone.

"Samir, that was Pat. The cops are on their way up here!"

"Fuck!"

As expected the doorbell rang.

"Nina, answer the door, and I'm not here," Samir whispered before heading into Nina's room to hide.

Once she was sure Samir had enough room to disappear into the room, Nina gathered herself and answered the door. "Hello, officers. Is there anything I can do for you?"

"Yes ma'am, there is," the shorter of the two officers began. "I'm Detective Parker, and this is my partner Detective Greene. Earlier today, there was a shooting, and it seems that a person fitting the suspect's description was thought to be seen coming into this building and heading up to your floor."

"Oh my goodness! No, no one's been here. It's just me and my wine in here." Nina prayed that outwardly she appeared nonchalant as opposed to her inward panic. "There's access to the roof and the back staircase from my floor. Maybe whoever it was used either of those routes to get away."

"Well, do you mind if we come in and look around? We just want to make sure you're safe."

"Actually, I do mind officers. I don't mean to be difficult, but my father's an attorney, and he would be furious with me if he knew I ever let an officer in my home without a search warrant," Nina smiled sweetly hoping that her lie would work. She learned in the past that just the mention of a lawyer often swayed the conversions with cops. "I thank you for your concern, but I assure you I'm safe."

"Okay understandable, but please let us know if you do see something or hear anything. Here's my card."

"Oh thank you. I most definitely will." Nina replied. "This is a nice building, and I wanna make sure it stays that way. By the way, what exactly would this fellow look like? You know, just in case I do see him?" Nina knew she was laying it on a little thick, but she had to ensure she didn't draw any suspicion.

"He's an African-American male, mid to late twenties, between six feet to six feet two inches tall and about one hundred and ninety pounds. And ma'am, he's considered to be armed and dangerous. So, call us if you see him and please don't try anything heroic."

"Thanks again for checking on me. Enjoy your night. Oh, and I hope you find that guy. He sounds dangerous." Nina closed the door with a sigh of relief and headed to her room to pull Samir out of hiding.

"You can come out. We're good."

"They're gone?" Samir had no plans of coming out of hiding until he was sure the cops were gone. He was a tough guy, but he had no intentions of being locked up in the 84th Precinct. He couldn't stand those stale ass cheese sandwiches and he for damn sure wasn't taking the chance of actually going to prison.

"Yeah baby, they're gone. I think I threw them off. Plus, the description they have is mad vague. It could be anyone. I think if you lay low for a bit and stay away from those guys, it should pass. You know what? Hold on a second."

Nina walked out to the intercom and picked up the phone. "Hello Pat, have the officers left the building yet? Okay, good." She headed back into the room to give Samir the news. "Pat said the officers not only left the building, but they pulled off already." She didn't expect cheers of joy, but at least she thought Samir would be happy with the news. He wasn't though; his face was still blank. "You okay?"

"Yeah, yeah. I'm good." Samir finally smiled. "Thanks, babe. You my rider. You just keep holding me down like you just did and we gon' be aight." Samir pulled on her hand gently. "Come over here and give me a kiss. Samir gently kissed Nina. "I love you."

"So, what you think? You think this gonna work?" GeGe ran her fingers through the short black wig. "Soooo..." GeGe turned from the mirror when Nina didn't answer her. "Your ass ain't even paying attention, huh? Nina!"

Hearing her name brought Nina back to the present. "What?!" Nina snapped.

"Don't what me chic," GeGe said with a laugh. "I've been asking for your opinion on which wig to wear for like ten minutes and you sitting over there in la la land."

"Oh my bad, I was thinking about something." Nina nodded her head to shake away the memory as it quickly once again replayed in her mind. "Yeah, I like that one. That cropped pixie looks really good on you, Ge. It's natural looking too. If I ain't know you, I would think it was your real hair. Once you add the makeup and big shades, nobody gonna be able to recognize you. Not now or later."

"Good, good. Aight! Which one are you wearing?"

"I'm wearing this one; da bad gyal one mon," Nina said in a bad Jamaican accent. She laughed at her own silliness. "The locks look mad real. Right?"

"Damn, they sure do," GeGe replied impressed. "I thought it looked good in the store, but up close the locks look real as hell."

Nina threw the wig on and started doing the Dutty Whine. GeGe couldn't contain herself, she burst out laughing hysterically and fell back on the bed at the sight of Nina trying to do the dance.

"What are you laughing at?" Nina asked mockingly.

"You, with your stupid butt. You're hilarious."

"You know me, always trying to make light of a bad situation." Nina's smile slowly faded as she sat down on the bed and took off her wig. "Ge, I talk a good one and I'm seriously down for whatever, especially when it comes to Samir, but I'm scared yo. Twice already, I've done things I shouldn't have and gotten away with it. I mean earlier we got away scot-free. You know what I mean? I'm leaving bodies all around like I'm a serial killer or something. I'm not a killer. I don't even know how I did it. I ain't know killing somebody was even inside me. I'm just thankful ain't nobody looking for me." Nina bit her bottom lip before continuing. "Nina, B ain't like these other dudes. He's a gangsta for real. If anything goes wrong tonight or if he thinks something's up for any reason, he won't hesitate to put a bullet in us." Nina exhaled deeply and walked over to her bedroom window. "What if something goes wrong this time Ge? What if one of us gets hurt? What if…"

GeGe placed a finger across Nina's lips. "Nina, stop that. It's gonna be okay. Don't put that negative energy out there." GeGe removed her finger from Nina's mouth. "We got the ability to speak things into existence, and we don't need that negative shit right now. We gotta keep our heads, aight?"

"I know what you're saying, but…" Again Nina paused. She turned her head finding it difficult to face GeGe.

GeGe continued to speak. "I'm scared too, but we in too deep now to quit. I got plans for the money we 'bout to get. I wanna build a better life for my daughter. I wanna leave my mom's house and know I'm stable enough to never have to move back in with her. Those dreams are what's driving me through all this crazy shit. GeGe grabbed Nina's hands. "Focus on the positive." She smiled sweetly at Nina and asked, "So, what you wanna do with your money?"

"Of course I want to do the typical things like treating myself to some nice things and putting some away for a rainy day, but what I really wanna do is take the LSAT. Nina looked at GeGe expecting an expression of ridicule. Instead, she looked encouraging. Nina continued. "I always wanted to be a lawyer for as long as I can remember, but managing up and coming artists came easy. Plus on top of everything, it was mad fun." She smiled remembering many of the good times. "My family never understood why I didn't try harder to become a lawyer. It just wasn't me at the time. Ge, I think it's finally time, though. I think I'm ready to go to law school. All I need is the money to start doing all the things I've always wanted to do."

GeGe stuck her hand out for a dap. "See, that's what I'm talkin about! Keep your head in the game and do what we gotta do and you'll get to take that LSAT. Now, get dressed and let's go." Before walking away to get her outfit, GeGe turned to Nina. "We gon' be straight. I promise."

"You're right Ge. I'm gonna think positive even though we doing some negative shit." They look at each other and burst out laughing. "I told you, I'm always trying to make light of any situation," Nina said laughing.

"You're a fucking clown, with your silly ass."

With the mood lightened and the mission ahead, Nina and GeGe got dressed in outfits that were nothing similar to anything they would ever wear and packed B's money in the briefcase.

"Y'all ready?" Samir called from the den.

The two women stepped into the den looking nothing like themselves. "What you think?" Nina asked.

Samir was genuinely surprised with how they looked. "Oh shit, I hardly recognize you, and I know you!"

"Good," they said in unison.

"You got the briefcase right?"

Nina nodded yes.

"All the money there?"

"Yeah, it's all here," Nina answered.

All three of them stood silent for a minute until Samir clapped his hands softly and said, "Aight, let's go!"

As the door clicked behind them, the familiar uneasy feeling came over Nina. "Damn, I hate this feeling. I feel like it's trying to tell me something."

GeGe sighed. "Nina we just had this talk. Don't do this shit again."

Slightly embarrassed Nina looked away. "I know, I know but.." Nina's volume dropped to almost a whisper, "but a black cat walked by me earlier today."

GeGe and Samir looked at Nina, then at each other and started laughing as they all stepped into the elevator.

"Come on now. It's not funny. Y'all think I'm joking, but you know I'm not. I take this type of stuff mad serious." Just as Nina finished talking the elevator doors open and they all stepped out into the lobby. Nina and GeGe went left while Samir went right. Nina's mouth fell open. "Samir! I just told you about the cat, and now you're gonna split the pole! Come on now," Nina whined. "This ain't funny; I'm serious. I feel like all of this is a sign."

"Girl, sign your ass over here and let's go!" GeGe giggled.

"How about this," Samir began, "if it makes you feel better I'll go back around the pole, but there ain't nothing I can do about that black ass cat."

Nina knew Samir was mocking her, but she couldn't take any chances. "Please?"

Samir walked back around the pole and joined the ladies on the left side of it. "Are we cool now?" Nina nodded yes. "Now that that's outta the way let's get back to business. This is gonna be real fast. We in and we out. Aight?"

"Aight," they replied and headed for the parking garage to the car.

Nina and GeGe sat in the front seat while Samir sat in the back checking and rechecking each of their guns. When he was satisfied all of the guns were good, Samir texted B to let him know 'Angel and Steph', his "cousins" would meet him to drop off the money, and they were on their way to him.

The car was quiet, too quiet for Nina's comfort. Despite GeGe and Samir's reassurances, Nina's nerves were shot, and she needed to shake them off. Nina turned on Anita Baker's greatest hits. The angelic melodic sound of her voice was exactly what Nina needed. Anita almost made Nina forget where she was going, at least until they pulled up about a block away from the projects where they were meeting B.

"Stop right here," Samir said from the back seat. "I wanna make sure you can't see me, so nobody can spot a nigga and two bitches rolling up. We don't want nothing to go wrong at the drop-off." Before Samir hid he checked the guns one more time and handed them to Nina and GeGe. "Go on and put these in your purse. Oh, and take the safeties off. Hopefully, you ain't gonna need them, but with B you never know." He tried not to look worried, he wanted to instill confidence in the ladies, but his shooting was still fresh on his mind.

Nina shifted the car into drive.

"Wait!" Samir couldn't send Nina into possible battle without showing her how much he appreciated her. He reached around the headrest and pulled her face towards him awkwardly and kissed her right beside her lips. "I love you," he whispered as he laid his forehead on her cheek. Samir wasn't usually the sentimental type, but Nina made him feel things he hadn't before, and he had no shame in showing how much he loved her in front of GeGe. "Be careful, aight?!" He squeezed GeGe's shoulder to let her know that he hadn't forgotten her and slid back into hiding.

Again Nina shifted the car into drive and drove towards B's. Once in front of his building, Nina and GeGe stepped out of the car and headed inside. "You good?" Nina asked without looking at GeGe.

"Hell yeah, let's get it!" GeGe kissed her thumb for good luck. It was a shared habit with her daughter that developed after GeGe told her thumbs were for kissing not sucking. It didn't make much sense, but ever since they kissed their thumbs as a silent way of saying I love you. *Everything's gonna go as planned.*

With one last look of solidarity between the two, Nina opened the door, and they headed up to B's floor.

"Ge, wait right here at the end of the hall. If shit goes bad or if I don't come back out in about 15 minutes you come get me aight. Come blasting if you have to!"

"I got you, without fucking hesitation, I got you!" GeGe said. Her gaze followed Nina as she moved towards B's door and knocked.

To Nina's surprise, a naked woman answered the door. *So not what I expected.* "I'm looking for B," she said in her most no-time-for-the-bullshit tone.

"Who are you?" the naked woman stared at Nina icily.

"Tell him Steph is here. He'll know what it's for."

"Wait right here."

The door closed in Nina's face. A few minutes later it opened again. "You got the money?"

"Yup, that's why I'm here."

The naked woman motioned her head towards the back room. "He's in the back."

Nina walked in the direction that she pointed and knocked on the door.

"Yo, come in," boomed a deep vibrating voice from the other side of the door.

"I got your money." Nina expected an immediate response or at least an indication that B heard her. She got none. He sat for a few moments staring at her until she became uncomfortable. She couldn't read him. He wore no emotions. When he finally broke the silence, it wasn't to ask for his money; it was to ask for her purse. *Oh shit!*

"Slide your bag over here and don't try no funny shit."

"Huh?"

"I'm only gonna ask you one more time, and you're lucky I'm even doing that. Now slide the fucking purse across the desk!"

How the fuck did he know? Nina slid her bag to B as he had instructed.

"Now you can sit. And your girl that was posted up in the hallway is in the other room. If everything goes the way it

79

should, and all my money is accounted for, both of y'all will get your guns when it's time for you to leave."

"Look I just had to protect myself..." Nina said as she tried to smooth things over.

"None of that matters, I don't give a shit 'cause you wouldn't even gotten a shot off." There was no need for him to elaborate, his message was clear. "Back to the matter at hand, if one dollar of my money is missing, it's you and your homegirl's ass."

A chill ran down Nina's spine, and she hoped that B couldn't hear her heart racing. "It's all there." Her voice was much more confident than she was as she handed over the briefcase. She prayed for her sake that Samir had counted the money correctly. He had counted and recounted, each time arriving at the correct amount. She knew this, but as she sat in front of B uncertainty filled her. B stood from his desk walked to a table in the corner with a money counter. B began placing stacks of money into the money counter. After the machine had counted one stack, he placed another one into the slot. Nina's eyes followed his every move, traveling back and forth between him, the money and the money counter. When the last of the money was accounted for, B calmly and silently walked back to his desk. Again, he was silent. He folded his arms across his chest and stared pointedly at Nina.

Nina began preparing for the worst and started to pray silently. *Father, please forgive me. I know I was wrong for all that I've done.* Her heart hurt more for GeGe's little girl than anyone else because she knew GeGe would meet her fate as well. *I'm sorry.*

"It seems that Samir is a man of his word. He paid what he owed, and I'm going to assume the extra ten thousand is for my troubles."

Thank God. Nina stood to leave. "Where's Angel?" B said nothing. "I need to get my purse and gun back, and her's too."

"Nah, not yet. The ladies will escort you and Angel out. Y'all will both get your guns back then." The way he said Angel let Nina know he wasn't buying their aliases. B tilted his head slightly to the side and tapped his finger above his upper lip as if he were thinking. "Let me ask you something, you looking for a job?"

Nah, I'm good."

He squinted somewhat but remained quiet. Nina could tell he wasn't used to hearing the word no. When he finally spoke, it was in a measured tone as an attempt to control his anger at the perceived disrespect. "That wasn't a good answer, especially not knowing what job I'm offering you. In my experience, I've learned you should listen to a proposition before saying no. She knew she wasn't interested, but listened anyway not wanting to appear disrespectful. "I know you saw the ladies out front?" Nina nodded yes. "They are making racks just bagging; nothing hard, nothing complicated. If you wanna put some of that bread in your pockets, I would be more than happy to put you on. I mean since you got a lot of heart, not to mention a nice body too.

Nina decided not to press her luck with the disrespect and tried a less harsh approach. "I appreciate your offer, but I'm good."

"Cool. What about your homegirl? She cute too."

"Nah she's good too. I assume my business is done here, right?"

"I don't know. That's up to you. You want it to be?" Nina could see where this was going and she had no intentions of putting herself in the same situation she had with Tee. *Fool me once; I'm nipping this shit in the bud.* Considering neither the rude or respectful approach was working, Nina tried to be as straightforward as possible. "I delivered the money and that's all this meeting was about. Since you trying to carry on with stuff that has nothing to do with this; I'm leaving now."

B smirked, he respected her heart. There were very few people who could get away with speaking to him like she had. "You gotta slick mouth. I like it, though." He pressed a buzzer and the same naked woman who let her in returned. "Escort her and her friend out." She signals with two fingers indicating that I was to follow her.

"My gun?"

B overheard her ask, and he laughed. "Oh, so you real with it huh? I see you not leaving here without your piece." He nodded to the naked girl who walked over to him. He handed her the purse. "Give her this outside my room. I hope to be seeing you again...real soon", he laughed.

81

Nina was handed her purse once she was outside of B's office, where she saw GeGe sitting on the couch impatiently waiting. She could tell just by looking at her that GeGe's patience had been tested to the point she could snap at any minute. Nina gave her a head nod letting her know everything went as planned and they could leave. GeGe stood from the couch and looked over her shoulder at the women behind her. "Gimme my gun."

A look of amusement crossed the woman's face. "Oh, this little thing? Here you go." She handed GeGe the gun and smirked. "Oh, so you tough now, huh?"

"Damn right! What you thought this was?" GeGe replied through gritted teeth.

"Oh trust me; you don't wanna know what I think, especially since I was holding you hostage with your own damn gun. Right?"

GeGe put the gun in her purse, smoothly handed it to Nina and punched the mouthy girl in the face. Nina was thankful that one of the other women thought like her and held the girl back before all hell broke loose right outside of B's office. Nina held GeGe back because it just wasn't the time or place for the bullshit. She hoped B had no idea what was going on, but there was no such luck as B burst out of his office.

He menacingly glared at Nina and GeGe. "You two bitches need to get the fuck outta here before it's a muthafuckin problem!"

"No disrespect meant to you, but your paid whores in here starting shit," Nina said.

"Look I don't give a fuck who started what, just get the fuck outta here. Now." B said calmly, which only proved exactly how serious he was.

Nina rolled her eyes in disgust. She grabbed GeGe by the arm and walked out of the apartment. She was fuming, but her mood lightened when she overheard B speaking through the door. "I need you bitches gangsta like that, or you can pound the fucking pavement. Got that?"

Although Nina's mood changed, GeGe was so angry she could barely keep her composure.

Samir could sense GeGe's mood as soon as they got into the car. "Yo, you good?"

Nina couldn't help but smile. "Yeah we good, but Ge was about to body a bitch in there."

Samir's eyes widened with surprise, and he laughed. "Say word!"

That was all it took to break GeGe's anger, and she burst into laughter. "Samir for real. You know I'ma calm, cool and collected kind of chic, but these so called boss bitches wasn't even about that life. In there talking shit like we don't give it up how we live."

"Aight gangsta boo!" Samir was almost in tears from laughter. "Y'all some new gangstas, but from what I hear y'all handled y'all business."

"Thanks," replied Nina and GeGe in unison. Nina started the car ready to head home.

"Babe, before you pull off hold up. I know y'all ready to go get some rest, but listen we got another stop to make before we call it a night. We gotta hit up my Spanish connect."

Nina felt a little let down. Just a few moments ago they were on a high from what they just pulled off. They wanted to keep talking about it, they wanted to relive the glory, but Samir cut their celebration short talking about another job. "Where are we going?" Nina asked.

As Nina drove to the Bronx as instructed, Samir laid out the details for what they were about to get into.

"Okay, so we gon' meet up with my connect Demario. I already talked to him, he knows what we need, but he could be the type to try and short you. Make sure that you get six keys. Aight?

Nina nodded yes.

"I heard mad shit about him, but this is only my second time dealing with son. Just in case, you need to be strapped and ready. From what I've seen lately, y'all ain't gonna have no problem handling yourself.

GeGe, who despite Samir's earlier interruption, was still hyped from the job at B's replied, "You damn right! I wish a nigga would try me this go around. B saved that bitch, but this go round I'ma be kicking ass and asking names later." GeGe clapped her hands. "It bet not be no bitches acting tough up in there because I swear I'ma smack the shit outta her and pray that somebody else wants it, so I can give it to them too!"

Samir and Nina laughed.

"Calm down Tyson. Damn." Samir said. "It shouldn't be that type of party. You just going to pick up the work, this should be easy as one, two, three. I just want you prepared 'cause he knows I been shot up. I don't want him getting no ideas. I already told him I was sending somebody to pick up. Since y'all already in disguises I thought we might as well get this outta the way. It's just one more thing to get us closer to the money."

Nina thought about what he said, and it made a lot of sense to her. "I feel you babe and don't worry it'll go smooth. GeGe's turnt up right now, but we got it."

"Cool. We pulling up to the pick-up spot now." Samir looked around surveying the surroundings. "Slow down a little." Nina did as he asked. "Good, good. Okay, park right here. I'ma stay in the car while you do what you do. When we back at the spot, I'ma start putting together a team, so we can get some real money. I got a few loyal no-nonsense dudes in mind that ain't got no problem pushing weight."

"Sounds like a plan. You ready Ge?"

"Hell yeah."

Nina leaned over and gave Samir a kiss. She looked out of the window and noticed Demario's place. It was obvious to anyone looking at his brownstone that he was getting money. Nina couldn't be too sure because of the street parking, but she was willing to bet the luxury cars that lined the block belonged to him too. Just being in the middle of all the expensive things confirmed to Nina they should be getting money like Demario. "Okay Ge, let's do this."

When they go to Demario's front door, Nina rang the doorbell and waited. After only a few seconds the door swung open. There stood a Puerto Rican man draped in all white linen.

"Hola chicas bonitas."

He had come to the door so quickly he took Nina off guard, and it showed on her face.

"Hablas Espanol?"

Luckily Nina remembered a little Spanish from her high school years. "Habla muy poco Espanol."

"Oh! Pensé que eras Dominicana!" He stopped himself short. "I'm sorry, I'm doing it again," he said with a laugh. "I thought you ladies were Dominican, my apologies. Please come in."

Nina wasn't one to usually stereotype, but this guy who she assumed was Demario, didn't seem like a drug dealer at all. He answered his own door, and from what Nina could see he didn't have any women or any other entourage hanging around the house. His home was pristine in a meticulous fashion. As they walked through the foyer, Nina noticed the smell of fresh paint and the echoed sound her heels made on the marble floor. The deeper they walked into the home, the more exquisite it became. Nina almost lost it when she saw he had original Basquiat and Warhol paintings. *Damn!* By the time they reached the living room, Nina saw things she had only seen in magazines. She was far from broke and owned nice things herself, but this was a different type of nice. As they continued to walk through all of the luxuriousness; she stopped to admire one particular painting. *Beautiful.* She could tell it was dearest to him by the way it sat alone perched on an ornate white easel. Nina was in awe of his home and art collection, as was GeGe. Nina politely and indiscernible as possible tapped GeGe, so she could close her mouth which still hung open in amazement.

"Ladies, can I get you some tea or perhaps a glass of wine?"

"Yes, I would love a full body red wine if you have it." Nina was going to call him by his name until she realized there had been no proper introduction. "I'm Nina, and this is GeGe. Demario is it?"

"Yes, you are correct. And you?" Demario turned to GeGe for her requested drink of choice.

"I'll have some Moscato please."

Nina could have died from embarrassment. Demario clearly had refined taste and GeGe's stood in front of him asking for some ghetto fab ass Moscato. She was glad that Demario had the good grace to reflect GeGe's faux pas.

"Well, I'm sure I have a beautiful tasting red wine, but not quite so sure about the Moscato. I'll do my best to search for some for you. Oh, and please don't be so formal. Call me Lazo; it's a nickname," he said as he walked off to get their drinks.

"GeGe what in the world is your problem? Asking for that kinda drink, knowing damn well this man ain't got no damn Moscato," Nina said noticeably irritated.

"Girl, I'ma keep it one hundred...I ain't never seen no shit like this! This some different kinda shit right here, not the typical hood rich bs I'm used to seeing. This man is wealthy, girl! Did you see that chandelier and the fucking white baby grand piano in the other room? It looked ten times better than all of the "good rooms" I've ever seen. You know which rooms I'm talking about, the one good room in your momma house that if you even thought about stepping foot in there, you gonna get the taste slapped outta your mouth faster than you can lick your lips."

"Yo, you stupid." Nina laughed and caught herself when she realized how loud she was. "Aight, let's get it together. We gotta give the impressions we are up to his standards if we want him to continue doing business with us. He's on some next level stuff, and I know he doesn't wanna do business with a bunch of hood rats. You know what I mean?" GeGe nodded yes. "Let's be professional, so we can keep him close 'cause there's no way I'm dealing with B again."

"Nina I got you, but damn look at..."

GeGe stopped short when Demario entered the room with a gold tray carrying two bottles. He popped the cork on the first bottle of wine and poured Nina a glass before handing it to her. "Thank you," Nina said and proceeded to swirl her glass in a circular motion while holding it by the stem. She softly smelled then sipped the wine. *Oh my goodness, this is one of the best wines I have ever tasted.* Nina gave Demario a nod to establish that it was, in fact, a great tasting wine.

He reciprocated with a smile while handing GeGe her glass. "I see the wine is to your liking."

"Yes, it is. It has the perfect balance of sweet and bitter."

GeGe raised her glass and took a sip. "Yup and my white wine is mad good too. It tastes like a good balance of white grape juice and the Welches Peach Orchard."

SHALONDA "SJ" JOHNSON

I'm gonna kill her, Nina thought. Again she was thankful Demario didn't acknowledge GeGe's lack of couth. She did notice, however, Demario kept his eyes locked on her.

"So ladies I'm sure you want to get to the business. I have six keys for you. Do you think you'll be able to handle that?"

Honestly, Nina didn't know if they would be able to handle it or not. She knew nothing about that life, and it sure seemed like a lot of product to move. But Samir said six, so she was getting six. She hoped Demario didn't pick up on her doubt. She was thankful that GeGe was too busy sipping her drink and checking out Demario paintings to register his question.

"Demario, I mean Lazo, the six keys will be fine. When do you need your turn around?"

"Well Nina, I am pronouncing it correctly, yes?

Nina smiled and nodded yes.

"As long as all business in conducted through you, only you, and not this Samir then I will give the option to choose your own turnaround date, within reason of course," he smiled. "Naturally, I would expect the date to be sooner than later, and I never want to have to come looking for you. Always maintain communication with me regardless if it's good or bad news because if I have to come looking for you, it will not end well. Keep in mind, while I'd prefer not to, I will hunt you down." Demario took a sip from his glass before continuing. "The purpose of the hunt is to locate prey and when that prey is found the intent is to kill. Yes?"

Fuck. He's a prettier package than B, but he's just the same. Nina's face must have indicated her internal thoughts.

"Nina, why the face? This is business." He smiled. "You're a lovely woman, who from my limited interaction, seems to have lots of potential in this business. Everything will be fine."

Demario gently rubbed Nina's arm then placed a small duffle bag filled with the six keys into her hand.

"Bonita take this, work your magic and call me in a week to tell me how things are going." He placed his hand on Nina's upper back and led her to the door. "Come, let me walk you ladies to the door."

GeGe joined them at the door. "Lazo your home is dope, and the paintings are crazy. I really like that Baskey."

87

"You mean Basquiat?"

Nina was amazed at his ability to remain polite and avoid being condescending to someone who clearly lacked the most basic of class.

"Yeah, yeah him. He's dope."

"I'm glad you like my home and my paintings." Demario stopped by a small painting. "GeGe I would love for you to have this Basquiat as a token of mucho dinero we will make together."

GeGe couldn't believe it. "Wait, are you serious?"

"Si, I am very serious."

"Thank you!" The look on GeGe's face was priceless. It was the happiest Nina had seen her in a very long time. "Look Nina; he gave me a Baskey. Thank you, gracey!"

Here she goes again, Nina thought once again embarrassed. Demario caught her look and winked. "It's muchas gracias Ge," Nina said politely. "Thank you Lazo, that was very nice of you." Nina lifted the bag slightly and said, "I will give you a call in a week."

"Yes, I will be awaiting your call," he responded then he whispered to himself "Te prometo que serás mía." (I promise that you will be mine.)

"Again thank you."

"Yeah, thanks Lazo," GeGe said as they both walked out of the house and headed to the car.

Samir wanted an update as soon as Nina and GeGe sat in the car. "Everything went good?"

Nina smiled, proud that everything had gone smoothly. "Yes, and it's all here, six keys." Nina handed Samir the bag.

"So what else he say and where the hell did GeGe get that ugly ass painting from?"

"First off this painting ain't ugly!" GeGe replied. Nina paused and decided not to go into details about the painting because she knew it was pointless. She switched the subject and said, "He told us to call him Lazo. Honestly, I ain't sure if that goes for everybody or just me and Ge."

Samir cut her off before she could say anything else. "Everybody like who? I know I ain't included in everybody. Who the fuck he think I am?!" Samir yelled. "I'm the one about to flip this shit and bring his ass mad money, and he thinks I'm everybody?!

"That's not what I'm saying. Nina replied. All I meant was he specifically asked GeGe and me to call him that. I'm saying if he didn't tell you to call him Lazo you should probably continue to call him Demario. You know, to keep good business." Nina could feel the heat coming off Samir and decided to deliver the last bit of information with a bit of a lie to make it easier to handle. "Oh and he wants to handle all future business with just GeGe and me. You know, continue how we started."

GeGe cleared her throat and pulled Nina's card. "Excuse me missy, but I clearly heard him say he wanted to continue to do business with you and not Samir. He didn't even mention my name."

Nina expected Samir to go through the roof, but he didn't. "I ain't tripping. I ain't stupid; I always use any advantage I can when handling business. He don't wanna do business with GeGe and me? It's cool. I can take one for the team. Demario's got a little crush on you. I mean he even gave GeGe that ugly ass painting and shit. It's cool though, that'll make it easier for us. I don't care how we do it just keep the business rolling and the money pilling. Capeesh?" He looked at Nina sternly. "Just keep it business Nina, strictly business. Be smart, don't be dumb!"

"Of course babe. Besides I got a man, I don't need another one." Nina switched the conversation to steer the attention away from her and Demario. "Well what happened with the crew, we gotta team or what?"

"Damn right! I just need a small favor from you two."

"What?" Nina and GeGe both responded.

Samir hesitated. "I need you two beautiful and kind ladies to bottle the work up for me."

"Oh hell nah!" Nina replied.

"Boy you fucking tripping," GeGe said simultaneously.

Nina was taken aback by Samir's request. "Babe you never said anything about all that. Come on for real. Damn." Nina sat silently for a minute; she looked at GeGe and looked back to Samir.

"This is gonna cost extra, and I mean extra."

Samir smiled knowing there was a good chance he would get his way. "How much?" "I don't know yet, but I'll let you know when we get it together."

"Aight, y'all know I'm good for it now that I'm 'bout to be back on top. Gimme a kiss." Samir looked at GeGe and laughed. "Not you GeGe, you can gimme a dap." The entire car erupted in laughter as Nina leaned towards the backseat and pecked Samir on the lips. "Now, keep your eyes on the road because everybody knows New York women can't drive for shit."

"Shut up boy!"

"Yo, we about to get paid!" GeGe high-fived Nina. "Girl, we about to change the game."

Nina looked at GeGe and looked at Samir through the rearview mirror then replied, "You ain't never lied."

CHAPTER THIRTEEN

After some convincing Nina and GeGe decided to bottle up the product as Samir had asked. Reluctantly, Nina had reservations about setting up shop at her place. However, after weighing the pros and cons, they all decided that with the heightened security of Nina's building her place was their best option. Nina and GeGe sat at a desk in the corner of her office working.

"Samir sure better be glad I like him 'cause this shit is boring as hell. Plus these little ass bottles are annoying. But I can't lie, when he mentioned the extra money my ass got in line real quick." GeGe laughed at her own joke and shoulder bumped Nina.

"You are such as mess."

GeGe blew Nina a kiss. "I know."

"I'm sure you do, Ge." Nina smiled as she remembered a past situation very similar to this one.

"Samir how long you gonna be? The movie starts in thirty minutes." Nina sat in Samir's den annoyingly flipping through channels while she waited. *This boy is slow as cold molasses.*

From the back of his apartment Samir yelled, "I'm almost done. Hold on; I'm trying to finish up now. I just need a little bit longer. Hey, why don't you come back here?"

Nina could barely hear Samir. "What? I can't hear anything you're saying," Nina yelled back. "Hold on for a second; I'm coming to you." She peeped into his bedroom. "So how much longer? You know I hate being late...and what in the hell are you doing?" Nina's face screwed in irritation.

"Nina chill, we gonna make it to the movie on time. I just had to bag up this work myself after I fired those sticky-fingered muthafuckas." Samir motioned to the seat next to him. "Yo sit down next to me and help me...please?"

"I'm not touching that! Besides, I thought you were getting out the game? I thought we had a new plan? Remember?"

"Yeah, I remember." Samir sat the bottle that was in his hands down on the table. "This is my last run, and then we gonna be set. Okay? So come on babe, help me so we can make this movie."

"I don't even know how to do this ghetto shit."

"Don't worry. Follow my lead, I'ma teach you. Cool? Samir looked at Nina hoping he said enough to convince her to sit beside him. "Plus, you never know when you might need this skill in the future. I'm giving life lessons here," Samir said with a laugh.

"Life lessons my ass!" Nina smiled. "We both know you're doing this because you might need my help again one day. Right?" Nina didn't wait for an answer because she knew that she was right. "I just hope it's not anytime in the near future."

"Yeah, yeah. Just sit your beautiful ass down and help me." Nina sat down, and Samir kissed her on her cheek. "You my rider baby, always remember that."

Nina mocked Samir's movements in her attempts to help. "Nina Baby, I appreciate you helping, but if you keep filling bottles like that I'ma be broke," Samir said with a laugh. "You're bagging too much in one bottle." Samir filled a bottle to show Nina how it's done. "Just this much. Okay? We want them to come back, but not bad enough to give shit away."

"Whatever Samir. You not even funny, just pass me another bottle."

"Pass me another bottle. Nina, pass me another bottle. Girl, you okay? You keep drifting off on a sista."

"Yeah Ge, I'm good. Here you go."

"Thanks. Just checking on you," GeGe said taking the bottle. "How you learn how to bottle up anyway?"

"Don't worry 'bout all that." Nina smiled letting GeGe know that she wasn't serious. "All you need to know is that me and

Samir been through a lot together. That's why I go so hard for him."

"So basically you saying Samir taught yo ass." GeGe laughed because she knew she was right. Nina laughed because she knew she had been caught.

"Shut the fuck up Ge!" Nina tried to keep a straight face but ended up laughing again anyway. "Did I say that? No, so just bottle the rest of this work up 'cause I'm tired as a motherfucker." Nina turned serious for a second. "I can't wait to give this to the crew tomorrow. I want my money back tenfold for all this manual labor that I'm having to do."

"Yeah you and me both. Yo, Nina you ever tried coke before?" GeGe continued without waiting for an answer. "I heard it's like a superhuman fun kinda thing."

Nina grabbed GeGe's hand and stopped her from bottling up. She wanted GeGe's full attention for what she was about to say. "GeGe don't you ever, and I mean ever in your fucking life touch this stuff or anything else! It will ruin your life and relationships, not to mention our friendship. This drug shit that we caught up in at the moment is to give us a better life, to get the things we never had or do the things we never had time to do. This ain't recreational or for the long haul; it's short term. This is where my business sense like marketing comes into to play. We'll keep our customers happy, increase profits and transition back into legitimate business when this is all over. And we ain't doing none of that strung out with habits shit. You hear me?"

"Well damn bitch, I was just saying…"

"Ge I'm not playing. Stay focused on this as a business. You gotta promise me you won't ever try this shit. I'm serious Ge, promise me."

"Girl I got you. I just asked a simple ass question, and you went all Dr. Phil on me and shit. Trust me, I ain't dumb. I got a daughter to raise."

Silence hung between them until Samir called them from the other room. "Yo, you two almost done? It's about that time to make some dropoffs."

Nina ignored Samir. "Promise me GeGe!"

"I promise girl!"

"That's all I asked." Nina leaned over and gave GeGe a hug. "Now let's get this done and shut his ass up," she laughed. "We're almost done," Nina yelled to Samir.

After about an hour, Nina and GeGe were finally finished. Nina sat back in her chair and stretched. "Well I guess it's about that time, but first we need to clean ourselves up. We look a hot mess."

"Speak for yourself girl, because GeGe is never a hot mess." GeGe laughed as she waved her hands over herself.

"Okay, well Miss Never-a-hot-mess, I'm getting in the shower and putting on some clean clothes."

GeGe laughed. "Yeah, well a shower wouldn't hurt."

Once out of the shower Nina pulled out the same briefcase she used to deliver B his money and perfectly filled it with bottles. She liked the briefcase because she felt it confirmed she was all business. "Everybody ready?"

"Let's get it," Samir replied.

"No doubt," said GeGe.

"Good. To Brownsville." Nina opened the front door to let GeGe and Samir pass. She hit the lights, and the door closed behind them.

The street team Samir assembled was waiting when they pulled up. "We gonna handle everything from the car. Keep the doors locked, and your windows rolled up. These niggas know me and what I am about, so it's better that I do all of the talking. Plus, I put nothing past no nigga. Keep your guns cocked just in case some shit pops off."

Nina and GeGe did as they were told. Samir was much more experienced in this game, so they had no problem letting him take control. Samir rolled down the window and summoned the lieutenant of the team.

"Here's the work," he said as he passed the briefcase over. "I'll pick up the money every day. There's too many stick-up kids out here to take chances." The lieutenant nodded. "When you out here, keep your eyes open and be on point. We taking over B's block and he definitely gonna have a problem with that. When him or any of his crew step to you, hold shit down and tell them to holla at me. Notice that I said when and not if. I know B and his crew gonna try you, but that's why I picked this team of soldiers. I know you able to hold shit down. With that said, none of y'all can leave the block without letting me know. I don't care if you gotta take a shit, you hit me and let me know. Y'all got a quota to meet every night, and it'll be hard to do if you ain't in place. Any questions?"

"Nah, I got it. I'ma put these boys to work and make sure they do it right." His lieutenant responded.

Samir appreciated the fact that he had chosen the right guy to be his lieutenant. "Good. Now let's get to work, it's already bottled up."

His lieutenant saluted and walked away as Samir rolled the window up. "Aight that's handled. We out."

Samir's words broke Nina from her thought. She had been mesmerized by Samir as he spoke to the team. Although his demeanor was stern towards them, Nina saw their admiration of Samir. She could see they were willing to do it all for Samir because they knew he would keep their pockets fat. Even as they drove away from them, the team immediately posted up for the sales. Nina was impressed, and it only served to heighten her attraction to him.

Nina looked at Samir through the rearview mirror. "That was kind of a turn on back there. Let me find out you a gangster for real." Nina said in a sarcastic tone.

Samir smiled. "I'm the realest nigga you ever met in your life, and you know that."

"Mmmhm." Nina looked to her left and noticed that GeGe was knocked out. "How in the hell did she fall asleep that damn fast? Let's just drop her off on our way home."

"That's cool, but you ain't waking her up 'cause your girl is out."

Nina laughed. "I'll wake her. Hell, I'll do anything tonight. I'm just glad I get a chance to breathe for a minute now that everything's taken care of. It's been non-stop for a while. All we gotta do is sit back and collect now. Right?"

"Yeah pretty much. We still gotta stay on top of the crew and you gotta re-up with Demario...you know what, fuck it, I'm calling his ass Lazo too! So yeah, we just gotta keep everything moving smoothly. If we do this right, we can leave this game and never go back to this street shit ever again.

"Yeah, that's what you said last time."

"What you say?"

"Oh, nothing. I didn't say nothing." Nina laughed as Samir poked her in the side as payback for the smart comment just as they parked in front of GeGe's mother's house. "Samir this girl is over here drooling." Nina laughed at the site of her friend sleeping so hard and softly shook her by the shoulder. "Ge wake up." GeGe's eyes opened, but Nina could tell she was still half asleep. "I'm just gonna walk her in and get her situated. Aight? It took Nina about fifteen minutes to get GeGe settled in and then she crept back down to the car. When she opened the door, the interior light showed a pissed off expression on Samir's face. "Baby, what's wrong? I'm gone for a few minutes, and your whole mood has completely changed."

"Yo, my bad Nina. I can't even lie, ever since I got shot I'm paranoid as a muthafucka. When it took you a minute to come out, I started having wild thoughts that maybe something had happened to you." Samir reached over and grabbed her hand. "For real, I was about to run up in GeGe's mom's house to check on you. I didn't know if someone grabbed you in that dark ass house or what."

"Babe, that's so sweet, but I'm good. Okay? You gotta chill."

"Nina…"

Nina reached up and turned the dome light off to make sure the car would stay pitch black when she pulled over into the dark, secluded spot. "Shhhhhhh. Don't say another word before you mess with the mood."

Samir raised his eyebrow as if to say 'oh really' and smiled.

As they drove looking for someplace to be alone, Nina slid her hand across his dick print and began to rub it until she felt his shit get rock hard. With her free hand, Nina pulled the car over and shifted it into park. She leaned over to him and unzipped his pants and unbuttoned his boxer briefs. Samir bit his bottom lip, closed his eyes and laid his head back onto the headrest in preparation for what he knew was coming next. Nina pulled his dick out and slowly stroked him until he stretched to full length.

It's sheer size never ceased to amaze Nina. She licked her lips in anticipation and slid his rock hard dick into her warm mouth. He grabbed the back of her head and wrapped his fingers in her hair. The car was quiet with the exception of his deep breathing and the wetness of Nina's mouth as it smoothly slipped up and down his dick. From the corner of her eye, she could see how much he was feeling what she was doing, and she took it as a challenge to give him more. She pulled his dick out of her mouth and began to slowly and teasingly lick up and down his shaft, while she gently played with his balls. Nina firmly grabbed the base of his dick and gently licked around the head before slowly deep throating all of him. Samir's breathing picked up, and his grip on her hair tightened. He loved how Nina's mouth felt as she switched speeds and took him deeper into her mouth until he pressed against the back of her throat. She knew this was her cue to let him take control. She stopped sucking and opened her mouth a bit more to keep her teeth from scraping against his dick as he pushed himself back and forth past her lips and down her throat. He let out a low groan as he nutted into her mouth. Nina swallowed his cum and kept his dick in her mouth until she felt him go limp.

"Damn girl!" Samir said as he buttoned his underwear and zipped his pants.

There wasn't a need for him to say anymore, Nina knew exactly what he meant. She smiled as she reached across him into the glove compartment for a water bottle to rinse her mouth.

"For real Nina, that was exactly what the fuck I needed tonight. I was mad stressed." Samir paused. "Let's just say, I ain't stressed no more."

"Good, now let's get back to my place, so you can return the favor," Nina said as she started the car and pulled back onto the street.

The ride back to Nina's seemed to take only minutes. They rushed through the lobby to avoid the crowd and hurried to Nina's floor. They couldn't keep their hands to themselves. Nina coyly laughed as Samir whispered in her ear how he couldn't wait to get inside. His breath was warm against the side of her face, and Nina felt herself grow wet as he said, "I'ma tear that pussy up!" They both knew he was still recovering from being shot. For all the things he couldn't do yet, there were still a few he could do very well. Samir pinned Nina against the door with hard kisses as he unlocked the door. The door swung open, and Nina walked backward into the room while Samir continued to kiss her.

"Take all of them clothes off!" He said in between kisses.

"Yeah, do what he said." Nina and Samir froze at the sound of the female voice.

"Who the fuck..." Nina stopped midsentence as the light came on and she saw Traci sitting on her couch. Nina was furious. "Oh bitch, I know you not up in my shit?!" Nina screamed, "I'm 'bout to fuck you up!" Nina charged towards Traci but stopped when she noticed the gun sitting on her lap.

Samir still hadn't moved. "Traci, what the fuck are you doing? How the fuck you get in here?"

Nina was so shocked Traci was in her home; she never thought to ask how she had gotten in. *Pat's ass is mine! I can't believe this shit!*

Traci ignored him. "So Nina, you better do what he said and take them clothes off."

"Traci, where is my daughter, while you up in here acting a damn fool?"

Traci face twisted in disgust. "Well looka here, now Samir is concerned about his daughter and her whereabouts?" She put her hand on the gun. "What about you Nina, you got any questions for me since it seems to be the question Traci hour?" Nina stood silently. "Nothing to say, huh?" Traci gripped the gun tighter as she grew angrier and she challenged Nina to ask her a question. "No, go ahead. Ask me a question and if I like the question I promise I won't shoot you. At least not yet anyway." Still Nina stayed quiet. "I'm waiting! Ask me!"

Nina took a deep breath to remove the anger from her voice. She was pissed but didn't want to give Traci any reason to turn the gun on her. "What do you want Traci?"

"Ding, Ding, Ding that's the million dollar question isn't it? Three gold stars for Nina." Traci smiled menacingly. "You know what I want Ms. I think I'm all that? I want you to come sit your prissy ass right next to me." Traci patted the space beside her on the couch with the gun.

Nina didn't move.

Traci lifted the gun and pointed it directly at Nina. "I'm not gonna ask you again. Get over here, now!"

"Traci come on, put the gun down," Samir pleaded. He knew Traci was irrational and he didn't want Nina to get hurt. "Nina ain't got nothing to do with the disputes we're having."

Traci recoiled as if she had been slapped. "Oh, you don't think so, do you? What about the fact that she fucked up our happy home? Huh?"

"Traci our marriage been fucked up for a minute now. Ain't no getting around that."

Traci slowly got up from the couch and walked towards Samir pointing the gun towards his chest.

Her tone was calm and cold. "See, that's where you're wrong. Our marriage might've not been perfect, but this bitch right here is the reason you couldn't focus on making things right with us. You were too busy fucking her and telling her you love her instead of coming home to your daughter and me, telling us you love us."

"Traci don't be disrespectful." Nina began.

Traci snapped her attention towards her. She walked over to Nina, leaned down so they were eye to eye and pushed the gun into the side of Nina's head. "Bitch, don't you ever cut me off when I'm talking! You think I really care about you asking me not to be disrespectful? Really bitch? You talking to me about respect when you been disrespecting me for years by fucking my goddamn husband?" Traci pushed the gun harder against Nina's head. "So, don't sit here and talk about some fucking disrespect. Bitch, I should shoot the shit out of you right now just for saying that dumb shit! And if you even think about parting your lips to say one more word, I'ma shoot your ass right in that big ass mouth of yours. Am I clear?" Nina said nothing. "Exactly, you better not say shit."

Traci turned her attention back to Samir. "Now, back to you. The one thing I don't get about you is how you tend to forget shit. That shit gets me tight." Tears welled in her eyes as she tried to keep her composure. "You wanna parade this bitch around and treat her ass all special like she's the one that's been riding with you all of this time. You must've forgot, but I

99

remember who was with you riding in the passenger seat of that raggedy ass '89 Ford Escort. That's right; it was my ass who was with you when you only had enough money in your pockets to buy one snack box from Kennedy Fried. Remember that? I do, 'cause we would share it. Or how about when you first started hustling and you ain't have no team, so I stepped up to the plate? You forgot? I didn't. It was me who put my life on the line standing on those corners selling weed for you. And when I got locked up, I sat my ass in jail for three days and never even thought about snitching on your no good ass." Traci stopped to catch her breath and rubbed her forehead. "What about the fucking loyalty Samir? Huh? You didn't even have the decency to respect the original team." Traci raised her voice, "I'm the fucking original team Samir, not this wack-ass side bitch!"

"Look Traci; you gotta chill the fuck out. Yeah, you right, you was there from day one, but I was there for you too. That's what being in a relationship is. You don't do what you supposed to do and ask for pats on the back. You supposed to invest yourself in the relationship, take a risk with your heart, go hard for that person and give your all. We both did that, but while you standing here lecturing me, you seem to have forgotten some things yourself. Not to mention you rewriting the hell outta our history. Your ass damn sure wasn't perfect! Don't act like your ass wasn't fucking mad niggas behind my back. Now I'm not saying two wrongs make a right, but Traci you know we were over. You had your's, and I had mine. So, don't sit here talking mad shit like I'ma no good ass nigga. You for damn sure not gonna play me like I'm not a good father either. I take damn good care of my daughter. Period! I'm out here every day grinding and busting my ass to pay her private school tuition and making sure she has every motherfucking thing she needs! Don't try that shit, Traci." Samir was so engulfed with proving his point that even the threat of Traci's gun couldn't stop him. "You know I want a divorce?! You knew for a while. The only reason you even acting crazy like this is because you know I'ma solid dude regardless of everything we went through."

Traci screamed and started punching herself in the head. "Samir why would you leave? You said we would never leave each other. Remember?" Traci begged. "You said you would always be there for me. Why Samir? Why you lie?" Tears began to stream down Traci's face. "You told me forever." Traci looked defeated and said in a very low tone, "I can't live without you." She wiped her eyes with the back of her hand. "I thought you couldn't live without me, but now..." She looked around Samir to get a glimpse of Nina. "I lost. I know that now, I'm done." The tears flowed freely once again as Traci recited the only prayer she knew by heart, "Now I lay me down to sleep, I pray the Lord, my soul to keep, if I should die before I wake, I pray the Lord my soul to take." She pulled the gun up to her head and pulled the trigger. *Click!* In the silence of the room, the click of the revolver as it failed to strike a bullet seemed to scream.

Nina stood silently staring at Traci.

Traci laughed sadly. "I was hoping this wouldn't turn into a game of Russian roulette." She shrugged her shoulders weakly. "I only brought two bullets and this ain't going as planned. These two bullets were for y'all."

Samir had long lost love for Traci, but he couldn't just stand here and let her kill herself. "Traci, you bugging! Give me the damn gun." He reached his hand out to her hoping she would give him the gun. "Calm down and let's talk about all of this without the gun."

Traci was not moved. In a voice barely above a whisper, she said, "If I can't have you then I don't want to live."

"What about our daughter Traci? Ain't she worth living for?"

"I ain't no good to her like this Samir. I want her to be happy more than anything in this world and if that happens because I'm not here to fuck her life up then, so be it." She once again looked at Nina. "Besides, Nina here will be able to play mommy real nice."

"Traci, come on now. Our baby girl needs her mother. She needs you more than anything."

"Bye Samir." Traci blew him a kiss then turned to Nina. "Fuck you bitch!" She raised the gun to her right temple and pulled the trigger. The bullet violently ripped through Traci's head spraying bone fragments, brain matter and blood across

Nina's living room before her lifeless body dropped heavily to the floor.

"Oh shit!" Nina and Samir said in unison before the room fell silent again.

Samir stood with this mouth open trapped in thoughts of how he would explain this to his daughter.

Nina repeatedly blinked her eyes in the silent aftermath curious about her fate with Samir. She wondered how far she would go for him and if it were possible for her to end up like Traci.

"I ain't think she was serious. I can't believe she actually pulled the trigger." Samir looked at Traci's body sprawled across the floor and a lump formed in his throat. He swallowed hard and pushed it down. "I'm sure someone heard the shot, we gotta call 911 immediately, so we don't get caught up in this shit." Samir looked around. "Yo, we gotta make sure there's no evidence of the coke around here. No product, no tools, no nothing."

Nina couldn't help but be a little selfish. "Damn why did she have to do this shit in my damn house? There's blood everywhere, not to mention it's gonna bring heat to my spot."

"No, it won't! As long as we make sure ain't nothing here to draw attention to anything other than Traci. When they look at the evidence, they gonna clearly see she killed herself. That's why I need you to call 911 right now."

"But, I'm sure once they run your name and see you've been arrested before they gonna start snooping around. Pretty soon they connecting dots and we gonna get busted!"

"Nina, look at me. Ain't nothing gonna happen! Okay? You trust me right? Right?"

"Yeah."

"Good, now please go and call 911 before it's too late."

Nina walked over to the phone while Samir checked around to make sure the house was good.

"911, What is your emergency?"

"Hello, yes I would like to report a suicide."

CHAPTER FOURTEEN

Nina was able to relax once the coroner collected Traci's body and the police left. Samir was right all along. They asked mad questions, but after surveying the scene and speaking to others in the building, they were pretty satisfied that Traci's death was at her own hands. Of course, an autopsy would be performed for final confirmation, but considering Traci had actually killed herself, Nina was sure her death would go down as another person unable to handle lost love. Nina made sure to pour it on thick when she was questioned. She wrung her hands together, filled her eyes with tears and went on about how she couldn't believe Traci killed herself because she had a daughter to live for. It's not that Nina intended to be totally phony. After all of the dirt she'd done lately, she wanted to make sure all of the police's questions pertained only to Traci. Her strategy worked, or at least that's how it appeared. About fifteen minutes later, she closed the door behind the police without answering any prying questions about herself. As soon as they left, Nina dried her fake tears and returned to her usual demeanor. She had a heart and felt bad that Traci took her life right in front of her. If it was between her or Traci, Nina was glad it was Traci.

On the other hand, she could tell Samir was genuinely hurt. She knew Samir didn't want to be with Traci anymore, but she was the mother of his child whom he loved deeply at one point in his life. He sat across from the bloody couch staring at the large stain with tears in his eyes. "She wasn't always a bitch. She was a good person too, not too long ago."

Nina walked over to him and hugged him tightly. "Everything is gonna be okay." She used the end of her sleeve to wipe the tears from his eyes and suddenly felt guilty for the fake ones she had shed.

"What am I gonna tell my baby girl? Traci's mother has her right now, but I don't know how I'ma look her in the eyes without breaking down. Traci was a shitty wife, but she was a good mom." The tears began to fall again at the thought of his daughter living without her mother. "Damn Traci." Samir hung his hand and wept.

Nina stayed quiet because there was nothing she could say, but seeing him like this softened her earlier attitude towards Traci. Still, she had no answers for Samir. The only thing she could do was hold him, and she did until he fell asleep. When she was sure she wouldn't disturb him, Nina started to clean up. Before she began, she stood above the spot where Traci's body laid hours ago and said a prayer for her. She promised she would make sure her little girl was well taken care of. Nina even apologized for loving Samir, and although she didn't know he was married, she apologized for distracting him from working out his marital problems. Cleanup was difficult, and several things would have to be thrown away. Just as well, Nina didn't think she could ever sit on that couch again. Samir woke up about ten minutes after Nina finished cleaning.

"Nina?"

Nina walked over to Samir and softly asked, "You okay?"

Samir looked down and quietly replied, "No, but I'll be aight." Then he continued, "baby I'll get you a new couch and rug okay? If your floors need to be refinished, I got that too."

"Samir, don't worry about that; it's okay. It'll get taken care of."

"Okay?"

After Samir replied in agreeance with Nina, she continued talking to him in a very soft tone to help keep his mind at ease. "Babe I was thinking, we've been through a lot these past few weeks, and everything is moving so fast."

Samir looked at Nina waiting for her to continue. "Okay. Go ahead."

"Let's just lay low for a while to wrap our minds around everything and make plans for the future. We can stay here, watch Netflix, order takeout and just enjoy being together."

Samir looked up with sadness still in his eyes, but behind it was a little bit of happiness with the thought of Nina's plan. "I feel you. There's been mad life changing shit going on lately; things that would send a lot of people to Bellevue. You right, we need to lay low for a while. Let's take the time to chill and worry about the rest of the world next week. The only thing is that I can't stay here the whole time. My daughter is gonna need me. Her mom just died. Don't worry though, 'cause every moment I'm not with her, I'ma be right here with you. Okay?"

"Sounds good," Nina replied with a smile on her face, happy to be there for him in his time of need.

A few days passed with Samir and Nina held up in her place. With the exception of his daughter, the rest of the outside world disappeared as they relaxed peacefully without a care in the world. They stayed up late talking about the future and spent all day making love and watching movies. Their first visit into the real world came the day of Traci's funeral. Nina felt funny being there, but Samir said he needed her for support. From everything Nina had ever seen or heard about Traci, she would have never imagined that she was loved by so many. The church was filled with people who wanted to pay their respects. The immediate family wore all white, and she watched quietly as a line of people passed by Traci's casket for viewing. Nina was surprised it was an open casket funeral considering Traci had shot herself in the head. The funeral home had done a great job disguising the wound. For the first time, Nina understood what people meant when they said that a deceased person looked good at their funeral.

Samir and Nina sat a few rows behind the immediate family. Many of the people who stopped to speak to the family offered their condolences to Samir as they passed. Nina could tell how others interacted with him that Traci never told anyone about their issues. No one even stared at him wondering why he was at her funeral sitting with another woman. There were no ugly glances or side eyes; they all gave him hugs and handshakes. Nina respected the fact that Traci didn't go out of her way to make Samir look bad and it was a clear indication her love for him ran deep.

Samir's daughter Layla, who was sitting with her grandparents, ran up to him and gave him a hug. She rubbed the side of his face and whispered to him, "it's going to be okay daddy."

Her strength almost broke Samir, and more tears threatened to spill from his eyes. "I love you, baby."

"I love you too daddy." Layla kissed Samir on the cheek before returning to her grandparents. Layla looked like a princess dressed in all white and a sparkling headband. She appeared so fragile and delicate; however, she was anything but weak. Nina noticed she didn't cry during the service. Her head hung low a few times, but never for too long. Layla was her grandmother's rock, rubbing her back to console her when she broke down, but she never shed one tear. Nina couldn't believe what she was seeing. Layla was incredibly strong and mature to be so young.

At the conclusion of the service, the family viewed Traci's body one more time before her casket was closed. Nina stood behind Samir as he said his final goodbyes. Her vision blurred, while her eyes grew inexplicably misty even though Traci had nothing more than hatred and disdain towards her. Nina took the opportunity to apologize once again to Traci and to reiterate her previous promise to take care of Layla. She couldn't explain why and was pretty sure it was her guilt speaking. At that moment, she believed Traci had forgiven her.

Samir took the funeral harder than he had expected and was in no shape to deal with the burial. Instead of sitting at the burial plot, Samir and Nina stayed in the car and watched from afar until Traci's casket was lowered into the ground. From where they sat, they could see two police cars continuously circling before the two cars finally parked nearby. As the casket was being lowered, Samir mustered enough strength to get out of the car. He and Nina slowly walked over and dropped a bouquet of flowers down to his former bride. "I hate funerals," Samir said almost as an afterthought. Then he placed his hand on the small of Nina's back and led her back to the car.

As they approached the car, Samir couldn't help but say, "the worst thing about a death in the family or death period is the fact that the world doesn't stop. The next day comes regardless of what you're feeling, and if you don't move with it, the world will pass you by. You gotta continue with your life as if you didn't just lose someone. There's no time to mourn, and that's the fucked up part."

Nina consoled him with her words of comfort as best she could. "It's so fucked up, but it's life. The reality of the situation is that standing still doesn't bring anyone back and moving forward doesn't mean that you didn't love the person who died. All it means is that you're still here and you gotta live your life."

Samir stopped just before getting in the car to let Nina's words sink in. "You right, Nina. If there's one thing I can take away from this is that you can be here one day and gone the next. I gotta live for me, and I gotta live for Layla. So that means getting out here and getting this paper, so my baby girl doesn't have to worry about a damn thing." Samir and Nina both slid back into the car. He sat in thought for a minute. "Since we out, let's hit the block and pick up our money. Once we get it all counted and see how much we're making, we can go hit Lazo and re-up."

"I'm good with whatever you wanna do," Nina replied.

Samir started the car and blasted the music once he exited the cemetery in an attempt to ease his pain. Nina leaned back against her seat as they drove to do their pick up. Though she knew him well enough to know differently, Samir drove like he didn't have a care in the world; fast but in control. She found it sexy. When they arrived in Brownsville, the street team was in position. Samir held back for a second and pointed them out to Nina. Keyshawn was the shortest. He had a babyface that fooled many into thinking that he was a good guy all while he was plotting their demise. Then there was Darion who was down for whatever and would give his left rib for the game. Blaze was the quiet one of the group. He was Asian and African American with the pretty boy looks that drove the women customers crazy. Last but not least, was Homi which stood for "Homicide" who was the shooter on the team. His name explained everything anyone ever needed to know about him. Nina knew all of this information and more from previous conversations with Samir, but considering he just buried Traci she didn't remind him.

"Sit tight. This should be quick." Samir hopped out of the car, sat on the hood and waved the guys over. Although they were posted up on different corners, each man peeped the signal and made their way over to the car. Nina cracked the window to hear the conversation.

"Aight so what's it looking like out here? What's the word?" Samir asked the team.

Darion was the first to speak. "Man all I know is that we getting this money and niggas is mad tight."

Samir wanted clarification. "What you mean? What they be doing?"

Darion continued. "A couple of B's niggas pulled up on some shit, talking about these they blocks. I told them, we ain't going no fucking where because we took over and these blocks ours now. You know they kept it moving. Ever since then, B's old ass been circling the block watching us and shit."

Homi's face screwed. "Yo Samir gimme the word my nigga and I'ma put a bullet in all they heads. You know how I get down! Just gimme the word."

Samir gave Homi the signal to chill and turned to Keyshawn. "What's good with you, you had any problems?"

"Please! These bum ass niggas mad corny. They ain't want no problems; they fucked up by trying to press me. I told them, fuck outta here and be glad we let them still work at all." Samir nodded his head proudly. "Well damn. I see you niggas out here handling your B I." He noticed up until now that Blaze had been quiet. "What's good with you Blaze? You mad quiet over there boy?"

"Yo Samir, I'm good. They be out here talking slick shit, but I just block they asses out. They be trying to get my mind off getting this money, but I ain't having that."

"Exactly!" Samir clapped his hands. "That's what I wanna hear Blaze. B and his team trying to use scare tactics and shit to get y'all off the block. Don't play into their bullshit ass games. If you lose your head out here, you just might lose your head. You get what I'm saying?"

Everyone nodded that they understood.

"B's been in the game for a good minute, and it's made him mad predictable, so I can tell you right now the stick-up boys are coming. And we gonna be ready. First, I'ma get you some back-up. I'ma make sure they posted nearby, but not close enough to be spotted. When the stick-up boys come, I wanna be able to get the drop on them. I don't want them fuckers to know what hit them. Feel me?"

Samir could see the wheels in Homi's head turning. "Yo Homi, I know you'll pop that thing in a second, so you probably thinking you don't need no backup, but I need you to handle the work. I trust you with my money, and I need you focused on that. Now don't get it fucked up, I ain't say don't pull your piece if you got to. For the purpose of keeping B's boys and other sucka ass stick-up kids in pocket, we gonna use another team for that."

All four men looked at him and nodded in agreement.

"The next thing we'e gonna do is give ourselves a little insurance plan. No more holding a lot of bread on you for extended periods of time. I'ma put a little system in place to keep the money in movement. It'll keep our money outta the hands of the stick-up kids and the cops. I'ma hit you later with the details."

As usual, Homi was cocked and ready to go. "Man, Samir I respect what you saying and all, but I wish a nigga would try me! It'll be the last time he tries anybody. Know what I'm saying?"

"Yeah I know, but we gotta stay focused on why we out here doing this shit. We don't need no type of heat from nobody especially the damn police. We already got B to worry about. We ain't making no unnecessary enemies. I need all of you to understand what we're doing. This game we playing right here ain't about egos and short-term money. We're building enough so all of us can go legit real soon without ever having to come back to these streets. I need y'all to hear me and hear me good. We ain't hustling for sneakers and whips or chains and hoes. This shit is an investment. We're hustling for homes, stocks and businesses. We doing it, so our kids don't ever have to touch this shit."

Keyshawn couldn't help but cosign Samir. "Hell yeah, boy!"

"So as tempting as it's gonna be to start flossing when the money starts rolling, you gotta stay humble. Let these other dudes think we're making pennies. If they don't know how much we're moving, we're gonna stay under the radar that much longer. I need you to be smart and not flex if you don't got to.

Look, I know y'all some of the realest dudes out here and y'all got more heart than a lot of these dudes, and that's why I handpicked each one of you for the team. But we don't want no problems that we don't need. Aight?"

A chorus of bet and aight rang from the small group.

"Good. Now all that's said, I'm here for the pickup. I know y'all only got today's bread on you 'cause I just popped up, so I'll take that for now. First thing in the morning I want you to meet me at the address I gave you earlier to hand off the money from the other days. When you get there, you can hang around for a second, and I'll hit you off with your cut." All four of the men nodded, smoothly handed their knots to Samir and headed back to their corners.

Before he got too far away, Homi turned around. "Yo Samir, I'm sorry to hear about Traci."

"Thanks my brotha," Samir said and got back into the car.

Nina could tell that the mention of Traci took him by surprise. "You ready?"

"Yeah, let's head back to your spot. Yo, Nina, we gonna be back on top real soon. You just wait and see."

Nina smiled. "We sure are baby. We sure are."

Samir started the car and drove silently back to Nina's condo. The silence didn't bother her because she knew he needed it, plus it gave her time to think. Nina was confident in Samir's abilities before, but after hearing him speak to the team, she was even more impressed. Everything he said made so much sense. In that short conversation, he showed how knowledgeable he was about the game and how it should be ran. He was one of the most intelligent hustlers she'd ever seen in her life. What made him most special was that he didn't mind putting people on to the game. He shared his values on life and drug dealing freely. His words and advice were highly respected, and people listened when he talked. Nina looked at him proudly and considered herself lucky to be with him. He was someone who could see beyond all of this hood shit. He wasn't complacent being a drug dealer and aspired to achieve greater heights in life. She loved this man more than he could ever imagine.

CHAPTER FIFTEEN

Nina woke up the next morning and decided that with Samir gone to meet the team now would be a good time to check up on GeGe. They usually spoke multiple times a day, but the whole mess with Traci had thrown Nina out of her typical routine. Under normal circumstances, the period of non-communication wouldn't bother Nina, but now that they were partners in crime, she couldn't let any more days pass without them speaking. Nina always believed one person knowing a secret was one person too much. She didn't want or need GeGe developing a conscience or running her mouth to someone. Nina shuttered at the thought of some busy body convincing her to go to the cops. GeGe was solid in her eyes, but the truth was you could never really know someone fully. She learned that one the hard way with her former best friend, Karen.

Nina would have given Karen anything or at least until she went single black female. By the time she was finally out of Nina's life, Karen had stolen her identity, tried to ruin her relationship, dirtied her reputation in the streets and even had several bench warrants out in her name. After her, Nina never let anyone else into her circle. As far as friends were concerned, GeGe was the last of the Mohicans, and although she loved her, Nina would never be blinded by friendship ever again. She didn't want to miss any signs or slip ups because that could be the difference between freedom and prison or worse; life and death.

Not too long after leaving home, Nina pulled up to GeGe's mother's house and rang the doorbell.

"Come in."

Nina always thought GeGe's mother was too trusting. She couldn't believe she was still leaving her front door unlocked and telling people to come in without checking to see who it is was first.

"How are you doing Mrs. Brown?" Nina said while hugging her. "Well if it ain't Ms. Nina," Mrs. Brown said with a sweet smile while embracing her with the kind of hug only a mother could give. She had a special place in her heart for Mrs. Brown because unlike most people, she always thought the best of Nina. "Is GeGe here?"

"Yeah baby, she's upstairs. It's so good to see you; I haven't seen you in so long." She stepped back to take a good look at Nina. "You look beautiful; look at you. Your hair looks healthy, your skin is glowing, and it looks like you've been kissed by the sun. How is everything?"

"You are too funny Mrs. Brown, but thank you! I'm doing just fine, staying busy as usual."

"I'm glad to hear it. I'm ok, just taking it one day at a time. How's the job? You still managing clients and turning them into superstars?"

"Yes ma'am, but I'm kinda taking a break for a little while. I'm branching out into some new business ventures that are more promising and lucrative."

Mrs. Brown smiled again. "Well, baby do your thing. You always have been one to go and get it. It seems whatever you touch turns into gold." She sighed lightly. "Just lay them hands on that child of mine upstairs. She said she's helping you with this new thing you're doing and that is all type of big deals and stuff. That's all she would say, though. She even came home with this painting that she says is very expensive. If you ask me, it just looks like some ole scribble scrabble crap," Mrs. Brown said with a laugh.

"Well don't worry, when we get everything squared away Ge will tell you everything. The only reason why she didn't go into details with you is because I asked her to wait until we've worked out all the kinks before sharing with anyone; you know first impressions and all."

"That does make a lot of sense. Lord knows people will nitpick your idea to the point of killing it if you're not careful.

So, it's good that you're keeping it to yourself for a while." Mrs. Brown paused. "Lord look at me, talking you to death. GeGe's upstairs. She's probably taking a nap since she was up all night and early this morning with the little one. You can head on up."

"Okay. Thank you, Mrs. Brown."

Although GeGe hadn't spilled any details, Nina was furious she had opened her mouth about the business at all. She told her not to say anything to anyone about anything at all. By the time she reached the top of the stairs, she was heated. Nina burst through the door ready to give GeGe a piece of her mind. "GeGe why in the hell would you tell your mom…" Nina stopped mid-sentence unable to believe what she was seeing. She blinked to make sure her eyes were not playing tricks on her. There's no way she saw GeGe doing a line of coke off of her nightstand. It just couldn't be possible. "What the fuck Ge?! I know I didn't just see you snorting coke?"

GeGe didn't miss a beat and nonchalantly replied, "Come in and close the door before my baby runs up in here."

Nina's head immediately started to hurt at GeGe's non-denial. She walked into the room and closed the door just as she was asked to do. *Here we fucking go.* Nina sat next to GeGe on her bed and rested her hands on her head. "GeGe you doing coke now? What the fuck?" She lifted her head to look GeGe in the face. "When you start doing that shit?"

"It ain't nothing but a little coke, and I don't even do it all the time." GeGe wiped her nose clean and sniffed deeply before continuing. "Yo Tee put me on to it. I'm telling you Nina, after a little bump the sex was amazing. Not to mention it made the good times just a little better. "GeGe smiled and waited for Nina to return it. She didn't, and GeGe continued. "So I do it from time to time," GeGe said dismissively. "It ain't nothing Nina. You're acting like it's heroin or something."

Nina pinched the bridge of her nose to calm herself before speaking. "So let me get this straight. You were playing me the other day when you asked me about the coke and if I ever tried it? What were you trying to do, feel me out to see if I was into it so we could share stories? Is that what that was? Because why the hell else would you ask me when you know I don't be doing that shit?" Nina waited for an answer, but none came. "You know what I can't understand is where all this came from? I mean we stopped smoking weed mad long ago because we wanted to stay in control plus it wasn't cute to be walking around smelling like weed."

"Well, this sure don't make me smell like anything." GeGe laughed at her joke.

"GeGe that ain't funny. You can get hooked on this shit, like for real. This ain't like weed. You get too far into this, and you'll be like every other junkie on the corner."

The smile dropped from GeGe's face. "First of all, I ain't addicted. Stop acting all brand new."

"Ge it ain't even like that. We've seen how this story ends too many times and it never ends well. I don't want that for you. You just need to stop doing this shit." A sudden thought came to Nina's mind. "Wait a minute; is this one of our bottles? You fucking stealing product?"

A look of genuine hurt crossed GeGe's face. "What Nina? Hell no! I ain't never been no snitch or a thief. You know that. I ain't never give you no reason to think like that. The only reason you even coming at me like this is because your grimy ass ex-homegirl Karen stole your identity. I may be a lot of things, but I ain't no thief, and you should know that. If you must know, I had a little bit left from last night when I went out with my homegirl. It's fucked up you would even think something like that." GeGe bit her bottom lip while holding a blank stare on her face. "I should kick your ass just for accusing me of something like that," GeGe said angrily.

Although Nina knew her and GeGe would never physically fight, she responded, "No, I should kick your dumb ass for doing this stupid shit."

"You ain't gon' do shit, Nina."

"Oh yeah? I got something even better. If you don't stop I'ma tell your mother." Nina paused for the dramatic effect and stood up from the bed. "In fact, I think I'ma tell her right now. Oh, Mrs. Brown!"

GeGe popped up off of the bed, covered Nina's mouth with her hand and lightly pushed her back onto the bed. She ran over to her bedroom door and peeked her head out to see if her mom heard Nina. She was thankful when her mom didn't respond to Nina's call.

"Girl that shit ain't funny. You know how my moms is. If she ever found out, she would be devastated and have me up in church every day all day."

Nina laughed hysterically. "That's where your ass needs to be, in church, because you're bugging right now."

"Aight Nina you got it. I'ma stop. Just keep this between you and me. Cool?"

"Yeah aight, whatever."

"So what's going on out there? Everything moving good in the streets?"

"Damn right." Nina nodded her head enthusiastically. "That's what I came over here to talk to you about. Yo Ge, we getting money and it ain't even been two weeks yet. Once we get the rest of the money and pay Lazo, then I'ma hit you with your share for your work."

GeGe waved her hand dismissively. "Girl I know you gonna break me off. I ain't worried about that. I know you good for it."

Nina nodded her appreciation and stood up from the bed. "Aight Ge, let me get out of here. I'll check you later."

"Aight girl, see you later." GeGe smiled. "You know your way out."

Nina forced a fake smile, so as not to betray her true feelings. She left more disappointed than she had ever been with GeGe. Before this morning Nina felt like the three of them were the perfect team. Now she knew it had to be just her and Samir because she could never trust GeGe wholeheartedly ever again. Not only would they have to worry about product, but they also had to worry about GeGe getting high and stepping out of character. She was liable to do anything if her judgment was impaired while under the influence. Nina just couldn't take that chance. She decided right then and there she would keep GeGe around just long enough for her not to get suspicious and wouldn't tell her anything else about business.

When Nina arrived home, she couldn't wait to discuss everything she just found out with Samir. He agreed with her plan to keep GeGe close. He thought she simply knew too much to piss her off. Samir tried to be gentle with his next piece of

115

advice seeing as he knew how much Nina loved GeGe. "Nina I know you asked her to stop 'cause you're only looking out for her, but watch how you ask her. Okay?"

Nina looked slightly confused. "What do you mean?"

"GeGe's grown Nina, but right now she's not thinking straight. The more you lecture her about quitting, the more she's gonna rebel and keep doing it."

Nina started to speak, but Samir cut her off.

"I ain't saying you can't try to help her, but she's not gonna stop until she's ready. So until then, all we got is us. Aight?" Samir stuck his pinky out, and Nina grabbed it with hers. He smiled as they both kissed their thumbs and then rubbed them together as their pinkies remained interlocked. "It's just you and me."

CHAPTER SIXTEEN

"So was it worth it? Huh, was it? What's wrong, cat got your tongue." A set of cold eyes stared daggers into Nina's soul. "Oh no silly me. Let me correct myself 'cause we both know it's Samir keeping you quiet, right?" A cold laugh broke through the air. "I guess you thought you were in control of everything, but it ain't take long to see that's not true. Right?" The laughter came again. "Poor stupid Nina, what you gonna do now? Doesn't feel too good not to have options, huh?" The eyes radiated pure hatred yet they mocked Nina. "You ain't learn yet that there not really choices if that's all that's given to you? I learned that lesson real quick when you came along. I had no choice but to be alone 'cause that's the only option I was given. You took away my choices. You took away my life, and I hope that fucking my man was worth it!" The last words hung in the air for an eternity. "So let me guess you thought I forgave you? Well, I didn't. You can keep your apology like you kept my man. We not good and we will never be good. Remember that. You took my choices, and now I'm taking them back." Nina saw a glint of chrome rise. "Now open up that mouth. You know, the one you use to suck Samir's dick with?! Open it up and taste this thirty-eight. Count to three, and it will all be over. One, two..."

Nina woke up in a cold sweat barely able to catch her breath.

"Babe you aight?" Samir asked concerned. He stood before Nina holding a breakfast tray. "Damn you soaking wet." He lifted the tray giving Nina a better view of its contents. " I made chicken and waffles with some fruit on the side. Your man even brought you some fresh squeezed orange juice," He said with a smile. "Now sit up and eat this gourmet meal a brotha put together 'cause it won't be long before it's time for you to link up with Lazo." He gave Nina a second look. "You sure you okay?"

"Yeah babe, I'm good. I just had another nightmare about Traci trying to kill me." Nina shook her head. "I had convinced myself that she had forgiven me. I'm starting to think my ass was wrong. This bitch is gonna haunt me for the rest of my life."

"Come on now Nina. Don't be like that. After all the shit we done and then seeing Traci kill herself..." Samir paused at the sound of Traci's name coming from his mouth. "Look all I'm saying is with everything that's happened, it's totally normal to have bad dreams." Samir grabbed her hand as he continued to speak. "I have nightmares too. I just deal with them myself because I don't wanna wake you. Your ass be sleep hard as hell, I mean knocked out for real." He laughed at his joke before continuing. "So I know what you're going through." Nina looked slightly away from Samir then gently turned her back to him. "Listen, look at me. The dreams will stop soon enough, but I'm here for you. Just know that. Okay?"

Nina hugged Samir tightly. "Thank you, Samir! You always have the right words to say. What would I do without you?"

"Let's not find out. Now eat up cause you 'bout to be late for the meeting with Lazo."

"Well damn! Can I relax and eat the breakfast you made for me? Sheesh!"

"You can relax when you dead."

Nina stopped eating mid-bite and gave him the side eye.

"Okay, I said that wrong. What I mean is that you can relax once we are officially back on top. So chop-chop missy, let's get this money!"

"Mmmhmm. Anyway, thank you for breakfast. Now if you give me a few minutes, I'ma throw it down real quick and get ready to go. I'm starving."

As promised, Nina ate quickly before jumping into the shower. With her hair clean and her body smelling right, Nina threw on a tight, black maxi dress. She looked at herself in the mirror and admired how it accented her shapely frame while hugging her every curve. Nina smiled at the thought of how much Samir loved her in this type of dress. If his reaction to her dressed like this was any indication, she would have no problems with Lazo tonight. *Now to finish the look*, she thought to herself. Nina ran some gel through her curls to tame them and dabbed a little concealer under her eyes to hide the dark circles courtesy of her many sleepless nights. Normally, Nina wouldn't care so much about small things, but tonight was different. It was important she always had her best face on when meeting Lazo. It was critical to her and Samir's operation to keep him turned on and constantly lusting after her. That was their best bet if they wanted to continue getting product at a discounted rate with negotiable repayment terms. While the rest of the chumps were out there scraping up money for their connects' outrageous prices, Nina and Samir were getting the lowest prices and making crazy profits. Nina had Lazo right where she wanted him and had every intention of keeping him right there.

Nina gave herself a final look in the mirror before kissing Samir on the cheek and preparing to head out. "I'll be back babe."

He looked at her intently, noticing how great she looked. "Keep it tight. Aight?"

Nina's face said it all. "Samir, you better be playing?! I ain't no thot or hoe, so you need to stop talking like you think I am. If you think I'd ever sleep with Lazo for a damn connect..." She inhaled to stop herself from becoming any angrier.

"Samir bit his bottom lip. "I trust you; I just don't trust him." He silently apologized by kissing her on the cheek. He opened the door and held it as Nina passed. "Be safe." Nina placed her hand on his shoulder and walked out.

Nina sat in her car for a minute to gather herself. She would never let Samir know, but the nightmares were starting to get to her. *Fuck you, Traci! Ole spiteful ass still bothering me from beyond the damn grave.* Nina started the car and put it in drive, then just as quickly put it back into park. *I can't meet Lazo in this mood.* "This will do the trick, it always has," Nina said aloud after shuffling through her music. Seconds later Lil' Kim's "Hardcore", specifically "Queen Bitch", blared through the speakers. Nina's mood immediately changed. The beat dropped, she shifted her car back into drive and pulled out feeling like 'that bitch'.

119

Several songs later Nina pulled up to Lazo's. He answered the door in the same manner as the last time, suave as ever. "Ms. Nina, such a pleasure to see you again. You look even more beautiful than the last time we met." He stepped aside motioning for her to enter. "Come in por favor."

"How are you doing Lazo? It's very nice to see you again."

"I'm well mi amor."

In a pleasant tone, Nina replied. "Lazo, please remember that I speak very little Spanish, so I would appreciate it if we could keep it to English, so I can understand what you're talking about."

"Yes, I understand. But with all of the business we will be doing together, it will be best for you to learn how to speak Spanish or at the very least you need to understand it. It would be to your benefit mi amor." Lazo smiled. "Would you like a glass of wine?"

"No thank you, Lazo." Nina inadvertently looked at her watch and handed Lazo a briefcase filled with the money he was owed.

"In a hurry?" Lazo asked. "May I ask the reason for such a rush?" Lazo looked questioningly at Nina. "Have I offended you in any way? Have my services not been up to par?"

"Oh no Lazo, not at all," she said sincerely. "I just have some other business to attend to today."

Lazo waited for a bit. Nina couldn't tell if he was offended or simply waiting to speak. When he finally opened his mouth his tone was even, but his words were measured. "I look forward to our meetings, and I expect you to schedule all of your other engagements, so they do not interfere with our time."

Nina nodded her head in compliance although she was beyond pissed. The only thing that kept her from flipping was her and Samir's end goal. As angry as she was, Nina would never let her ego get in the way of their plans. They have a connect who was providing some of the purest product out there for an unheard of price. There was no way a little bit of pride was going to stop them from staying on good terms with Lazo.

"Lazo, please understand I meant no harm."

Lazo raised his hand for Nina to stop. "My precious, there's no need to say anymore. What can I do for you to make sure that both our business arrangement and meetings run as smoothly as possible?" His sly smile communicated his true intentions.

In the brief time they had known each other Lazo never hid his attraction from Nina. In fact, she had no problem using it to her advantage. However, she was slightly irritated that it was creeping into every second of their conversation. She spoke sternly, yet sweetly. "Lazo, I'm here to handle business, and while I enjoy your company, I don't want or need any favors that require sexual encounters as thank you's. I want to have a great professional relationship with you, one where you respect me and one where we can both make money hand over fist."

"Say no more mi amor." Lazo smiled authentically. "However you must know that I am a gentleman and being as such I will always treat you like a lady. So although I will always respect you as a colleague, I will respect you as a lady first." He walked over to the briefcase that Nina just delivered to him. "Let me give you a gift to commemorate our new found understanding of each other." He opened the briefcase and counted its contents. He then took some and closed the case back. "The one hundred and twelve thousand you just gave me; I'm giving back twelve thousand of it." Nina's heart began to race while Lazo continued. "I will also, for this one time only, when it is time for you to make your next purchase I will give you the standard six keys for twenty thousand each instead of twenty-eight. How does that sound to you?"

It took Nina a moment to respond. *This cannot be real.* "Lazo are you sure?"

"Yes, Nina I am very sure."

"And what exactly would you want in return for this nice gesture?"

"Nina, I think we have both made ourselves very clear. I assure you I want nothing in return, but my money. Of course minus the amount that I have just given back. I only have two conditions. My first is, as I stated earlier, I don't want our meetings to be rushed. From this point forward our meetings will not have designated end times. They will flow naturally and unrestrained. The other is that whenever you need any assistance, whether it's business related or not, all you have to do is ask. Are we in agreeance?"

Nina stood silently, still in shock by what she just heard.

"Nina?"

"Lazo, I just find it hard to believe that you are parting with such a large amount of money without any expectations," she responded in a questionable tone.

"This is not a game of trust; I know that, but I've told you what I expect. It's up to you whether to believe me or not. You see, I don't take my money lightly. I get what's owed to me and will not hesitate to punish those who steal from me. Please understand that money is not my primary motivation in life, it's my respect. Again, I am a gentleman, and it would be a pleasure to give such a beautiful woman gifts and anything else you may need in the future. For now, I'm sure a glass of my finest red wine should suffice."

"Thank you, Lazo. I sincerely appreciate all that you have offered, including the wine, but let's handle the business with the product first."

Lazo laughed and smiled. "Nina I like your style, always business before fun. I like that about you. You remind me of myself when I was younger."

"Thank you. I apologize. I just always find it's easier this way."

"No no. No need for apologies. I completely understand and respect it. Please sit here, and I will be back in a bit." He began to walk out of the room but turned shortly before his exit. "I can tell that your mind is elsewhere, so we will cut this meeting short as you initially intended. Let's say we meet again in a month and pick up from where we left off. Agreed?"

"Yes, agreed! I'm just not..."

"Shhhh. No need to explain yourself any more mi amor." He left and returned with the product.

"This is the same as last time, six keys. Since you have accepted my gift, I will simply take it as a sign that business will run smoothly." Lazo popped open the case he'd just brought in and turned it towards Nina. "Please look inside and inspect that everything is bueno."

She looked inside and found everything as it should be. "Yes everything is good or should I say everything is bueno."

"See this is what I mean about you. Such a beautiful spirit and a witty personality, you're exceptional!" Lazo walked closer to Nina, gently grabbed her face and placed a soft kiss on her forehead. "Enjoy your day Nina."

"Thank you again, Lazo."

"Please let me walk you to the door."

Nina grabbed her things, the product and followed Lazo to the door.

"Adios, Nina. See you in a month."

"Yes, see you then."

Nina left Lazo's wondering what she had gotten herself into. There was no way in hell she could tell Samir just how much more than business Lazo wanted with her. He would be furious at the most, and at the least, his pride could potentially cause them to lose their connect. There was no doubt in her mind he would insist on being the new point man even if it cost them the discounted rate. There was no way Nina was letting that happen. She rationalized that there wouldn't be a problem because she wasn't fucking Lazo. It was just a little innocent flirting to get what they needed.

CHAPTER SEVENTEEN

While driving home, all Nina could think about was Samir. She wanted nothing more than to spend the rest of the day lounging in front of the television and pigging out. It was the best way she could think of to celebrate how well things were going after the hellish week they previously had. Nina felt like they could finally breathe again and with the low prices they were getting from Lazo, she could clearly see the better life away from the game she envisioned for them. She knew life was unpredictable. At the moment, everything was so perfect she couldn't see how it could ever go wrong again. Nina caught a glimpse of her reflection in the car beside her and liked the smile she saw. Even though she had a large amount of money and product in the car, her day was going so well she felt confident enough to stop by the grocery store.

Nina arrived at her front door and was startled when Samir opened the door before she could. "Boy you scared the mess out of me," she said as she gathered herself. "Hey, can you do me a favor and get the rest of the groceries outta the car for me?"

"Aight. It's not a lot, is it? I'm kinda in a rush."

"Nah, it's just a few bags." Nina walked inside and called back to Samir, "Hey, where are you going?"

"I got things to do and people to see." Samir flashed a smile.

"Boy don't play with me. Like I said, where the hell are you going?"

"Come on Nina, calm down." He dropped his voice down to a loud whisper. "Even though I love it when you get feisty. It turns me on."

Nina threw an empty bag at him. "Samir!"

"Nah, but for real, I'ma swing around the way to pick up some money. Is that okay with you, Ms. Nina?"

"I hate when you try to be all secretive about your whereabouts that's all. So, now that I know where you're going, please go and pick up our money."

"I knew if money was involved your ass would be okay with it," Samir said with a laugh.

"Whatever! Don't be too long I'm cooking dinner and I'ma find us a good movie to watch."

"Okay babe." He walked over to Nina and gave her a kiss on her lips before smacking her on her nice bubble shaped ass. "Keep it tight!"

Nina winked and rubbed herself where she'd been popped. "Ouch! Samir you smacked my ass too freaking hard. You know I hate when you do that!"

"Mmhmm, you love it! I'll be right back with the groceries and then I'ma go handle that B I."

When Samir pulled up to the block in Brownsville, the first person he saw was Darion. Samir hopped out of the car and gave him dap. "Yo my dude, what's good? How's everything looking today?"

"Boss man you already know money flowing like water out here. We're keeping the faucets on at all times. You feel me?"

"Damn right that's what I love to hear. Come holla at me." Samir nodded his head towards his car on the corner.

Darion knew what Samir was saying without him saying it. As soon as they sat in the car, he reached into his stash and handed Samir a knot of cash. "Here's your bread."

Samir took the cash at face value. He would count it when he was someplace secure, and if there were any shorts, which he doubt there would be, he would handle it then. "Cool, any more problems with B or his goons?"

"Nah, no problems here." Darion paused while he weighed whether or not to say what was on his mind. 'No snitching' had been drilled into him for years. Not to mention both Homi and Samir were his boys and he was loyal to both of them. However, Samir was the boss and what he knew could potentially screw with the business. *Fuck it,* he thought. "Yo, Homi's been talking to that nigga."

Samir's eyes narrowed at the news.

"Every time he passes by, Homi be all up in his face and not like going at him neither. They be straight up talking about shit and Homi be having mad shit to say. And when B pulls up in his car..." Darion shook his head in disbelief. "Yo, he stay at that nigga window for mad long too son. Shit's crazy!" He expected Samir to say something, but when he stayed silent, Darion continued. "But look you ain't hear none of that shit from me. Aight? I ain't no snitching type nigga. I know it sounds ill, but I'm not here for all that. So, I just thought I let you know that something don't seem right with them two. I could be wrong, but in this game, it's better safe than sorry. Feel me? It could be nothing. Just make sure you peep the situation yourself." Darion stuck his fist out for a pound. "Aight let me get back to work, see you in a few days."

Samir bumped fists with Darion, nodded to him and watched him walk away. *Fuck*! I don't need this problem he thought as he popped the trunk of the car. With a lot on his mind, he hopped out to stash the money Darion just passed him in the hidden compartment of the trunk for safe keeping.

"Samir, ayo Samir!"

Samir turned to see Homi waving for him to come down the block to meet him.

Samir's attitude towards Homi was icy. It didn't help the situation that Homi was yelling his name down the street for any and everyone to hear. *Here we fucking go! What in the hell does he want and who in the hell does he think I am?!* Samir threw his hand in the air as an indication that if Homi wanted to talk he would have to come to him.

"Yo, I gotta show you something real quick."

This fucker is gonna piss me off if he keeps yelling. Samir sighed in frustration. He knew Homi was up to something; he just didn't know what. He decided right then it would be in his best interest to act normally around Homi until he could figure out what exactly was going on. Samir was no fool. He knew if he were backed into a corner, even by someone he considered a friend, Homi would have no problem living up to his name. And since he had every intention to keep collecting his money while he straightened things out, Samir cooled his temper and walked over to Homi to see what was up. "What's goodie? What's up with taking a break from the corner?"

Homi shook his head no. "Nah no breaks here, boy," Homi replied. "I'm waiting for this dude who don't like to meet and exchange shit out in the open. He's a good customer and is always copping, so I do him a solid by meeting him over here."

"Oh aight." Samir got straight to the point. "What you gotta show me?"

"Yo, I said it wrong. It's something I gotta speak to you about. I gotta proposition for you."

Samir shifted. He still wasn't one hundred on Homi, but he was willing to listen if money was involved. "Well aight let me hear it. I'm all about more money."

Homi rubbed his stubbled chin. "See this plan involves more than just you and me."

B stepped around the corner. "Well, well, well. What's goodie my G? We meet again."

"What the fuck you want B?" Samir said angrily.

B continued to talk as if he hadn't heard Samir's question. "I don't need to ask how you're doing. Do I? I hear you becoming the man out here. You got everybody wanting your shit." B let out a gravelly laugh meant more for himself than anyone else. "Funny thing is, you messing with my bread. I've been hustling since before you sold your first nickel bag and ain't never let nobody fuck up what I had going on. One thing is for sure; I'm damn sure not gonna start now. You understand what I'm saying, son?"

"I ain't your fucking son!"

Again B talked through Samir. "You do remember I'm the one that put you on when you was trying to get on, right? And I was the one you turned to when you needed a come up." B didn't wait for an answer. "Exactly! Me that's who and don't you ever forget it." B walked in closer to Samir. "So listen up. I say we go into business together. Since this here is my block I get seventy percent, and you get thirty. Hell, I think that's fair. So what's up?"

Samir couldn't believe what he was hearing. "B you gotta be outta your fucking mind! You got some damn nerve standing up in my face and offering me the chance to give a larger cut of my block. You're fuckin crazier than I thought if you think I'm giving you a percentage of my shit at all. You must got me fucked up?!" B closed the gap in between them.

"I'm the one with the product everyone wants. Me!" Samir pounded his chest. "I paid you what I owed you, and that's where our fucking business ended. So don't stand here and act like you doing me any goddamn favors. Fuck outta here!"

B drew his gun and pointed it at Samir's chest. "Ninja I'm doing you a huge motherfucking favor by coming to you to talk and not putting this bullet in your dumb ass right here, right now," B growled. "I hate dumb ninjas like you. You think you got it all figured out, but you don't know shit. You still wet behind the ears boy." B spat Samir's name like it was covered in shit. "Young ninjas like you always think you're running the game. When they finally realize they ain't, they come to their senses, and they come right on over to me. They always come. So see, you ain't nothing special ninja. You out here thinking you some golden child or some shit, but I'ma show you better than I can tell you. From now on, just run them pockets whenever I see you."

Samir made no move towards his pocket. The memory of being shot was still fresh on his mind, but there was no way he would let B break him. "B, let me tell you something. You can wave that wack-ass .380 at me and think I'ma be scared if you want to. You got me fucked up. I ain't scared of you son. You up here talking and ain't saying nothing. You mad pussy. Your washed up bum ass should've exited the game years ago just to save face." B felt himself growing angrier the more Samir spoke. "I would've had more respect for you if you had just left. No, you just gotta have something to prove. You wanna show everybody you still got it. Right? You ain't shit boy! You feel me?" Samir yelled. "And I ain't giving you shit! Not outta my pockets or my business. If you don't like it, you might as well shoot me 'cause ain't nothing moving on this end. Fuck you!"

Samir looked over his shoulder to Homi. "Yo, we're done?! Your snake ass is through over here too."

Unfazed by Samir's words, B slid his gun back into his waistband and smirked. "My man Samir. You're a funny dude. You're not too smart though, but you got a lot of heart. I knew you would be a tough nut to crack when you made it passed Tee."

Samir heart pounded loudly in his ears at the sound of Tee's name, but outwardly he remained unmoved. *So, B was behind that shit?!* He angrily said to himself.

B began to walk away. "Make no mistake about it; it's war. The only reason you still standing here is 'cause I let you. Don't let today make you believe I won't fill your ass full of holes and leave you leaking." B quickly turned the corner and was gone. Samir called behind him. "Yeah what the fuck ever chump!" Samir shouted back to B. Samir looked at Homi with pure hatred in his eyes, then walked away.

As he got close to his car, he heard Homi calling from behind him. "Yo Samir, hold up."

Samir didn't bother to turn around. "Man fuck you! You mad wicked!"

Homi jogged to catch up with him. "Yo son I ain't know B was gonna do all that. He just said he wanted to talk to you and shit." His voice was sincere, but Samir wasn't trying to hear any of it. "I was trying to make our team stronger. I just wanted us to get all the money out here."

Samir couldn't take it anymore. "Save it, my dude. I ain't fucking stupid! What you thought was gonna happen was B was gonna press me into partnering with him, and you was getting a better position on his team. Now you see that shit ain't happen, so you wanna come back over here on this side. I saw the look on your face when B came round the corner." Samir spoke so hard he spat. "You think I'm dumb enough to let you clock my moves, so you can line me? Boy, fuck you! Fuck outta here! You made your fucking choice when you called me over here. Now live with it."

Homi knew Samir was on to him, but he would die before he admitted it. "Well fuck you too then nigga!"

Samir made sure not to let Homi see how much he had hurt him. After everything he did to put together the best team, this guy turns around and stabs him in the back in less than a month.

I took his dirty ass in and gave him an opportunity to make real money, instead of that nickel and dime change he was getting from selling garbage weed. He couldn't believe Homi had set him up like that. He had proven himself loyal in the past, but it was obvious things had changed. The only words he could say in response to Homi were, "Yeah, aight." On the way back to the car, Samir passed Darion and gave him a pound again. "Good looking my brother. You proved yourself. I owe you one."

Darion nodded.

By the time Samir made it back to his car all of the emotion he had tried so hard to contain came spilling out. Behind the tinted windows, where he was sure no one could see him, he banged on the steering wheel until his fists hurt. *Get your shit together.* He said to himself with pain in his heart. "Aight Samir, new plan," he said aloud to himself. It didn't escape Samir that B just admitted to trying to set him up. He knew there was no turning back for either of them and their problems went way beyond beefing over territory. Now, it was all personal. There could be no more assuming anything was safe. Samir would have to stay strapped and keep a team of shooters on the lookout if he wanted to be able to make moves around the city. He silently thanked Darion for warning him about Homi and was glad he had shown his cards sooner than later. His only issue now was Nina. She would be a nervous wreck if he told her what had just transpired between him and B. She would be constantly looking over her shoulder and lose her edge. Samir didn't want to do that to her. He would just have to find a better way to keep her safe and out of all of this. *I got something for B's ass, though.* Samir started the car and pulled off blasting 2Pac's throwback, *Hellrazor.*

CHAPTER EIGHTEEN

"Ahhhhhhhh." Samir sat in up in bed swinging wildly.

"Samir! It's okay." Nina gently shoved his shoulder. "You're having a bad dream baby."

Samir opened his eyes, and the room came into focus. B and his shooters were no longer in sight. He wiped his forehead, which was drenched in sweat. "My bad Nina. Between the two of us and these nightmares, we ain't never gon' get no sleep around here." Samir halfheartedly laughed at his joke.

Nina's face was stone. If his nightmares were anything like her's, she didn't find anything funny about it. "You okay?" she asked concerned.

"Yeah, just give me a second."

"What happened?"

"Nina don't worry about it. I'm good. Okay?"

She sat up and rubbed his back. "Samir what happened? What were you dreaming about?"

Knowing she wasn't going to let it go, he exhaled and started to speak. "It was B. He was trying to kill me." Samir looked away slightly ashamed.

"Babe, why are you letting him get to you like this? You already know he's not smarter than us. There's no way he can out think us." Nina smiled in her attempt to reassure him. "He's the one that should be having sleepless nights about how we're taking all of his customers."

Samir felt a pang of guilt for not telling Nina about what happened with B and Homi. He hated to lie to her, but he felt it was the best way to protect her. "I know babe; I'm bugging." Samir stared out into the room to stop himself from sharing his real concerns. "I know this sounds dumb as hell because at the end of the day this shit is killing the community, but I just want to give the people what they want."

He looked at Nina expecting to see a confused look on her face. It wasn't there.

"Look I know we should be ashamed of selling it to our people, but if we don't someone else will," Samir rationalized. "If they're going to do it anyway, why shouldn't we make us some money in the process? It's all a business. All I do is provide a product that the consumer decides whether or not to use. I ain't forcing nobody, you know?" Nina sat quietly as he finished his thought. "These tobacco companies do the same thing. They sale a product that everyone knows is bad for you, that everyone knows can kill you and no one says shit to them. You want to know why?" He didn't wait for an answer. "It's because everyone knows it up to the individual whether they want to smoke or not. I ain't no monster Nina; I got a conscience. It's just business." He scratched his head wondering if he was trying to convince Nina or himself. "You know in the beginning, when I first started hustling, I wouldn't sale to pregnant ladies, young kids, or first-time users." Samir didn't finish his thought. It wasn't necessary. He knew he was wrong and there was no justification. In his heart of hearts, he knew that none of it mattered to him. All that mattered was Nina and Layla. If he had to sell drugs to hold them down, he would; without apology or regret. Besides, like he said, he never forced anyone to buy what he was selling. "Yo, it's cool Nina, don't worry about it. I got it." For the first time, he noticed the time. "It's early, go back to sleep."

"Okay, babe. You try to get some rest too."

"Yeah, I'll try."

Nina's buzzer rang before either of their heads had a chance to hit the pillow.

Samir looked at Nina. "You expecting someone?"

"Nah. Let me go see who this is." Nina walked into the living room. "Hello? Yes, yes. Send them up."

By the time she hung up, Samir was standing behind her. "What was that about? Everything good?"

"It was actually for you. It was your mom."

"My mom?"

"Yeah, she'll be up here in a minute." Nina looked down at herself and realized that she did not want to greet his mother in her lingerie. "I'll be right back. I'ma go slip something on."

As she walked out the room, the doorbell rang.

Although Samir loved his mother and usually enjoyed her company, he was concerned that she was at Nina's early and unannounced. "Ma, what's wrong? What are you doing here?"

His mother greeted him with a warm smile. "Hello, Samir. Baby fix your face. Nothing's wrong. Okay? I just think that it's time for you to start taking care of your daughter."

It wasn't until then that Samir noticed Layla peeking out from behind his mother.

"Layla, baby girl! Come give your father a hug." Layla ran in and hugged him sweetly. "Hey pumpkin, I need a favor. Let me and Grandma talk for a second. Okay? I bet there's a really good cartoon on. What do you think?"

Layla nodded and laughed. "I bet there is daddy."

"Okay, good. You see that table beside the couch over there? "Yes."

"Well, the remote is sitting right there. Do you think you can turn it on by yourself?"

"Yes, daddy. I'm not a little baby." Layla giggled as she ran towards the table.

"Your favorite channels start on twenty-three. Okay?"

"Okay, daddy." Layla sat on the couch. Seconds later, her face was illuminated by the glow of the television. Samir turned to his mother. "Come on in Ma. Let's go to the kitchen and talk."

Mrs. Wright followed Samir into the kitchen. "You need something Ma? Something to drink or anything?"

"No thank you, baby."

Samir pulled a chair away from the table and offered it to his mother. He sat across from her.

"Now like I was saying a few moments ago, you need to start taking care of your daughter. Since her mother passed, it's like you're afraid to be around her." Mrs. Wright lovingly placed her hand on top of Samir's hand. "Baby, I know it's hard. I understand right now that Layla probably reminds you a lot of

Traci and the things that went wrong in your marriage. That's not her fault. She's already lost a mother; she doesn't need to lose her father too."

"Ma, it's not like that."

Mrs. Wright raised a knowing eyebrow, and the weight of Samir's selfishness hit him like a ton of bricks. He knew he had taken the easy way out and that his visits with his daughter weren't enough.

"Ma, I'm not running away from my daughter. I swear I'm not." His voice cracked a little. "It's just, I've been taking care of some things that have kept me moving around, and I wanted Layla to have a little more stability. That's all."

"Samir, I've raised you. You are my child. I love Layla to death and would do absolutely anything for her, but she's your child. I'm too old to start again."

"I understand Ma. I'm grateful that you have helped me out this long, but I have her from here.

"That's my boy." Mrs. Wright smiled and kissed the back of his hands. "You know I love you right, baby?"

"Yes Ma, I know." He couldn't help but smile. "Did you bring any of her things?"

"Just the things that were at my place while she was staying there; it's all in the suitcases by the door in the hallway."

"Now Samir, you know if you or Layla need me, I'm always here to help; just one phone call away."

"Yes Ma, I know." Samir grabbed his mother by the hand and led her back into the living room. "Thanks again for everything. I love you."

"I love you too baby." She hugged her son tightly. "Oh, I almost forgot. Nina said it was okay for the desk attendant to send this mail up here with me."

"Thank you," Samir said as he grabbed the mail from his mother. "Layla come say bye to Grandma."

"Bye Grandma. I love you!"

"Love you too baby girl. Oh Samir, please tell Nina that I said hi since I didn't get a chance to see her."

"Will do, Ma. See you later." Samir closed the door. "So, baby girl are you hungry?"

"Do you have any cereal?"

"I think so. What kind do you want?

"Cheerios. Do you happen to have any of those? They're more of a healthy heart choice."

"Well damn. I see that the money I'm paying for private school is paying off. You're eating healthy and speaking properly." Samir nuzzled Layla's cheek. "So how are those grades?"

"Dad you know I make straight A's." Layla giggled as Samir beard tickled her face. "I think you're just being silly right now."

"I know baby girl. I'm just making sure. Come on; let me get your cereal and then I'ma go check on Nina."

"Okay, dad."

Samir walked into the bedroom just as Nina finished getting dressed. "So what's up? What does your mom need? Everything okay?"

"Yeah, yeah. Everything is cool. She had to leave, though. She told me to tell you hi."

"Oh okay. Maybe I'll get to see her next time."

"Yeah, maybe." Samir sat on the edge of the bed. "Nina come sit down beside me, I have to talk to you about something."

A chill ran down her spine. "What is it Samir? What happened?"

Samir heard the panic in her voice. "Babe it's nothing like that." Samir rubbed his chin. "Um, my mom came by to drop Layla off. She thinks that it's time I go back to taking care of her full time." Samir began to ramble. "You know my mom is getting up in age and she's raised..."

Nina interrupted him. "Babe stop, it's fine. "Why are you trying to sell me on the idea of Layla living with us. That's your daughter. I assumed that it was gonna happen eventually and I'm honestly surprised that it took this long." Nina finally sat beside him on the bed. "Look Samir; I understand she's your main priority. Now she's mine too. Okay? We will just have to rearrange a few things and stagger some schedules." Nina smiled warmly. "We're going to be aight."

"Damn girl! As if I needed another reason to love you. You're amazing. You always got my back." Samir rubbed her thigh. "Promise me you'll never change up on me."

"Cross my heart." Nina drew an exaggerated x across her chest and laughed.

He kissed her on the forehead. "Cool, let me get dressed, so I can run Layla to school. Oh, and my mother brought up the mail from the desk attendant. I put it on the table near the door."

"Okay, thanks."

Samir quickly dressed and headed out to drop Layla off.

Nina walked into the living room to check the mail. *Bill, bill, bill, another damn bill and more damn bills.* The last letter in the pile was a plain envelope without a return address.

She ripped the envelope open and out fell a handful of pictures. Nina bent down to pick them up and immediately recognized herself in one of them. *What in the hell?!* Her heart raced, and she grew warm as she flipped through the pictures. They were all of her. There was even one of her walking to her car after she killed Tee. "Oh shit!" *Someone is playing games. Who could have taken these pictures?* Nina ran through every scenario possible in her mind and couldn't think of any time she noticed anyone following her. She thought she had been so careful. Sure GeGe knew, but she found out after the fact. *This shit cannot be happening.* Nina pulled her cell phone from the pockets of her sweats and dialed Samir's number.

He picked up on the second ring. "Samir, where are you?"

"Not far, but I figured I stop by the block before heading back in. Why? What's up?"

"You gotta come home now! Something ain't right. I can't get into it over the phone, but trust me we need to talk ASAP."

"Yo, I'm on my way!"

Nina sat on the couch and nervously waited for Samir. The pictures taunted her as they sat on the table. The pictures called on her to keep looking at them even though she knew doing so would only make her feel worse. *Someone's trying to blackmail me, I just know it.*

Just then, Samir burst through the front door. "Nina, what's wrong? You're scaring the shit out of me. You okay?"

Nina slid the pictures across the table. "Look at these."

"What's this?"

"Just look please." Nina was broken to the point of whining.

"Nina, what are these? I got better things to do than look at some damn pictures. I was about to make some money when you called me to come back. Now, what's the problem?"

"Samir, just look at the damn pictures!" Nina screamed.

He finally did as he was asked. "Oh shit!"

Nina pointed to the picture on the top. "This one right here is from the day I shot Tee! Someone was following me that day. Hell, they could still be following me now!" Nina was frightened, and there was no hiding it. "What the fuck are we going to do Samir?"

"Calm down. Calm down. It's gonna be okay."

Nina looked at him like he was crazy.

"Let's just wrap our heads around this and do some investigating of our own. Okay?" Samir tried to reassure Nina, but the look on her face said that it wasn't working.

I'ma head out to the block and see if anyone is talking. I'ma see what I can find out." Samir's ringing phone interrupted him. Samir's face twisted in confusion at the weird number on the caller ID. "Hello? Hello?"

"Yo, it's your boy! A nigga just got out."

Samir looked at the phone to check the number again. He thought he recognized the voice, but the number was throwing him off. Considering the pictures he just saw he had no plans of making any assumptions. He wasn't taking any chances. "Who is this?" He asked.

The voice on the other end laughed. "Damn boy, I only been locked up for five years and you forgot about my ass already? That's fucked up. I thought I knew you better than that."

There was no question about it now; it was exactly who Samir thought it was. "I know this ain't my cousin, Wolf?"

"Ding, ding, muthafuckin ding. You finally got it right my nigga."

"Yo Wolf!" Samir was happy to hear his cousin's voice. "Man, I definitely didn't forget about you son. I knew you were getting out soon; I just didn't expect for you to be calling my phone from some weird ass number."

"Well I'm out and I ain't on no papers either. When shit went down, I told them to give me my sentence day for day cause I wasn't coming home reporting to no muthafuckin body. You feel me? Anyway, how 'bout we link up tonight? We gotta do something. It's been a minute since your boy been on the streets and I'm looking to pop some bottles and fuck a bad ass bitch."

Hearing Wolf's voice made him forget about the pictures. "Cuz, I know just the spot. Let me get some things worked out and I'ma call you back with the address. You can just meet me there. Cool?"

"Yeah, but I ain't driving nowhere tonight. I'm trying to get fucked up."

"Aight, I got you. Where you want me to pick you up?"

"You remember where Tayesha, my third baby momma, stay?"

"Yeah, I remember."

"That's where I'll be. You can scoop me from there."

"Aight cool. I'll be there around 10 o'clock. Ayo, Wolf this number you calling from good, right? I can call it if I need you?"

"Yeah, it's good cuzzo. I'll see you around ten and man we gotta talk. I hear you the man out here."

"We'll talk when we see each other."

"Bet!"

Samir hung up the phone with a smile on his face. "Nina baby, find something to wear, we're going out tonight."

Nina didn't respond immediately. She was shocked at his sudden change in mood. "Babe do you think that now is a good time to be going out. I mean, did you forget the pictures?"

"It's a perfect time. We ain't gonna find out nothing sitting up in the house. I was about to head out to put my ear to the street anyway. Besides we can use the opportunity to show whoever sent the pictures that we ain't scared. We gonna show them that we're still doing us." He hoped Nina wouldn't give him too much resistance on this because he hadn't seen his cousin in five years. "Look we're just gonna lay low, pop some bottles and observe? Okay?"

"Samir we don't even do the club like that. What in the world made you want to go to the club tonight? And did you forget we have Layla now?"

"Yo, Wolf is out, and I want to show him a good time. And, nah I didn't forget about Layla. I didn't get a chance to tell you because of how things popped off, but she's spending the night with a friend tonight. When I dropped her off at school this morning, one her friend's mom invited her over. That's why tonight is the perfect time to take Wolf out!"

"Wait you mean Wolf, shoot'em up at any given moment Wolf?"

"Yeah!"

From everything Nina heard about Wolf, he wasn't one to blend in. " Samir, how in the hell are we going to be low key with him. He's everything that we're not. He's loud and flashy. He's going to bring mad attention to us, and it could be bad attention."

Frustration began to show on Samir's face. "Nina, I got it. Can you please just find something nice to wear tonight, okay? That's all I want you to worry about. I'll handle everything else. If it'll make you feel better, I'll head out to ask a few questions before we go out. Will that help?"

Nina decided to put her trust in Samir. "Okay babe, I'm down, and yes, that will make me feel better. Thank you."

As promised Samir left to gather information on the pictures, while Nina tried to make the best out of her new situation. She called GeGe. "Hey Ge, I need you to come over and help me out with something. I'm going to the club, and you're coming too. So, I need to find the right thing to wear."

Nina could hear the shock in GeGe's voice. "The club? Bitch, when you start going back to the club?"

"Don't worry about that, just know I'm going with Samir and his cousin Wolf," Nina said laughing.

"Fine ass Wolf? Girl, the things I would do to him just off the name he got out here."

"Girl, calm your hot in the pants ass down. I'll be there to pick you up in a minute, so you can help me pick out some fly shit."

"Aight, I'll be here."

Nina hung up the phone questioning if it all would have been different had she not asked her to be part of their team. GeGe was still her homegirl, but since she had a coke habit, Nina wasn't sure if she was keeping her involved with their business. Nina would never turn her back on her, but it was time some changes were made.

CHAPTER NINETEEN

Nina stood in front of her full-length mirror examining herself. She ran her hands along the front of her dress, smoothing out any wrinkles. She imagined what she would look like in full hair and make-up. "What do you think about this one?"

"First things first. Is Wolf still fine as shit or what? I'm telling you I heard some things about him, girl. Oooh, I just thought about it, if he's been locked up all these years I know he got a dope ass body." GeGe was already infatuated with anything pertaining to Wolf. Just the mention of his name sent her into a frenzy. "Girl tell me something good. Inquiring minds wanna know."

"Ge, I told your ass already that I haven't even seen him yet. I'ma see him for the first time when we go out tonight. Now I'ma ask your crazy ass one more time, what do you think about this one?" Nina spun around giving a full view of the dress that she was wearing. "You think it's too tight?"

Nina looked good in the dress. There was no denying it. "Girl bye. With a body like your's, there ain't never a thing as a dress being too tight."

"I just wanted to hear you say that." Nina stuck her tongue out at GeGe, and they both laughed. "But for real Ge, I wanna make a good first impression. I don't want Wolf thinking Samir is out here dating some wack-ass chick. Plus, this is the first time a lot of people will be seeing us out together since he started doing his thing again. I can't make him look bad. You know it's all about that look?!" Nina looked at GeGe pleadingly hoping she understood how serious this was.

GeGe did. "Nina trust me, you don't have nothing to worry about. If you're wearing that dress, you'll definitely represent for Samir tonight."

The sincerity in GeGe's voice put Nina at ease, and she finally released the nervous breath she had been holding. "Thanks." She chose her next words carefully. "And Ge, I'm not trying to be your mom or nothing, but please stay away from that shit tonight. Okay?"

GeGe's eyes rolled back in frustration. "Nina, I hear you, but you gotta stop acting like I'm a crackhead or some shit. I told you I only do a little when I wanna have some fun. I ain't addicted."

"For now," Nina mumbled under her breath.

Oblivious to the insult, GeGe kept talking. "Besides, I know you don't do it, so outta respect for my girl, I'm not doing any tonight anyway."

"Okay Ge, but…"

"Nina, chill. Aight? I'm good."

Nina decided not to push the issue and changed the subject. "Hey, are you hungry? You wanna go pick something up to eat before we go out tonight? Samir is gone and Layla's at a sleepover, so I don't plan on cooking. If I would've been thinking, I would've done it earlier when I picked you up."

"Yeah, I could go for something. So, Layla's living here now or just visiting?"

"Since Samir has moved in and that's his child, she's living here too."

"When did all of that happen? You ain't tell me about none of this." They discussed Samir's daughter in the past, but this was the first GeGe had heard about her living with Nina. Her feelings were slightly hurt. The information just slipped out, and Nina had opted not to freely share the news with her.

If Nina noticed her friend's hurt feelings, she didn't let on. "It happened just this morning."

"Oh okay." GeGe stood from the bed and grabbed her purse. "Well, let's go 'cause as soon as you mentioned food, I realized I was mad hungry."

Nina and GeGe dashed down to the takeout spot down the street. While they sat in the car waiting for their orders to be ready, Nina noticed a black Mercedes S550 with darkly tinted windows parked a few spots behind them. There was nothing special about the car that made it stand out. It looked like every other S-Class in the neighborhood, but there was something about it that held Nina's attention. *Just another hustler I'm sure.* "Ge, you think the food's about ready?"

GeGe looked at her watch. "Yeah it should be, it's been a minute. I'll go check." GeGe hopped out of the car to get the food. As soon as she got out something strange happened. The Benz started, and the back door swung open. Nina noticed someone begin to step out of the backseat. However, they quickly jerked back inside and closed the door when GeGe walked out of the restaurant. The car then slowly pulled away from the curb and crept by Nina's car before merging into traffic. Suddenly, the car didn't seem so innocent.

GeGe hopped back into the car with their orders. "Girl, I'm glad I went in when I did 'cause the food was sitting there waiting. Hopefully, I got it before it got cold. Man, I hate cold ass food." She looked at Nina waiting for some type of response. "You okay girl?"

"Ge, don't think I'm crazy, but I swear this car that was parked behind us was up to something. It's hard to explain, but I know what I saw."

"Girl, why would I think you're crazy? I believe you," GeGe replied sincerely. "You think it had anything to do with you?"

Nina paused to think for a second. "Honestly, I'm not sure. All I know is it was mad suspect and creepy as hell."

"Well, then the best thing we can do is stay on point. The reality of the situation is with everything that's going on we never know who's watching or what's gonna happen. So, all we can do is keep our eyes open and be mad careful." She knew GeGe made a lot of sense. "Should I tell Samir?"

"Yeah, but not right now. You know Samir will pop off at the thought of something happening to you, so we need to be sure something is up before you tell him. He got a lot on his plate right now, so this would just get him even more paranoid."

143

Everything GeGe said was true. Samir truly had too much going on to worry about something that may not even be an issue. "Yeah, you're right Ge, but something just feels wrong. I'm definitely gonna be on point from now on, though." Nina started the car and tried to lighten the mood. "Now let's get this food home while it's still hot 'cause a sista is ready to eat."

Nina and GeGe sat at the table quietly eating. "You know what we need?" GeGe asked.

Nina stopped mid-bite and looked at GeGe skeptically. "What exactly do we need, Ge?"

"This." GeGe pulled out her cell phone and scrolled through her playlist. "You ready?" She smiled broadly before pressing play. "You ain't ready for this." Seconds later 'I Wanna Be Down' by Brandy played.

"No you did not!" Nina jumped from the table and started dancing. "Yo, this was my shit!"

"Your's and everyone else's." GeGe began to dance along with Nina while singing off key.

"Ge you sound like an electrocuted cat." She laughed at her joke and started to sing herself.

"Forget you."

The two were having such a good time the thought of today's events seemed far away. The mental images of the strange car were enough to drive her mad, but at this moment, dancing to Brandy with her bestie, Nina was good. Nina's phone rang. "Hello. Okay, we'll be ready." She put the phone down and kept dancing until the song went off. "Ge, that was Samir. He wants us ready by ten."

"Ten!

"What? That's early as shit. What is this a day party or something 'cause I ain't never heard of nobody in New York City getting to the club by ten."

Here we go. Nina's patience ran immediately thin. "Well, a day party would have to be in the day time genius."

GeGe narrowed her eyes, unsure if Nina was joking or not. "Duh. It was a freaking joke, but for real we leaving out dumb early."

"Let's just get ready Ge. Especially you 'cause your ass move mad slow."

She smiled because she couldn't deny the accusation. "True and you already know I gotta put my face on right tonight. You never know who I might meet. Maybe even the one that sweeps me off my feet."

"Well let's do the damn thing then."

After a few hours, the ladies were showered, dressed and primped. Nina looked at her reflection and said to GeGe, "we some bad bitches!" Both of their dresses were tight in all the right places and covered everything not meant to be seen.

"You ain't never lied," GeGe replied.

As if the timing was perfectly planned, the intercom buzzed with a message that Samir was ready and waiting downstairs.

Samir stood by the passenger side of the car when the ladies reached the front of the building. When they approached the car, he licked his bottom lip and stepped back to get a better look at Nina. She was beautiful. "Damn girl!" He stepped aside and opened the door for Nina. Samir kissed her cheek as she sat down and closed the door.

GeGe dramatically cleared her throat.

Samir was so mesmerized by Nina he almost forgot she was there. "GeGe you look nice too." He laughed and opened the back door for her.

"Aight y'all two ready?"

"Yes," they responded in unison.

"Cool, let's get it. We gotta pick up Wolf and then we gon' be on our way." Samir started the car and drove away.

Wolf's name was like music to GeGe's ears. "Yasssssss I been waiting for his fine ass all night."

"You ain't shy at all, huh?" Samir laughed. "Well, Ms. GeGe he is off limits tonight. My boy just got home and don't need to be locked down on his first night out." He tried to be nice. He didn't have the heart to tell her that Wolf didn't want a cokehead for his shorty."

She was not deterred. "Aww come on Samir. Don't be a hater. You all fronting on my love life. That shit ain't right. I ain't have no ass in a minute, and I'm sure the same thing can be said for Wolf."

Samir decided to take another approach. "Come on now Ge. You know damn well if you two start fucking and something happens it's gonna end badly. I can't have the two of y'all beefing and fucking up my money. I ain't got the time for issues in the inner circle when we're already battling people on the outside." He conveniently skipped over the fact she wasn't as close to the inside as she thought. "So to sum it all up, you two are friends, colleagues, or partners. Take your pick, but you ain't in love and you ain't fucking; bottom line."

Until now Nina just listened. "Yeah Ge, I agree. Plus you don't want none of the problems Wolf gonna bring." She shifted in her seat so she could face GeGe. "I know you Ge. You're gonna sleep with him one time and be in love, regardless if he tells you he doesn't want a relationship. Trust, you don't want that heartache." Nina hoped she was listening. "And it's like you said, he hasn't had any ass in five years. Can you imagine the whores he's gonna be running up in just to make up for lost time? Probably raw at that, it ain't worth it. Just chill, okay?"

GeGe sat with her lips pursed allowing everything she just heard to sink in. "I fucking hate both of y'all. You couldn't even let me dream. Fucking dream crushers."

"Don't be like that. We're just trying to save you from the bullshit girl."

"Mmmhmmm."

"Ge?"

"Yeah."

"It's in the best interest of everyone." GeGe's disappointed tone tugged slightly at Nina's feelings. "Just remember what we said."

"Yeah, I remember. I remember the two of y'all are some fucking dream crushing haters."

Nina and Samir burst out laughing. "Girl bye. You my bitch, but I just can't with you right now," Nina said.

The car pulled to a stop. "Aight, we here. I'll be right back."

Nina watched as Samir went to the front door and rang the buzzer. She was shocked when the door swung open, and Wolf charged out. The two men hugged and laughed loudly. Even from a distance, she could tell they were both happy to see each other. They looked so tight that it momentarily scared Nina. She knew Wolf always had a big influence on Samir, but she wasn't sure how it would be now after five years. It made her nervous that he could potentially mess up the smooth flowing system they worked so hard to establish.

Samir walked back to the car alone with a huge grin on his face.

"Babe, where's Wolf? He still coming?"

"Yeah, where Wolf at? Please tell me he still coming." Even though she knew he was off limits, GeGe still wanted to spend some time with him.

"Oh yeah, he's coming. He just had to run and get something." Samir looked out the window over Nina's shoulder. "Here he comes now."

"Wooh, that man is fine. He lives up to every story I ever heard about him," GeGe said excitedly.

"Look fast ass, don't get your panties all wet. Remember what we just said."

GeGe playfully tapped Nina on the shoulder. "Shut up, hooker!"

Wolf soon stopped outside of Nina's door, and she stepped out of the car. "Nina what's good?! It's nice to finally match your beautiful face with your name and voice." He leaned over and hugged her. "Yo, I appreciate you looking out for my cousin and for all those times you put money on my books. Good looking out." At that very moment, GeGe caught his eye from the backseat. Nina followed his stare.

"It was no problem at all, Wolf." She stepped back into the car and gestured towards GeGe. "This is my homegirl GeGe."

"Nice to meet you." GeGe smiled seductively. "Make sure you don't forget that name."

Wolf nodded catching her hidden statement. "Word? And I guess you heard by now I'm..."

"Wolf. Yeah, I know your name." GeGe slid over allowing Wolf to sit beside her in the backseat. "Glad you out. What's it been, five years right?"

He looked a bit taken aback. "Damn shorty you know it all, huh?" Wolf took GeGe's forwardness all in stride. "Yeah, it's been five years. Now that I'm home, me and Simmie 'bout to get it in. If you know what I mean?" He nudged Samir on the back of his shoulder. "Right cuz?"

Despite the answer being obvious, Nina asked, "Who in the heck is Simmie?"

"Yo, that's Samir's nickname I gave him years ago. Back when we we're shorties, this one right here fell in love with a semi-automatic grip. I called him Simmie ever since."

"Simmie? I'll remember that," Nina said.

"No, the hell you won't," Samir said and smiled. "You keep calling me Samir." He looked over his shoulder at GeGe. "You too!"

"Aight, aight Simmie," Wolf laughed. "So you people ready to get it in tonight, because I am. It's been too damn long." He tried to remain cool, but his excitement was unmistakable. "Yo, we getting a table and first round of bottles is on me." The smile on his face intensified. "We getting fucked up and having a good time tonight."

"Hell yeah!" GeGe held her hand up for a high-five and Wolf reciprocated.

"Hold up. Ain't no way in hell you buying anything tonight cuzzo. I got you! I don't want you to worry about nothing, but a good time. Understood?"

Wolf appreciated the love. Prison was a jungle, and he almost forgot what it felt like to have someone look out for him without an ulterior motive. "Aight Simmie, you got it." Then to himself he said, *Look at my lil cuz all grown up, giving orders and running shit.* Wolf was proud of Samir in a way he would never say. Samir was always about his business, but he was a man now. Better yet he was 'the man' now.

"For real though Wolf, I just want you to have a good time tonight. I don't want you even thinking about money. The only other thing I need from you is to not get too fucked up. We, which now includes you, have an image to uphold. We can't be sloppy out here."

"No doubt cuz. I got you, boy. Say no more." Wolf fully understood the importance of maintaining the proper image in the game. He had no problem playing his part.

On the other hand, GeGe took the opportunity to make jokes. "Here he goes again ladies and gentlemen, Simmie the dream crusher!"

The car erupted in laughter, and the mood stayed light. For the rest of the ride, the four of them reminisced, shared stories and just enjoyed each other's company. The vibe between them was undeniable, and with the exception of GeGe's questionable new habit, Nina was confident they would be unstoppable.

When they pulled up to the club, all eyes were on them. Male, female it didn't matter; they had everyone's attention. If this moment were in a movie, their theme song would have been 'Clique' by Kanye West. Although the plan was to stay low-key Nina couldn't lie to herself, the attention felt good. She loved walking passed the line and straight into the club because their names were on the list. She could feel the lust from the men as they watched her and GeGe's asses as the group of four were escorted to their table in VIP. She felt the same energy coming from the jealousy of the other women. It was at this moment Nina knew they were doing something right in the game because of all of the attention. Whether it was love or hate, it was a direct reflection of their new status. They didn't let any of the unwanted attention affect them. They were there to show Wolf a good time, not to get caught up in other people's insecurities. As soon as they sat down, a bottle girl appeared and set-up four shots.

Samir was the first to pick up his glass. "Yo, this is to my cousin Wolf. I wish you much success and prosperity. Welcome home bro!"

"To Wolf," they said in unison and threw back their shots.

Soon others began to approach the table showing love to Wolf. Nina also noticed how these same people made no secret of how much they seemed to genuinely respect Samir. It was like nothing Nina had ever seen in real life. It was some ole kiss the ring, Goodfellas type of respect. Samir took it all in stride. It was obvious he appreciated the love. His only goal for tonight was to celebrate Wolf and to keep gold-digging whores at bay. That was Wolf's weakness.

Nina also had a mission for the night; keep GeGe's nose clean. She could see the coke calling her at that very moment.

She would periodically need to go to the bathroom, but when Nina wanted to go with her, she suddenly didn't have to go anymore. Nina was lost in her thoughts of keeping her girl's nose clean when she felt the mood of the table shift. She looked up to see Samir pointing across the club and followed his stare until she found B. Nina's stomach dropped, and she leaned back in the chair hoping he wouldn't recognize her or GeGe without their disguises. Her breath was caught in her throat as Samir and Wolf walked towards him. She knew security checked for weapons at the door, but if B came in VIP as they had, it was possible he bypassed security with a gun on him. Nina's eyes stayed glued on the three men. She watched as they grew closer to each other and was curious when Samir and Wolf stopped before reaching B. She prayed that nothing popped off.

Samir leaned in close to Wolf ensuring he was able to hear him over the loud music. "There go B right there. Oh, but you know him right?"

"Of course I know that snitch nigga. I did a little business with him way back in the day." Wolf's face twisted in anger at the bad memory. "The nigga broke every street code out there just to try to be on top." Wolf shook his head. "When I found out he murdered his own cousin just to take over his block, I knew shit was getting too real. I mean that was his lil cousin. From everything I saw they were close like we are and that nigga killed him for territory. Shit is fucked up son, but I charged it to the game. I don't know if there were underlying issues between them. All I know is he's a fucked up dude. But I stopped fucking with the nigga once he snitched on his first baby moms and got her locked up, so he ain't have to go up north. What's even more fucked up is he set up his older brother too. I mean this dude was his blood brother, and he did him filthy. His brother was cool people and just wanted to do business and keep family separate. B didn't like that shit at all. Once his brother started making more money than him, B had two street cats put a few bullets in the back of his head. His own damn brother! Can you believe that shit?"

Samir was as real as the next man. He was more loyal than most, so hearing B had his brother killed made chills run down his spine.

"Say word!"

Wolf looked him straight into the eyes. "That's word to my mother! I ain't never lied on no street shit. For real my nigga, son mad grimy."

Samir processed Wolf's words. *Shit, that bullshit in the alley is making mad sense now.* He turned solemnly to his cousin. "Yo, I'm kinda having an issue with his ass right now." Wolf quietly waited for Samir to finish, but the anger in his eyes was obvious. "I told you I was back in the game, but what I didn't mention was I took over his block. So, since I basically shut his shit down, he stepped to me about partnering with him. Long story short, since he know I ain't budging, he wants to go into business together 60/40."

The music seemed to stop, and the crowd disappeared as Wolf's focus rested solely on B. "Yo, if that nigga thinks he fucking with my cousin he got another damn thing coming. I will rock his shit, for real," Wolf growled. "I'm home now ain't none of that shit going down. That's our block. I wish a nigga would try and make a move. Yo, me and you got this shit! You take care of the money end and I'ma take care of the problems." A sly smile crossed Wolf's face. "You know what? Let's go ruffle that nigga's feathers. Let's go say what up."

"Word! Let's do it." The two men closed the small distance between B and them.

Wolf was the first to speak. "Yo, what up B?"

B remained as cool and calm as ever. "Wolf, my ninja!" To anyone watching the interaction between the two seemed sincere and the history between them was barely noticeable. B stuck his fist out for a dap. "Damn, how long it's been? Glad to see you out, my guy."

Wolf played the game and stuck his fist out. "I see you still doing your thing out here in these streets." He looked around at the entourage that surrounded B. "You living the good life and all. I see bottles and bitches everywhere."

B grinned and accepted the compliment regardless if it was bogus. "Yeah you know how I do, still maintaining. Your boy Samir should know that," B said for the first time acknowledging Samir's presence.

B's predictability and ego led him exactly where Wolf wanted him. He promptly replied as he smiled. "Oh, this ain't my boy," he said patting Samir on the back. "This is my cousin, my blood cousin." His smile stayed fixed, but Wolf's eyes raged. "Yeah, me and him real tight. I'ma be helping him get this money. You heard?"

"Oh, word? I ain't know that was your cousin." An almost imperceptible look of understanding passed across B's face.

"Yeah, he is, and I got his back. You know what I mean?" Wolf didn't wait for B to answer because he was sure he understood him completely. Wolf and Samir began to walk away, but before they got too far, Wolf looked over his shoulder at B. "You still in the Ville, right?" Again, he didn't wait for a response. He said, "I'ma see you," as the two of them disappeared into the crowd.

Nina caught sight of them as they exited the crowd near their table. She wasn't sure what happened on the other side of the room, but their faces let her know both Samir and Wolf were pissed. Even with their angry expression, Nina was happy they were away from B. She began to relax. "Glad that shit is over," she said as she turned to GeGe. *Oh shit!* Nina had been caught up in the men's drama and failed to notice GeGe was no longer by her side. She pulled out her phone and sent a text asking where she was. Minutes passed without a response. Just as Nina was about to start looking for her, GeGe popped up. "Bitch, where the hell you been?"

GeGe recoiled as if she had been slapped. "Girl damn! You're acting like a parole officer. I just went to the bathroom." She rolled her eyes. "Nina your ass need to chill. A bitch is having some fun that's all. You need to loosen up and have some fun your damn self!"

Nina couldn't help but be suspicious and regretted tricking herself into believing everything was all good. "I bet you are having a good time after your bathroom break." Nina couldn't hide the sarcasm is her voice, and GeGe chose to ignore it.

"So what's up with Samir and Wolf? You've been watching them all night."

"Not so fucking loud Ge. Here they come right now." Both men sat down and immediately took a shot. Nina looked back and forth between the two of them. "Y'all good?"

Samir glass clanked against the table. "Yeah, everything's good."

She turned to Wolf. "You good?" Wolf didn't answer. He was lost in his thoughts.

"Yeah, he good," Samir said answering for his cousin. "You know what. I'm not even in the fucking mood anymore. Let's get outta here."

GeGe was visibly annoyed. "Right when everybody is having some fun, the dream crusher strikes again."

"Yo GeGe the jokes is getting fucking old," Samir said coldly. He pointed at everyone else at the table. "The three of us, we leaving. You can do what the fuck you wanna do. So if you wanna stay here and have fun, do it, but shut the fuck up talking shit to me!" Samir stood up from the table but paused when he noticed Darion walking towards them. "Boy, what the hell you doing in here?" Samir smiled.

"Shit, I came with my peoples," Darion said pointing to the dudes standing behind him. "We ain't been in here in a minute. I heard it was lit tonight, so I thought I would swing through."

Samir's face turned. "So, who's watching the block?"

Oh shit! Darion didn't know how to answer and stood silently.

Samir suddenly smiled. "Nah, let me stop fucking with you. I'm bullshitting you. I know you work hard, so do your thing and have some fun. The first bottle is on me." He pulled out a couple of bills and handed them over.

The acknowledgment felt good to Darion. "Aight boss man; sounds good to me."

"Before you dip, let me introduce you to my man Wolf. He's gon' be working with us."

Darion stuck his hand out to give Wolf dap. All of a sudden, his face twisted as he screamed out in excruciating pain and fell to the floor. Then, a blur of black shot passed them.

"What the fuck?! D you good boy?"

Darion's sounds of agony became more and more silent as his lips moved, but no noise escaped his mouth. Only a small

REDEMPTION & REPERCUSSIONS

trickle of blood seeped through his lips. Samir bent down to help him when he noticed the knife sticking out of his back.

Fuck!" Wolf was suddenly at his side and Darion's boys, with the exception of one, took off behind the blur.

Wolf scooped Darion in his arms. "Yo, we gotta get this nigga to the hospital!" He turned his attention to the only one of Darion's boys that stuck around. "Yo, where you parked?" Darion's boy moved towards the exit with Wolf following closely behind. Samir, Nina and GeGe weren't far behind him.

"Shouldn't we call an ambulance?" Nina asked frantically as they all exited the club. Luckily someone had the same idea. As soon as they hit the sidewalk, the paramedics were pulling up in front of the club. Wolf rushed over and laid Darion on the gurney the paramedic pulled out. Together the two medics stabilized Darion and prepared to take him to the hospital. Wolf looked at his boy. "Yo ride with your man, we'll meet you there."

As they ran to their car, Nina couldn't help but notice the same black S550 that was at the restaurant earlier. She silently passed it off as a coincidence until she saw B and his crew getting into the Mercedes. *Oh shit! Please tell me this is not happening.* Nina couldn't shake the feeling it was B who sat parked behind her earlier. She knew she had to tell Samir. There was no way around it, but she rationalized now wasn't the time with his man fighting for his life.

The car ride to the hospital was dead silent. No one spoke until they reached the emergency room. Stressed was etched across Samir's face, whereas anger was on Wolf's.

"Nina, I need you and GeGe to go check on Darion for me. I gotta holla at Wolf for a second."

"No problem, babe." Nina looked at GeGe. "Come on girl."

When they were alone, Samir began to speak. "Yo Wolf, this got B written all over it." He stared at the flashing lights of an ambulance that pulled in beside them before continuing. "I know he had something to do with it. I'm sure word on the block is that Darion is my eyes and ears when I ain't there. He did this shit cause he knows Darion is my main guy."

"This is most definitely some B shit! I told you that nigga a snake." Wolf sat quietly thinking for a second. "Yo, on the real, I don't even think it was some planned shit. I guess he got tight after our conversation, so he sent one of his dirty ass fuck boys over to send a message. He tried to let us know he ain't the one to be messed with, but he fucked up. That nigga must've forgot who the hell I am." Wolf gritted his teeth and balled his hand into a fist instinctively. "I don't even know Darion, but he's part of this team. So if it's war this nigga wants, it's war he gonna fucking get!"

Again Samir's attention was drawn to the flashing lights outside of the car. He nodded slowly as he replayed all of B's foul moves in his head. As the interior of the car flashed from red to white matching the rhythm of the ambulance lights, a quote Samir once read crossed his mind. *Life is a one-way street, and we aren't coming back.* "Wolf find out who did this shit."

"My pleasure cuz."

Samir looked Wolf in his eyes and said, "I'm gonna get them back myself."

CHAPTER TWENTY

A few days later, Nina watched Samir from behind as he stood looking out over the city from the terrace. She could tell Darion's stabbing still weighed heavily on him and wanted nothing more than to know exactly what was going on in his head. He had been in his thoughts since that night at the club. Nina peeped her head outside. "Samir that movie you wanted to watch is coming on in few. Why don't you come in and watch it with me?"

He spoke to her without turning around. "I'm good; I'll catch it the next time it comes on."

"You sure?"

Samir took longer than usual to respond. "Yeah, I'm sure. I'm leaving out to meet with Wolf and handle some things."

"Like what?" She asked even though she knew the answer. Samir simply looked at her, and she decided to change her approach. "Look, I know Wolf is your cousin, and you two are mad tight, but..." she paused to make sure she didn't offend Samir "...you can't let his shoot'em up mentality influence you." She looked at him to make sure she hadn't lost his attention. "We have to stay focused on business. I'm not putting him down or anything, but Wolf doesn't handle things like we do. He acts on impulse instead of thinking shit through. Hell, he's partially responsible for the shit that popped off in the club. If he hadn't been talking shit to B, Darion probably wouldn't have been stabbed." Nina composed herself after noticing she had begun to yell. "That could've been you," she said softly.

Samir remained unmoved. "Nina, you gotta relax. Nobody is out here doing nothing stupid, but this life ain't no fucking game.

We can stay to ourselves, and it's all good, but when problems come, we gotta nip 'em in the bud. If we don't, we're food!" Samir's tone softened slightly. I know you worried, but you gotta trust me. If we don't handle this and I mean now, we gon' definitely have problems."

She didn't want to, but Nina saw his point. "Aight babe. By the way, how's Darion holding up?"

"He's good. That boy right there is a fucking soldier. It's only been a few days, and he already wants to get back to the streets. I had to convince him to chill, especially since we ain't pinpoint exactly who poked him. We know it was one of B's boys, but still. I don't want whoever it was to come back and try to finish the job."

"Well, I'm glad he's okay."

Samir grabbed his keys and kissed Nina on the cheek as he passed her. "I'm out. Aight? I'ma talk to you a little later. Kiss Layla for me."

"Okay I will, but babe, be safe out there. And don't let me forget to talk to you about something when you get back."

"Aight," Samir responded half-heartedly as he walked out the door.

An hour later Samir pulled up to Wolf's and saw him sitting out on his stoop. Wolf wasted no time as he immediately stood and walked towards Samir's car. "Yo, what up boy?"

"Ain't shit." Samir got straight to the point. "Get in, let's go for a drive and tell me what you heard."

Wolf began to relay all that he found out. "So check it, word on the street is some kid they call Homi is the one who stuck Darion. You heard of him?"

Homi's name hit Samir like a ton of bricks. "Yeah, I know that fuck boy! He was on the team at one point. In fact, he's the one who set me up to meet B that day."

"Damn boy. Well, it looks like he's doing more than setting up meetings now."

Samir was furious, more at himself than anyone else. He couldn't believe he let Homi's grimy ass on his team. He thought Homi was solid and never would have thought he would turn like this.

Wolf caught Samir's expression and knew exactly what he was thinking. "The streets is saying, Darion got into it with Homi over some shit that happened on the block. Homi wanted Darion to stop selling on his corner. Being the little soldier he is, Darion told him to eat a dick in front of mad people. Now, you know as well as I do that pride is a muthafucka. I guess he poked him as payback. At least that's the word out here. I'm not one hundred if that's how it all went down, but the info I got was from a reliable source." Wolf gave Samir time to process the information he just dropped on him. "So, what up? What's the plan?"

"It's simple; we gotta get Homi out of here. He's a loose fucking cannon whose only loyalty is to the dollar."

The wheels began to turn in Wolf's mind. "Yo, when I was out there getting info and shit, this stripper bitch I know told me he be going to this strip club called...what did she say the name of that joint was?" Wolf was momentarily stumped. He could not remember the name of the strip club. He snapped his fingers hoping it would jog his memory. "Sues Rendezvous! That's the name. He be hitting up Sues out in Mount Vernon blowing all his bread."

"Oh really," Samir replied. "Let's ride out there and see if he's there."

"I can do you one better." Wolf pulled out his phone and scrolled through his contacts. "I'ma call the chick I was telling you about and ask her if he's there tonight. She be on my dick, so she'll do whatever I ask."

Samir sat back and watched Wolf work his magic.

"Hello, this Diamond? Yo, I need a favor. You know that dude Homi right?" Wolf got all of the details he and Samir would need to get Homi.

They moved across the city in silence as they prepared for payback. Samir grew more anxious as they crossed the Triborough Bridge. Nina's earlier words reminding him not to do anything stupid rang through his mind. He struggled with his allegiance to her concerns. Samir knew Nina had a point, and he should move differently than Wolf, but if Homi wasn't dealt with now, he might not stop until he killed Samir.

When they arrived outside the strip club, Wolf called his girl Diamond again to make sure Homi was still inside. She confirmed he was and Wolf gave her detailed instructions on how to drive him out of the back door. "Good looking," Wolf said hanging up the phone. "Aight cuzzo, this is how it's about to go down. Shorty gonna have her friend create some drama that's gonna make everybody run. She gonna block the front entrance when he gets close. He ain't gon' have no choice, but to run out the back door. Right where we'll be waiting for his ass. You know exactly what he looks like, right?"

"Yeah. I told you the fucker used to be down with me."

"Aight good. Everything is going down soon." Wolf looked at his watch. "It should be about thirty minutes. Let's wait in the cut for this nigga."

Despite everything he knew, Samir began to have doubts if he was ready to take Homi out right here, right now. "So, what are you thinking? We still need to kill this nigga, right?"

Wolf looked at Samir as if he was crazy. "This gotta be done, boy. And it gotta be done before he wilds even more." Suddenly, his expression softened. He knew Samir had gone through it in the last months, and he couldn't be around to help, but it was different now. He was home. "Look Samir, I know you. I know you got more heart out here than any of these niggas. I'm not gonna think you're pussy if you can't pull this trigger. Sometimes we gotta trust our gut and if your gut is telling you to chill, then chill. My gut is telling me to kill the nigga, and that's what I'm gonna do," Wolf said with a sinister smile.

Just then, shots rang out from the club, and the crowd burst through the back door. Samir and Wolf stood to the side waiting for Homi to break from the crowd to avoid the possibility of hitting an innocent bystander. They saw their chance when Homi stumbled and fell. Samir made the move to grab him and pulled him into the alley, but stopped short when the back door was kicked open. Samir slid back into the shadows of the alley. Two men walked out of the open door and stood above Homi.

"So, you think you can get away with not paying me my fuckin money? Well, that was the wrong move my mans," one of them said to Homi. "In this game, there ain't no second chances." The familiar smell of gunpowder and fresh blood filled the air after the sound of four shots were released into the night.

"Damn," Samir and Wolf said in unison.

"Come on let's get the fuck outta here! I don't wanna take the chance of being caught out here when someone calls the cops." Samir looked to Wolf who had walked over to Homi. "Man we ain't got time for that. Come on!"

Wolf turned to walk away when Homi whispered through the blood that filled his mouth. "Fuck you."

"What the fuck did you say, nigga?" Wolf walked back to where Homi laid.

With the little strength he had remaining, Homi lifted his head and said, "Fuck you. B still gon' get you." He coughed spitting blood everywhere. "Shit ain't over, pussies." Wolf pulled his gun and squeezed the trigger letting off two shots into Homi's head.

The next morning Samir woke up from yet another nightmare. "Shit!" He looked around to gather himself and was relieved to see he was safely lying on Nina's couch. "When did you get home?" Nina asked standing above him with a concerned expression. "I guess you had another bad dream." She gently wiped sweat from his forehead.

"I'm good babe. My bad about the couch. I got in late and didn't want to wake you up, so I just passed out here."

Something in his tone raised questions in Nina. "You didn't do anything stupid last night, did you?"

"Nina, please stop asking me questions you know I don't wanna answer. We had some business to handle, and it got handled. That's all you need to know. Okay?" He looked at Nina with pleading in his eyes hoping she understood and not ask him any more questions.

Nina sighed loudly. "Look Samir; we're partners in this shit. It seems like since Wolf came home you're leaving me out and keeping secrets and shit."

Samir knew she was right, but he was only trying to protect her. He had already gotten her more involved in his bullshit than he ever intended. She killed for him and had his back when no one else was there. At the very least, he owed her the truth about what was happening in the streets. "Homi got murked last night. The crazy part is that we went there to do it, but somebody else beat us to it."

Nina's eyes widened. "Damn! But I guess it's good y'all didn't have to do it."

"Yeah, I guess so. In the end, he was talking mad shit, so Wolf let off two in his head to speed everything up." A blank stare came over Samir. "The funny thing is, at one point Homi was my little mans. I know dudes be flipping, but I never expected money to change him."

Nina sat down beside him. "Yeah, anybody is liable to change when money is involved, especially when they have a maniac like B in their ear."

"I know. It's rough out here."

"Yeah." Nina rubbed Samir's back. "Well, I'm about to run out for a hot second." She leaned over and stuck her cheek out. "Gimme a kiss." He gently pecked her. "Love you."

"Love you too," he said as Nina walked away.

Samir sat on the couch thinking about Homi's last words, and he had a point. There was no way B was going to stop. He would just keep sending people until Samir was either dead or his partner in crime. *I'm gonna have to deal with him one way or another*, he thought. His ringing phone broke him from his in-depth thoughts. The caller ID said it was Wolf.

"Hello. What up boy?!"

"Yo, ain't shit. I'm around the corner."

"Where at?"

"On Myrtle and Ashland," Wolf simply replied.

"Oh, word? Aight here I come."

Samir told Layla to put on her jacket so that they could leave. Then, they headed for the elevator. Shortly thereafter, he pulled up to Wolf who was leaning against his car.

"What's good cuzzo?

"Chillin. Chillin."

"You good? Wolf asked. "You ain't have much to say on the ride home last night."

"Yeah, I'm good. I just had some things on my mind."

"Good. Good. But peep this, I heard a couple of things you might be interested in. Word is B ordered the hit on Homi."

Samir was shocked. "Get the fuck outta here!"

"Yeah, that nigga found out he was getting work from someone else and had his own hustle on the side. B's crazy ass lined him to get robbed, so he wouldn't be able to pay his debt. Everybody knows what happens when you ain't able to pay for the product you got fronted."

"Yo, B is ruthless! I'm telling you Wolf; I'm 'bout to get this money and get my ass all the way out the game. I'm going legit and be done with this street shit."

"I feel you Simmie, but I ain't going nowhere. This street shit as you call it, is all I know. So, when you and your lady living out in the burbs with the white picket fence, my ass is still gonna have to deal with B.

Samir looked at Wolf waiting for his point.

"I say all of this to let you know that B's ass has to go. No question. So, while you're out here getting money and saving up for the house on the hill, I'ma be plotting on getting this nigga the fuck outta here. Feel me?"

Samir nodded his head.

"Aight, so let's get the team to the top of the game, so you can skate off with your queen and I be king of the muthafuckin streets. Bet?"

"Bet!"

CHAPTER TWENTY-ONE

Nina was thankful for the few drama-free months that passed; however, she had the distinct feeling something was about to change when GeGe called asking for a ride. Nonetheless, Nina found herself driving down a strange street, reading house numbers and looking for the address she had been given. *I think this is it;* she thought as she pulled out her phone to call GeGe. "Ge, you ready because I'm out front waiting in the car for you?"

A few minutes later, GeGe ran to the car and yelled at Nina to leave.

"Huh?"

GeGe snapped her seatbelt over her chest. "Bitch go! Just go! Get me the fuck outta here before that nigga wakes up!"

Nina sped away. "Ge what the fuck have you done? I don't have time to be caught up in your bullshit!"

GeGe was oblivious to Nina's tone. "Girl, I got him for all his shit," she bragged. "I got a key of coke, some cash and even his jewelry."

"This is what you been up to these last couple of months?" She tried not to sound too judgy, but Nina couldn't believe what she was hearing.

"Whatever Nina, I'm getting mine. What your square ass been up to?"

"Nothing outside the typical, but this new mom thing is wearing me out." And it was. Nina had been on her own for so long; she had forgotten how exhausting it was being responsible for the care of another person. She began to elaborate but stopped cold when GeGe poked her pinky into the stolen key and deeply sniffed in the white powder. "Now Ge you really bugging. Yo ass got a problem if you're doing that shit all out in the open! What the fuck Ge?!"

GeGe remained unfazed. "Girl relax. It ain't even like that, but look, check out the bracelet I got off son." She pulled up her sleeve allowing Nina to see the bracelet and so much more. "This shit is dope right?"

Nina looked passed the bracelet to the fresh track marks that lined GeGe's arm. Her eyes stung with tears that she refused to let fall. "What's that on your arm Ge?"

She smoothly rolled down her sleeve and pretended not to hear Nina's question. "I think this shit is 18 karat and the diamonds are mad clear! Bitch, I came up with this bracelet!"

There was no need to push the issue. Nina knew what she saw. "Yeah, it's nice, real nice."

Nina's heart hurt at the thought of her best friend turning into an addict right before her eyes. Bile rose in her throat as it occurred to her she probably played a part in GeGe's downward spiral. It was her that brought GeGe into the life of murder and drugs, and all without a thought of what it was doing to her. Nina had been so caught up in her own nightmares and occupied with Samir she never stopped to think about what GeGe was feeling. Sure, she never forced her to take drugs, and she even tried to discourage her from doing them. At the end of the day, Nina felt she had opened the door. Now her girl was sniffing coke, and shooting Lord only knows what into her arm. Her mind was cloudy as she realized it was only a matter of time before GeGe was like every other crack whore in the hood. "Drop you off at home, right?"

"Yeah, that's good."

With the exception of the radio, the car ride to GeGe's was quiet. When Nina pulled up to her house, GeGe hopped out. "You coming to get me before you head to Lazo's, right?"

"Yeah, I'll be back." The lie flowed smoothly from her mouth.

Nina cried all the way home. She wondered if the money was worth any of it. She was losing her best friend, and she nor Samir was able to sleep through the night without waking up in a cold sweat. The worst of it all was they were losing themselves.

Nina would never admit it aloud, but she could see them slowly becoming heartless and even worst, soulless. She reconciled this was a necessary evil to live the life she and Samir had planned for themselves. *It's all for a better life. Put your big girl panties on and do what needs to be done.* Reality suddenly set in and she wiped her tears with the back of her hand. She checked her face in the rearview and ran inside to get ready for her meeting with Lazo.

Three hours later, Nina stepped onto Lazo's block looking like sex and smelling like Gucci Guilty. The pencil skirt, low cut blouse and thigh-high Louboutin boots were just what she needed to ensure she and Samir continued to get the discounted rate from Lazo.

"Buenas tardes Nina." Lazo stood in front of Nina dressed much like he always was, but this time he showed glimpses of his slim, yet toned, chest by way of his unbuttoned shirt.

"Hola Lazo," Nina responded as she entered his home.

"It's always a pleasure to see you, Nina. You look lovely as ever." Lazo gestured for her to follow him into the dining room. "I have prepared a nice dinner, so we may eat while discussing matters. I've prepared Mofungo, my mother's recipe."

Nina didn't realize she was hungry until dinner was mentioned. "Why thank you, Lazo."

Lazo pulled a chair away from the table. "Please sit, I have to go freshen up. I would like to show you something before we dine. You'll find a glass of red wine waiting for you."

Nina sat at the table and savored the glass of exquisite red wine. After about twenty minutes, Lazo returned dressed in a smoker's jacket, paired with silk pajama pants. Once again, it exposed his toned chest. He approached her with his hand extended. "Nina come, I want to show you something." She took his hand and followed him into a bedroom.

The room was elegantly decorated as the rest of Lazo's home; however, it wasn't the decor that caught Nina's attention. Positioned in the middle of the room was a large canopy bed beautifully draped in sheer white silk fabric. On the bed sat two women, completely undressed and kissing.

Nina's face flushed. "Lazo why in the hell are you showing me this? This is not how I get down! I'm not having sex with you or these two bitches!"

"Please calm down," Lazo pleaded gently. "First of all, I would never disrespect you by placing you in a situation you are not entirely comfortable with." He moved closer to her and in a voice barely above a whisper he said, "besides, I would never want to share you with anyone else." His voice rose back to a conversational tone before he continued. "However, these women are in fact here for you." Nina began to protest, but Lazo raised his finger, silently asking her for a moment to explain. "I want you to watch and imagine it is you I am inside of. I want you to see how I make both of these beautiful women have orgasms. Envision what it will be like when you and I finally make sweet love."

Damn. Nina didn't realize she had been holding her breath until she felt a rush of air gently flow over her lips. "Lazo, I don't know."

He placed his finger across her lips. "Shhhh. Sit." She did as she was told.

Lazo stripped and climbed into the bed. He softly wrapped his hand around the smaller woman's neck. In one smooth move, he turned her around and pressed her face against the mattress. He wrapped her hair around his hand and pulled, while slowly kissing on her spine. The woman let out a faint moan, and Nina's breath quickened. He continued to kiss her until he reached the small of her back. Then, he slipped his fingers inside her, forcing a deep arch in her back. Lazo loosened his grip on her hair and with his now free hand motioned for the other woman to join them. She knew exactly what he wanted and took his rock-hard penis deep into her mouth. His hips pumped back and forth going deeper into her throat. The deeper he went, the harder he fingered the smaller woman. Nina's panties moistened from the built up juices flowing between her legs as her clitoris increasingly pulsated. She became more aroused by the most sensual sex scene she had ever seen. She bit her bottom lip and took in a deep breath as the trio changed positions. Lazo had the smaller woman sit on the other woman's face as he wrapped her legs around his neck. He firmly lifted her hips and slid forcibly inside her. With each thrust, the woman moaned louder and louder with sounds of passion. Both women moaned together. Nina mimicked them in a hushed tone, trying to conceal her enjoyment. Unbeknownst to her, Lazo could hear her, which made him stroke deeper and harder. He turned and stared directly into her eyes. She tried, but could not turn away. She was mesmerized by his sensual back and forth motions as the skin to skin contact made a melodic sound that filled the air. "Nina," he whispered.

Nina's name sounded foreign to her ears. It was the sexiest shit she ever heard, and it made her uncomfortable. Being as it was not Samir's voice calling out to her. She couldn't take it any longer and walked back into the dining room. Minutes passed before Lazo joined her.

He stood before her with questioning eyes. "Nina, mi amor, did I offend you?"

If only he knew. "No, I wasn't offended at all. I stepped away, so you and your girls could finish."

"Oh okay. Shall we eat now?"

"I'm sure after all of that you must be starving."

Lazo smiled genuinely. "I love your sense of humor Nina, but yes, I did work up quite an appetite."

Nina secretly loved the way he could make light of the most uncomfortable situation using only his natural charm. It made dinner go smoothly. They ate and conversed as if the earlier incident never happened. At the end of dinner, Nina thanked Lazo, and they conducted their business. As per usual, Lazo gave Nina the product at a discounted rate. However, this time he gave it to her for lower than the wholesale rate; she couldn't believe it.

"Lazo are you sure?" she asked.

"Yes, Nina. Consider it my investment in your future. I see something in you, something someone once saw in me. You see Nina; I am a very wealthy man. I can afford to give you this price, and I hope it allows you to grow your wealth. All I want is for you to have the best and to be independent."

Nina couldn't believe what she heard. "I don't know what to say."

"Say thank you."

"Thank you," Nina replied quietly.

"My pleasure." Lazo led her to the front door. "Nina, it is always a pleasure. Hasta te veo otra vez mi amor. Until I see you again my love."

"Again, thank you Lazo."

Nina left Lazo's feeling conflicted. Even though she had done nothing but watched, she felt a little dirty. However, on the other hand, she could not deny there was something about him. If it had been anyone else who pulled such a stunt, Nina would have kicked their ass for being disrespectful, but with him, she didn't feel violated in the least. Instead, she was merely appreciative for him wanting the best for her. No one had ever given her anything. Nina worked for everything she ever had. Lazo was handing her a new life.

Thinking about Lazo brought the sex back to mind, and Nina arrived home wanting Samir, but as usual he was out running the streets. *Damn! I guess I better take care of myself.* Nina was headed to the room when her phone beeped alerting her to several news updates. Out of habit, she clicked each story. The first story was about a murder at a strip club named Sue's Rendezvous. The police had several possible leads. A chill ran down Nina's spine. *Please don't any of this lead back to Samir and Wolf.* "Could this shit get any worse," she asked herself aloud. Seconds later she had her answer. Further down in the story about the strip club murder was a paragraph outlining Tee's murder. Nina's heart began to beat hard against her rib cage, but she forced herself to keep reading. The article stated there were suspects in question after an extended period of no leads. Nina's mind immediately jumped to the pictures she previously received. *What if the pictures were sent to the police? What if the person who took them is cooperating with them?* She fought against instinct and tried to remain calm. For all she knew, the police were lying trying to smoke someone out. Nina scrolled to the next article, and she thanked God it had nothing to do with her or Samir. The man, named Carl, who had been murdered lived and died in Jersey. Although Wolf had family out there, she knew Samir didn't frequent the state. *Thank God that's one thing I don't have to worry about.* Nina decided to call Samir to fill him in on the latest on both Homi and Tee.

Unfortunately for her, the conversation was cut short by Samir. Nina barely had the opportunity to form a sentence, when he reminded her certain things were never to be discussed over the phone.

"Yo, we'll talk when I get home," he told Nina and hung up the phone. Seconds later, his phone rang again. It was Wolf. "Yo, what up cuzzo?!"

Wolf didn't sound like himself. "Simmie, yo they got him! They fucking got him!"

Samir was confused. "Wolf, what the fuck are you talking about? Got who?"

"They got my cousin Carl, my lil cousin Carl!" Wolf yelled. "You remember him, right? My Uncle Rick's son. He used to always be around Jamal and me."

Samir continued to be lost while Wolf described Carl until Samir realized who he was. "Oh shit! Yeah, I remember him now. I ain't know him like that, but he seemed like a real good dude. So what the fucked happened?"

Wolf relayed the story of Carl's murder as he had heard it. With each passing sentence, he grew angrier and angrier. It was the general consensus in the streets, Carl had been set up, and it fueled Wolf's thirst for revenge.

Although Samir vaguely knew Carl, he was fiercely loyal to Wolf and offered his help. "Yo cuz if you need anything just let me know for real."

The appreciation in Wolf's voice was apparent, but he didn't want to get Samir involved. "It's gonna get real ugly cuzzo and I don't want you getting your hands dirty. You just stay focused on business, and I'll handle this."

"Aight cuz, hit me."

"Bet."

Samir hung up with no doubt his cousin was about to do something stupid. *But who am I to judge? I have people doing stupid shit a lot lately.* The reality was there was no stopping Wolf when family was involved. With him, it was family over any and everything and Samir knew there was nothing he could do to deter him from avenging Carl's murder. *Man, these streets are disgusting, and here I am with my girl all caught up in this shit!* On his drive back home Samir couldn't stop thinking about how he needed to concentrate on getting out of the game sooner than later. The longer he stayed, the more he put Nina and Layla at risk.

As the sun sank, Samir returned home. "Samir?" Nina called from the kitchen when she heard the front door close.

"Yeah, it's me."

Nina walked out of the kitchen to greet him and could immediately tell he had something huge on his mind. "Babe, what's wrong?" She asked concerned.

"While I was out, Wolf called and told me his little cousin was murdered out in Jersey last night."

Nina's eyes widened as she recalled the news alert she read on her phone earlier. "Wait, was his name Carl or something like that?"

"Yeah, but how you know about that?" Samir asked curiously.

"Remember when I called you earlier?" Samir nodded yes. "Well, that was one of the things I was gonna tell you about. I ain't think much of it, and I probably wouldn't have even paid it any attention if it hadn't come through at the same time as the alert about Sues Rendezvous. Oh yeah and I still gotta tell you about that. But how is Wolf handling it?"

Samir sat down and rubbed his forehead. "That's the thing. I know he gonna be all up in that shit Nina. He doesn't play when it comes to family. And to make matters worse no one knows why they took Carl out, so Wolf is out there looking for a head to take off."

Nina hated to sound selfish, but she had to make sure Samir stayed clear of Wolf's drama, even if he was family. "You ain't getting in the middle of this, are you?"

A pang of guilt rang in Samir's chest. "Nah, Wolf said he got it, plus he doesn't wanna get me involved."

Thank goodness! "I agree. I think it's best that you stay outta of it." Nina switched gears and filled Samir in on the information on Sues Rendezvous and Tee. "So you think the police really got leads on Tee's murder?"

Samir hopped up from the couch in frustration. "Them fucking cops ain't got nobody in questioning, and they don't know shit! If they had something or somebody, then you wouldn't hear nothing because they'll already be locked up. Come on Nina, don't get worked up over the bullshit." Samir turned to her and became serious. "I hope it never happens, but if it ever comes down to it and they got you down there for questioning, remember you don't know nothing. You make them fuckers work and still don't give them any information. Don't give them nothing! Even if they lock you up for obstruction or some other shit, it's better to be locked up for a couple days or months then to tell on yourself and go to prison for wild years."

"What about the pictures Samir? They think they got somebody that knows something, or at least they think they do.

"Yeah, someone is definitely fucking with us. If none of those pictures show you with the gun in your hand or you covered in blood, they can't prove shit. So, it's still like I said earlier, if anything happens don't say a fucking word! If you do say something, it better be you asking for your lawyer." Nina decided to put all her trust in Samir. "Aight. I just wish I knew who it was that sent those pictures, so we could take care of that real quick. Well on a lighter note, I made a pickup today, and Lazo gave us four keys for the price of two.

Although Samir loved getting product at a discount, he wondered at what cost he was getting it. "Nina, you fucking this dude?"

She shot him a hate-filled look. "Why the fuck would you ask me a question like that?" She felt like slapping Samir. "You being real disrespectful right now. I'ma assume that you under a lot of stress right now and it's making you a little paranoid. I tell you this though, that's your last time asking me some stupid shit like that. Especially, considering you were the one with the secret wife and child. Plus, I'm not a fucking prostitute!"

Nina and Samir continued to argue about Lazo until they were interrupted by Nina's ringing phone. "We gon' finish this conversation later." She looked at her caller ID and saw it was GeGe. "Hey girl, what's up?"

GeGe was frantic on the other end. "Nina I just got pulled over by the fucking cops and...look Nina, I fucked up for real, I'm not even gonna lie. I'm high off that shit, and I got a good amount of weed stashed up in here 'cause I was heading to make a sale real quick." GeGe's voice cracked in fear, and she sounded as if she were on the verge of tears. "I don't know what to do?"

Nina was pissed because she knew as soon as she saw GeGe sniffing there would eventually be a major problem. She tried her best to keep the anger out of her voice. Now wasn't the time to yell. "Just stay cool Ge. They might not even search the car if you don't give them a reason to. If they do search it, just let them. Don't do anything to make matters worse or maybe even get yourself killed. Just relax and don't tell them nothing."

"Nina, he's coming to the car. What do I do?"

"Calm down Ge and don't hang up the phone. Just lay it down, so I can listen."

Nina heard a deep masculine voice. "License and registration, please."

She heard paper rattling as she assumed GeGe retrieved the requested documents. Nina cringed when she heard her reply with a bit too much snark.

"Here."

"Do you know why I stopped you?

"No."

"You didn't make a complete stop at the stop sign."

Again, with too much attitude, GeGe said, "I did stop at the stop sign."

Nina wanted to jump through the phone. *Why is she making this more difficult than it has to be?!*

"Ma'am you did not come to a complete stop. I'll be right back." Nina heard what she assumed were the officer's footsteps as he walked away from the car.

"Ge, you gotta chill. Yes, the cop is being an asshole, but you gotta remember you ain't exactly clean right now. Don't say shit else when he comes back. Just take the ticket and be out."

"Here he comes Nina."

Nina's heart skipped a beat when she heard the cop say, "Miss you're going to have to come with me."

Oh shit!

"All because of a damn stop sign?" GeGe asked incredulously.

"Please step out of the car and place your hands on the hood. You have a warrant out for your arrest."

Oh shit! "GeGe!" screamed Nina as she tried to get her friend's attention. "GeGe!" she screamed once more until she heard the door slam, and then two sets of footsteps grow faint as they went farther away from the phone. Nina, then loudly screamed out Samir's name as loud as she could. "Samir!"

Samir could tell by the tone of Nina's voice something was seriously wrong. "What's wrong bae?"

"GeGe just got locked up! She had a warrant, and it's only gonna get worse if they search her car because she had a lot of bud stashed in there."

"Fuck! This shit cannot be happening! Her ass has been a liability from jump!" Samir paced back and forth while all of the possibilities ran through his mind.

"I told her don't say shit no matter what they say," she said it as if she could read his mind.

"Let me tell you something, all of that keep your mouth closed shit don't mean shit when somebody in the hot seat and their freedom on the line! Only time gonna tell if GeGe keeps it a hundred. Let's just wait and see."

Nina tried her best to ignore the sinking feeling in her gut, as she replied, "Yeah that's all we can do is wait and see."

CHAPTER TWENTY-TWO

Several days passed and Nina started to worry when she didn't hear anything from GeGe. She expected not to hear anything over the weekend being as she got locked up on Friday and would have to sit until Monday. Today was Tuesday, and she still hadn't heard a thing from her. Nina began to imagine the worst, and it was taking a toll on her. The stress was unbearable, so she decided to go into the office to distract herself. Nina felt at home walking into the office. Although it had been a few months since she had been to work, everything was exactly as she had left it and running smoothly. She silently congratulated herself for training her assistant thoroughly.

"Where to start?" Nina questioned herself as she sat down at her desk. *Shasha*, she thought. In Nina's eyes Shasha, or little Beyoncé as she liked to call her, was the next big thing. She had the look and voice; she was the truth. As it stood, Nina's assistant was booking her paid gigs here and there, but Nina knew she would eventually want more, rightfully so. Shasha was an exceptional talent. All Nina had to do was put her in front of the right person at the right time with the right song. Nina gave Shasha a call and scheduled a meeting for two o'clock to discuss her future.

Hours passed, and it was two o'clock before Nina knew it. Her assistant's soft knock on her office door alerted her that Shasha had arrived for their meeting. After a few moments, Shasha walked into Nina's office with a big smile on her face and with open arms, waiting for a hug.

"My manager. I missed you so much."

"I missed you too boo," Nina responded sincerely. "I had to take a leave of absence to handle some personal business." She held her hand out motioning for Shasha to take a seat. "I hope my assistant was helpful and attentive to all of your needs while I was away."

"Yeah girl, she was very helpful, but she just ain't you." She shifted in her seat confidently. "Look, you're back now, and I got a lot of ideas I think will make some things happen."

Nina politely interrupted her. "Slow down Shasha. We both know you have what it takes, but we have to remember we only get one chance to make a first impression. These smaller gigs have a purpose. They prepare you for the big showcases that will be in front of the right people." Nina spoke earnestly. "Shasha I have all complete faith in your talent, but this is a fickle business where people with talent fail every day. I just want you to make the most of your opportunities and be ready when you get your shot to blow. You don't want to become the latest industry punch line or worst; just ignored." She hoped her words had reached Shasha, but Nina could immediately tell they had failed.

Shasha sat silently with her lips pursed before speaking. "Nina I been ready and quite frankly I don't understand why you can't see it. I'll tell you this; I'm tired of waiting. I'm knocking these little ass performances out the park; getting standing ovations and shit. Hell, I even have other managers approaching me, but I stay loyal to you."

Nina took a deep breath to stop what she was thinking from escaping her lips. Shasha had no idea how close she was to getting cursed out. "I sincerely appreciate your loyalty more than you know, I just need you to trust me."

"Trust you, huh?" Shasha responded incredulously. "Aight then, bet. Epic Records is having a showcase in a couple of days. Mad producers, industry people and record label executives are going to be there looking for the newest, hottest shit out. That's me all day. I'm the fucking best thing out here! So, I want you to get me into that showcase. You want me to trust you? Well, make that happen."

Shasha's request didn't seem unreasonable to Nina. "Okay, sounds good. I just need to see you perform the songs…"

Nina was immediately cut off by Shasha. "Fuck that, Nina! I've been performing and busting my ass for too long now. Especially, for these past months when you were too busy to be in place. If you wanted to see me perform the songs then you should have learned to separate your personal and business so that you could've been here instead of your assistant!" Shasha was livid, but her voice suddenly dropped to barely above a whisper. "I'm not asking you anymore. I'm telling you to get me in that showcase."

I know damn well this girl isn't standing up in my office talking to me like this! Nina tried hard to maintain her professionalism. "With all due respect Shasha, I know how to do my job, and if you haven't noticed by now, I'm the best in the business. So you have two options, go at my pace, under my direction or find someone else who can simply do as you say."

Shasha stood coldly from her seat and placed a manila envelope in front of Nina. "You know what Nina? You're right, but see if this helps you see things my way."

Nina let the envelope lay on her desk without acknowledging it.

Shasha was not deterred. "My cousin Tee was murdered out in the pj's not too long ago. The strange thing is, these photos," she tapped the envelope, "seem to show you walking out of his building around the same time." She leaned in closer to Nina. "See what a lot of outsiders don't know is that a very paranoid resident that wants to keep tabs on his business has the whole joint wired with surveillance cameras." Shasha innocently twirled her hair around her finger while wearing a sarcastic smile. "So basically, on the night Tee was murdered you walked in with him, but came out by yourself. In fact, he never walked out at all because somebody killed him around the same time you were there. These right here are the proof." Shasha walked back to her seat. "I don't even gotta ask what the hell you were doing in his building, 'cause you already know. Crazy, right?"

Nina sat at her desk stone-faced. She refused to let Shasha see her sweat. *Just remember what Samir said. These pictures are all circumstantial.*

"So, let's talk about how this showcase is going to happen."

Nina slowly and deliberately picked up her phone and directed her assistant to hold her calls until further notice before calmly addressing Shasha. "So, you think you can blackmail me because you have pictures of someone who looks like me outside of your cousin's building?" She leaned back into her seat and drummed her fingers slowly on her desk. "Girl, I don't know what type of games you're playing, but you don't have to resort to such nonsense because you feel like I'm not paying you enough attention."

Shasha wore a look of uncertainty. This was not going as she intended, but she quickly recovered. "Two plus two is always four regardless of the bs you're talking about Nina. So, like I said, get me in that showcase."

Nina inhaled deeply and admired her manicure, never betraying her inner panic. "Shasha I think it's cute that you've come up in here with a nonsensical murder mystery story trying to force my hand with the showcase." She laughed light and airy. "Even had the gall to bring along some obviously bogus pictures with a look-alike in them."

Shasha stared at her while she spoke, but Nina could see her confidence was shaken. *Good.*

"Honestly, I should kick your ass outta my office and rip up your contract for even attempting such foolishness, but for some reason, I am slightly impressed at your gumption." Nina paused and stared at Shasha intensely. "Slightly. The way I see it if you put half as much effort into the showcase as you have in this trash ass story; you should impress a lot of people. Now be clear, I don't think you're entirely ready, so if you mess this up, there will be no second chances. This is it."

"I better get in that showcase, Nina. I'll contact you in a few days. When I do, all I want to hear is the time the showcase starts."

Nina walked over to Shasha and leaned close to her ear. "Please do not get any of this misconstrued. I'm getting you into this showcase because I think you're kind of ready, not for any other reason. Don't think otherwise. Oh yeah, if you ever threaten me again, I promise it will not end well for you. Now leave." Nina stood up and straightened her already immaculate skirt nonchalantly before sitting back at her desk.

"I ain't pl..."

Nina pointed to the door and Shasha silently walked away, now unsure of her plan.

As the door clicked softly closed, Nina felt her hardened exterior crumble. It was all she could do to hold it together after Shasha placed the envelope on her desk. *Shit! If Tee's ass had never tried to rape me, I could have waited until we were in a more secluded spot and none of this shit would be happening! Now Shasha's snake ass has pictures!* Nina's mind raced. She had to talk to Samir, but the office had too many ears. She desperately wanted to run to him immediately, but today was her first day back at work after months, so leaving early wasn't a realistic option. Nina sat in meeting after meeting, all while replaying her encounter with Shasha over and over. By the end of the day, she realized she only had two options, kill Shasha or turn herself in. Suddenly Nina's grandmother's words rang in her ears. *Baby, never let people in this crazy world make you believe you have to repent to them. You only owe God the truth. You make sure you repent to the Lord for your sins. He is your deliverer, and He is your forgiver, not no judge or jury.* She believed every word her grandmother ever told her and this was no different. There was no way she was turning herself in; her repentance was only to God. *If Shasha keeps going in the direction she's headed, I may have to repent for the things I'ma do to her*, Nina thought with a smirk.

When Nina arrived home, she was pleased to see Samir so they could discuss what happened with Shasha earlier in her day. "I am so glad you're still here because boy oh boy do I have some shit to tell you!" Nina looked around for Layla before going into her story. "Where's baby girl?"

"She's in the room doing her homework. I wanted to make sure it was done before I ran out. But, what's up?" Samir noticed the look on Nina's face and sat down and prepared himself for a story.

"Well, I found out who sent the pictures."

She had Samir's full attention now.

"Who?"

"My client Shasha. Supposedly, Tee was her cousin. This bitch had the nerve to walk up in my office today with the pictures and tried to blackmail me into booking her for an upcoming showcase!"

"Oh shit, that's crazy! What did you say when she showed you the pictures?"

"See here's the thing. I never looked at them in front of her. I didn't even touch them. I played the whole I don't know what you're talking about role. I can tell it surprised her that I didn't react as expected, but she's still pretty confident she has one on me."

"Nina, we can't let her go to the cops with those pictures! I think you need to get her in that showcase she's talking about. Even if it's just to keep her quiet."

"I know that Samir," Nina said slightly frustrated. "I know better than anyone. It's my face on the pictures, not your's or anyone else's. I'm just concerned about my career. And before you say it, yes I know that if I'm in prison, I won't have a damn career to worry about. I get it, but I've worked too hard to earn my reputation. If she's not ready, it's going to ruin both of us!" She paused waiting for Samir to respond, hoping he would understand her point of view. He sat silently. "I know she's talented, but in the months I was away, she grew cocky and complacent. She thinks she's too good to practice." Nina softened her approach and tone. "This business is so unforgiving."

"I get it, but it's nothing else you can do. Sounds like she made it mad clear what's gonna happen if she doesn't get what she wants," Samir countered.

"Yeah, but what if she never stops? What if it's never enough? What if every time she doesn't get her way, she pulls out the pictures?" Nina's exasperation was obvious. "I can't live like that."

"Nina, I can't answer that for you, but I'm with you. Trust me when I say I understand." He paused for a second to think. "How 'bout this? Why don't you get her in the showcase to buy us some time? Just til we figure out how we gonna handle this bitch. Honestly, I'm not too worried about the pictures because they're weak without any other evidence. Plus, I got an attorney that can poke holes in their little bit of evidence and beat the breaks off any DA. We just can't take the chance of the photos giving the cops any ideas of looking at us more closely. So far, we've stayed under the radar, and I want to keep it that way."

"Ugh! I just hate to do anything for this bitch after the mess she just pulled, but again I get it. I'll get her booked into the showcase."

"Just this once. Okay? We'll get it handled, don't even worry." Samir did his best to comfort Nina before leaving to meet Wolf.

Later that evening, Samir pulled up to Wolf's place and asked him to go for a ride. "Cuz my main man! What up son?" Samir greeted his cousin as he sat in the passenger seat. He could tell Wolf understandably had a lot on his mind.

"I'm good Simmie. Just wrapping my mind around the fact they got Carl over some dumb shit."

"You got word already on what went down?"

"Yeah, but for real, it's too many stories going around. You know how shit is. Everybody knows something, but don't nobody know nothing. Most of the shit doesn't even make sense because I know what type of dude Carl was. These niggas out here telling stories and in each one he ain't even have his gun. Come on now. He would've never been posted up on no corner, whether he was hustling or chilling without his gun. It's a fly in that fucking milk for real. Yo, Carl was always gripped up unless he was mad comfortable. You know like, when he was chilling with family. That's why the only story that kinda makes sense is that shorty lined him."

"These birds ain't shit! Yo, that is seriously fucked up. Shit is mad wicked out here."

Wolf's face turned as if he'd eaten something sour. "Yeah, some bitch named Shia, Sasha, or Shasha. Some dumb shit like that."

Samir's eye widened in disbelief. *This shit is all connected.* "Was it Shasha?"

"I don't know for sure. I'm just working with what I was told. All I know for sure is that she roll with that strip club hoe that helped us line Homi."

"Word?"

"Word! The craziest part of all was that even though Carl was a street cat, he wasn't no thug type. He ain't ever do nobody dirty in any type of way. The only reason he carried a piece was for protection, and I had to drill that in his head. I ain't want nothing to happen to him, and he still got popped." Wolf cleared his throat in an attempt to cover his crying. "I swear, I'm coming for this bitch, and whoever else was involved. I don't play no games when it comes to family." He banged his fist against the dashboard.

"I feel you son," Samir replied as they drove slowly down Dekalb Avenue.

An hour passed as they rode in silence; Wolf thinking about Carl and Samir thinking about Wolf. The silence wasn't broken until Wolf asked Samir to make a left turn onto the street they were approaching.

"What's this way?" Samir asked curiously.

"Samir I don't even wanna get you involved in this right here. Just drop me off right here at this park aight."

Samir shot him a look. "Wolf."

"Come on Samir. I told you I ain't want you in this. I got it."

Samir said nothing and continued to look Wolf in the eyes.

"Yo, this is where they say the nigga that pulled the trigger be at. I'm about to pop his ass and move on to the girl after that."

Samir couldn't believe his ears. He looked around making sure he was seeing everything clearly. "Cuz, you gotta chill! For one, it's broad daylight, and there's mad fucking kids out here. I know you wanna get this dude back, but you ain't never been one for taking out innocent people. You're gonna feel like shit if you accidentally hit one of those kids. Hell, you might even hit one of those young dudes on the court."

"Yo, I'ma roll up on him close enough to look him in the eyes. I ain't hitting nobody else. Trust me on that one."

"Wolf, listen to yourself son. You're bugging right now. You know damn well that's not how bullets work. Come on now. On top of that, you telling me you're willing to risk going back to jail for this nigga? I see more than twenty witnesses, and you know at least one of them gonna snitch." Samir laid his hand on his cousin's shoulder. "You're working off emotions right now. You gotta use your head; you gotta be smart about it."

Wolf took his hand off the door handle. "Damn cuz! For real, that's why I love you. You always tell me what I need to hear, not what I wanna hear. So, I'ma chill for now. I'ma get this nigga and that bitch too! I'ma have to do this the smart way. I ain't about to risk my freedom."

"My man." Samir stuck his fist out for a dap. "Let's get outta here. You got something else you wanna do since we already out?"

"You know what? I hadn't thought past putting one in his head, so I'm pretty much free", Wolf said with a sheepish grin. "I could go check out my man C; he just got out. Since the team is down one because of Homi's punk-ass, I figure we could use a soldier like him. He's good people, but I still gotta feel him out. You know what I mean?"

"Now, that's the Wolf I know, thinking about that dollar," Samir said with a smile before starting the car. "So, tell me what's good with C."

"Honestly, I ain't seen him in a minute, but before he got locked up, he was cool as a cucumber. People change, but if he's anything like he was; he's good people. A real soldier and loyal as hell."

Thoughts of Homi crossed Samir's mind. He remembered when he thought the same about him. *It's fucked up man.* "Sounds good, but after the shit I just went through with Homi you can't blame me for being cautious. But at the end of the day I trust you, and if he passes your test, then he's good with me."

Wolf shook his head indicating he understood Samir's point. "Fair enough. Trust me, if I vouch for this guy and he's not official, I'ma handle him personally for fucking up my name."

"I already know cuz."

Samir followed Wolf's directions to meet C and left him to handle the business. "You good here? You need me to come in with you?" he asked as Wolf stepped out of the car.

"Nah, I'm good." Wolf walked away, but quickly returned to the car and tapped on the passenger side window. "Yo cuzzo, good looking for earlier. I appreciate it, boy."

Samir nodded. There were no further words needed. He and Wolf read each other perfectly. He started the car and watched Wolf in the rearview mirror as he pulled off. When Wolf disappeared from his view, he called Nina. "Babe, you ain't gonna believe this shit!"

"What happened? You okay?" Nina asked in a panicked tone.

"Yeah, yeah I'm good. I'm Gucci!" Samir regretted starting the conversation the way he had. It completely slipped his mind she was totally on edge today. "My bad baby, I ain't mean to scare you like that. I just got put onto some shit about Shasha that I'm sure you wanna hear." He could hear her exhale with a sigh of relief.

"What is it?" she asked.

"You ain't gonna believe this, but it seems like Shasha is a line queen?"

"Shut up!"

"I was talking to Wolf about his cousin Carl and the word is some girl named Shasha lined him to get popped. Now, I gotta keep it one hundred. He wasn't completely sure of the name, but as soon as he said Shasha, I knew it was her. How many bitches out here named Shasha?"

"True," Nina softly cosigned.

"Nina, I'm telling you this bitch is a snake!"

"Aight. I'ma show this two-bit blackmailing whore how to play this game. She thinks she can walk up in my office and make demands and shit. The first thing I'm doing is canceling her spot in the showcase. The next thing I'm doing is inviting her to my office so that I can tell her face to face."

"Yo baby that's cold-blooded," Samir laughed.

"I am so serious Samir. I'll even record it for you, so you can hear me wipe that shit-eating grin right off her face." Nina laughed a full-bellied devilish laugh.

If he didn't know where her laugh was coming from, it would have sent a chill down his spine. "You enjoying this too much," he laughed. "Do your thing and I'll holla at you later."

Nina felt pure satisfaction after she canceled Shasha's performance. She laid it on a little thick for Epic Records. Nina profusely apologized for her client's escalating drug problem and refusal to practice. Even though she was on a mission, Nina had no desire to talk to Shasha, so she emailed and arranged a meeting at nine in the morning, sharp. Thinking she had the upper hand, she couldn't help but respond smugly.

Shasha wrote, "I knew you would see it my way. This just proves, in fact, you or someone you know killed my cousin." Nina couldn't believe her eyes as she continued to read. "At this point, I still think it might be best to pass the information along to the right people. Not the police, just my family and his homeboys. You know, just to let them handle it."

"This bitch," Nina screamed at her computer screen. She started to type out a response and immediately trashed it. *This will leave a definite paper trail. I have to write this email with the expectation that someone will read this in the future,* she thought. Nina typed out the most professional denial she could. She was sure to seem shocked at the allegations and betrayed by Shasha's accusations. Nina even fell on the proverbial sword and promised to do the best job ever for her client, despite how she was being treated. The icing on the cake came when Nina sent her condolences for the loss of her cousin. She closed the email reminding Shasha to be at her office first thing in the morning to discuss her upcoming performance. *If I didn't know any better I would believe me,* Nina thought before clicking send and heading to bed satisfied.

The next morning she awoke refreshed and in a good mood. She hummed her favorite tune, while she cooked breakfast for Samir and Layla. She kissed them both as they headed out for the day. *Game time,* she thought before heading to get dressed. Nina walked into the office feeling unstoppable. *An hour to go.* She sat at her desk reviewing and returning emails until her intercom buzzed precisely at nine. Nina reached over and set her iPhone to record, so she could capture every moment that followed. "Let her in," she said to her assistant.

Shasha walked in oblivious to what awaited her. "Hey, Miss Manager. I assume everything is in order today." Nina noticed she wore the expression of a happy child. "I'm so excited to do this showcase. I know I'm going to shine, Nina. I'm going to mesmerize them all and finally get a record deal." She clapped her hands together, smiled broadly and let out a small squeal. "I can't believe it! It's finally my time. You know what Nina? I'm so ready."

Nina momentarily felt bad for what she was about to do. In Shasha's eyes, she saw the ambition, the struggle and the chance to prove herself finally. Nina knew what it was like to go for something you wanted and to finally get your break. The sight of it all almost put water in her eyes. Until she remembered, Shasha was a bitch who was currently attempting to blackmail her.

"I always knew you had the talent Shasha, but there were so many times I believed in you more than you believed in yourself. Hell, I even use to have to drag you in the studio and record. But, that's all in the past now. You're..."

Shasha cut her off. "You're right, Nina. I know I've been shitty in the past, but I'm ready now. Trust me. I'm willing to do whatever it takes. That's on everything." She looked embarrassed as she heard the last few words out of her mouth. "Look, I didn't mean no harm by all that shit I said about you and my cousin. I just saw my opportunity to get what I wanted when I wanted it. It was just perfect time for me and piss poor timing for you to be in the wrong place at the wrong time." They both burst out laughing. "So, you got that itinerary for the showcase?"

Nina's smile quickly faded. "Nah."

Shasha was clearly confused. "Are you emailing it to me or something?"

Nina smiled wickedly. "Shasha, I'm releasing you from your contract. There is no showcase, at least not for you."

Shasha remained clueless. "Nina stop playing. For real give me the info," she said laughing.

"I just did. You're released from your contract. All the paperwork is the mail and should arrive by tomorrow." Nina turned her attention away from Shasha but continued to speak. "And here's a little advice. Be selective of whose dick you suck to make it to the top. Oh, and insist on a condom being used when you're riding whichever music exec's dick because he promised you the moon and the stars. Be sure to make a good friend. You'll need her shoulder to cry on when you get ran through and played out. Now please, exit my office. My assistant will validate your parking."

Nina's words finally sank in, and Shasha was furious. "Oh, so you trying to play me? Well, bitch the joke's on you! I think it's time for Tee's boys to check out that footage." She noticed Nina didn't flinch and began to worry.

"Please don't embarrass yourself any further little girl. This pathetic and desperate attempt to blame me for your cousin's death is getting old. I think it's pitiful you would take your cousin's death to try and exploit me with it."

"What the fuck are you talking about?"

"You know damn well I didn't have anything to do with Tee's murder."

"Well of course not and neither did I."

"However, you did line Carl to be killed."

Shasha's eye grew as large as dinner plates. "I, I don't know what you're talking about."

"I'm sure you don't, but you see how easy it is to throw around baseless accusations?" Nina hoped she was bright enough to read between the lines. "So you see Shasha, it's not very nice to involve a person's good name in such dirt. I mean just imagine what could happen to you if someone overheard this conversation about Carl? We both know the type of people he hung around are more thorough than Tee's boys. They're even more feared than the NYPD."

A flicker of recognition flashed in Shasha's eyes as she stood up to leave.

Nina continued, "It could be disastrous. So how about we keep each other's names out of each other's mouth? You know? So, no one gets hurt or killed. That would be a shame. Don't you think?"

Shasha lowered her head and walked towards the door. "You dead wrong Nina. I thought we were cool. I thought you looked at me like a little sister?"

Nina let out a sarcastic laugh. "Get the fuck outta my office and don't ever show your face around her again! As a matter of fact, if you see me in the streets, don't even speak to me. Cause if you do, I won't be so concerned with being professional." The door closed with a click as Shasha left. Nina smiled proudly as she thought to herself. *Not bad Nina. Not bad at all.* She managed to let Shasha know what time it was and gave her a healthy fear of retribution without incriminating herself in any way.

In the midst of her personal congratulations, Nina's phone reminded her today was a half day for Layla and parent-teacher conferences were at twelve. *Motherhood*, Nina smiled. She was still getting the hang of things, but she felt she was doing a decent job, all things considered. She pulled up her appointments for the rest of the day, shuffled them around and made moves to find Shasha's replacement. Before she knew it, it was time to head to Layla's school.

The parent teacher conference went well. As expected, Layla received rave reviews from all of her teachers. Nina walked out of the school with her chest puffed out, as she had birthed Layla herself. She grabbed Layla's tiny hand and began walking to the car. "Come on baby girl, let's go tell your father how great you're doing in school." Nina's heart skipped a beat when she noticed the black Mercedes, just like the one outside of the restaurant and club, sitting in front of the school. Her heartbeat sped up. It beat so loudly, she could barely hear the world around her. Nina picked up her pace, hoping to make it to her car before anything could happen. She fought hard to maintain control, out of fear Layla would catch on that something was wrong. "Just make it to the car safely," she whispered to herself. She looked slightly over her shoulder and released her breath. She didn't even realize she had been holding it until she noticed the car was gone. *I'm bugging! I'm sure it was just another parent.* "You ready baby girl?" Nina asked before pulling away.

"Yes, Nina," she said with a slight giggle.

As Nina sat at the stop light, the nervousness she felt from earlier had all but disappeared. Sade's smooth voice playing through the sound system had a healthy hand in that. The worries of the day fell to the wayside as she caught a glimpse of Layla sleeping in the back seat. Nina was at peace, but not for long.

Glass shattered, and the hood of Nina's car crumpled like aluminum foil. She was violently pushed into a fire hydrant on the other side of the intersection. Nina's head throbbed, and blood oozed from a fresh cut above her eye. Her face burned from the impact of the airbag and the white powder stung her lungs as she tried to catch her breath. The world spun in a blur as Nina yanked on her seatbelt, but it didn't budge. *Calm down, Nina. You have to calm down and gather yourself.* The seatbelt finally released her. "Layla! I'm coming, baby! It's gonna be okay!"

Layla silently nodded.

Nina looked around expecting the accident to draw a crowd, but surprisingly found the intersection empty for this time of the day. She felt around for her cell phone but stopped short when she heard the roar of a racing engine. Suddenly, she smelled burning rubber. She saw the black car come to a halt beside her before she had a chance to react. *Oh shit!* Nina knew this was not good. She prayed her engine was not damaged and pushed the start button. Thankfully, the car started. Nina reached down to shift the car into drive, but it was too late. A black figure stood over her. It quickly and powerfully punched her in the face. Nina's head rang, and her face grew warm as it quickly swelled. She prayed she wouldn't be hit again. *Please, God protect this baby and me.* She winced as the figure grabbed her by the hair and attempted to bang her face against the steering wheel. She fought him as best she could, but was outmatched. *Pepper spray!* Nina reached into the center console and sprayed her attacker directly in the eyes. He immediately backed off, but in the midst of his coughing and screaming; he lunged for the backdoor of the car. *Layla!* Now free, Nina picked up the flashlight that had slid from under the seat in the commotion and wildly swung it at him. She could barely see, but once she felt the flashlight connect, she continued swinging. Nina could hear Layla screams as the man pawed at her attempting to pull her from the car. Layla fought as hard as she could. She kicked, clawed and bit each time the man touched her. Nina refused to let Layla down. She gathered all her strength, focused her blurry vision as best she could and swung the flashlight with all of her might. The assailant fell backward out of the car and onto the pavement. Nina used the last opportunity to spray him with the pepper spray again. This gave her the few seconds she needed to shift the car into drive and get away.

Badly bruised with a swollen eye and blurred vision, she didn't stop driving until they were in her parking garage. Even then, she didn't stop moving until they were safely in her home. She grabbed Layla and hugged her deeply, letting go only to make sure she wasn't hurt. "Baby, are you okay?"

Layla nodded.

"I know that was scary, but we're home now." Although Nina was still petrified inside, her only concern was making sure Layla was okay. "You can tell me if something is wrong. Does anything hurt at all, even a little bit?"

"No, I'm not hurt." Tears began to well in Layla's eyes. "I'm scared Nina. I'm scared for you! That man was hurting you, and you're bleeding."

Nina kissed Layla's forehead and wiped away the tears threatening to spill. She hated to lie, but she did not want to make baby girl more upset. "I'm okay Layla. I know I look a mess, but everything is okay. You hear me?"

Layla didn't sound convinced. "Should we call daddy to take you to the emergency room?"

Nina knew that was a good idea, but she had to appear strong for Layla. "Since I'm okay and you're okay, how about we get cleaned up and order some pizza?"

"Nina?"

"Yes, baby."

"I don't want to lose you. I already lost my first mom."

Nina's heart shattered, and she fought her every instinct to break down. "I'm not going anywhere baby, I promise. Now, how about that pizza?"

189

CHAPTER TWENTY-THREE

While Nina and Layla attempted to recover and enjoy some pizza, Samir was across the borough waiting for Wolf outside of the barbershop. He was oblivious to the ordeal they just experienced.

"Look at this smooth muthafucka here," Samir joked as Wolf hopped in the car.

"Shut your ass up," Wolf laughed. "Yo, you busy for the next little bit?"

Samir shook his head no.

"Cool. So check it. I found out where the nigga is that popped Carl. I ain't trying to wait no longer to get him. It's dark out, and he might not be with his crew right now. So, I need you to take me up there real quick. Now, I ain't asking you to do nothing but drive."

Samir started the car. "You already know." He followed Wolf's directions until they saw his target.

Wolf jumped out of the car. "Yo cuz, drive around the block and wait for me over there by that alley. I'll meet you back over there in a sec."

Although the conditions were better than at the park, Samir still had his doubts. "Yo Wolf, you sure about this right here? Right now?"

Wolf pulled a gun from his waistband. "Wait right there."

Samir did just that. From where he sat, he could see Wolf approach the front of the building, and a split second later he saw the flash of a muzzle. The sounds of gunfire pierced through the noises of the busy city street. Samir began to worry when he noticed the change in the tone of gunfire indicating there were now two guns being fired. He could only assume the two were now trading shots. *Wolf's gotta make it back,* he silently prayed. After what seemed like an eternity, Wolf came running back towards the car. Samir was relieved when he didn't wear any of the signs of being shot.

"Let's get the fuck outta here before somebody calls the cops," Wolf shouted.

Samir's only response was to shift the car into gear and speed away. *Slow down,* he reminded himself. He knew it was best to get out of there, but not so fast to avoid drawing attention. He waited until he heard Wolf's breath return to normal before speaking. "What the fuck happened out there?"

"I dropped my man from the rip, but then one of his homies came around the corner blasting. I hated to do it 'cause my beef wasn't with them, but I had to put a couple of shots in him too. Feel me?"

"You did what you had to do." Samir looked at Wolf out of the corner of his eye. "You good, though?"

An expression of satisfaction and peace crossed Wolf's face. "I'm more than good. Now Carl can rest in peace knowing I took care of shit for him." He looked at Samir solemnly. "Yo keep this between you and me. Aight? Don't even tell Nina. This was strictly for Carl. I don't want no stripes for this one. I ain't even mentioning it again." He kissed his pointer and middle finger, then threw up the peace sign. "That one was for you baby boy!"

Samir understood fully. "I got you. I ain't saying shit."

"I know, that's why I ain't ask nobody but you to help me with this shit. On an another note, I need to talk to you about some other business."

"Go." Samir was taken off guard about how Wolf switched up so fast. If he said it was done, then it was done. He was willing to talk about whatever his cousin wanted.

"My man hit me and had a proposal for us. He knows where we can get our hands on some free product. All we gotta do is run up in this nigga spot and take it. We're gonna split it with my man, take our cut and get rid of it as we see fit. Ain't no paying back, ain't no mysterious connects...just a straight jux."

"Word? No catch or nothing?" Samir was skeptical because there was one thing he learned long ago, that nothing in life was free. "You sure your boy not on some lineup shit? Better yet, who spot we runnin up in? Because every stick-up job ain't that easy."

"Names ain't important, but so far it's looking like it could be an easy in and out job. You know your boy got a few tricks up his sleeves."

Samir weighed his options and mentally calculated how much faster he could leave the game behind if he was hustling for straight profit. "My connect gives me a hell of a price, but shit, you can't beat free. If your man is serious and it ain't no funny business, let's do it."

"Cool. We can run by the spot right now to check it out. We're not far from the address. I just wanna check some things out. You know, see what we're working with. I just need you as an extra pair of eyes." Wolf's attention was drawn to the house directly across from them. "Yo, I think this is the spot right here."

"You think?" Samir eyebrows raised in question.

"Nah this is it," Wolf confirmed. "That shit is nice!"

Samir studied the house. "The whole house his or is it separated into apartments?"

"The whole house is his."

"And how exactly do you know all of that?"

Wolf smiled mischievously. "You know a brotha keep a grimy bitch by his side tossing me info. So, home boy's girl can't seem to stay away from me. She cool and all that, but the best part is that she can't hold water. This bitch done told me everything from the layout of the house, who be running in and out of there and where the stash is at. I'm just making sure everything she said is on point. Plus, I wanna check out the foot traffic going in and out the crib. I don't want no fucking surprises."

Wolf continued to go into details about their mark's movements. After a few hours of staking out the house, he noticed the house was entirely too still. "Ain't nobody been in or out the whole time we been out here. I gotta hit shorty to see if I got the address wrong."

Truth be told, Samir had grown tired of waiting. "So you wanna be out?"

"Might as well. We can come back out after I hit shorty to check the address." Wolf's eyes darted to movement across the street. "Hold up, don't start the car yet. I think this is the right address after all."

The house had been still for the past hours; suddenly there was a crowd of people walking in and out. Both men agreed that the traffic at the house was too unpredictable and decided it would be best to hit them when they were transporting from one location to the other. With the jumping point of the plan in place, Samir and Wolf drove off mentally preparing for their next move.

After dropping Wolf off, Samir suddenly realized he hadn't talked to Nina all day. He found it weird he hadn't even received a text from her either. He rationalized, she more than likely had been busy at work and headed home to rest after Layla's parent-teacher conference. *Let me get home and check on my babies.* He sped home blasting Jay-Z, Kanye's and Rihanna's *Run This Town.*

When Samir pulled into the parking garage, he was relieved to see Nina's car parked in her designated parking spot. Nina had parked her car with the front towards the wall, so he never saw the badly damaged front end. Just the sight of her car parked exactly where it should be gave him confirmation she and Layla were safely upstairs. It was the little things that gave him peace of mind since he had drawn her into his life of crime.

The place was dark when he walked in, but he could see Nina's silhouette laying across the couch. "You sleep?" he whispered softly, not wanting to wake her if she was.

"No, I'm up. I just fell asleep for a little bit after we pigged out and watched a couple of movies." She sat up slightly hoping to hide her bruises in the shadows. She failed miserably.

Samir let out an audible gasp at the sight of her face before his face contorted into anger. His eyes burned with angry tears as he looked at the black and blue areas that covered Nina's eye and face. "What the fuck happened to your eye? Yo, your face! Who did this shit?" He walked towards her and gently pulled her face closer to him for closer inspection. "Who fucking did this to you?" he growled deeply through gritted teeth again. "I swear I'ma kill 'em! They're fucking dead!" His eyes widened in panic when he remembered Layla was with Nina for most of the day. "Layla? Layla! Layla! Where is she? She okay?"

Nina laid her hand on his chest to calm him down. "Samir Layla's fine. She's in her bed sleep. She was a little shaken, but she's okay now. Not a scratch on her. Trust me."

Samir was unsure if Layla was truly fine, so he ran to her room to check for himself. Once he saw her lying sound asleep without any noticeable bruises, he then reverted to questioning Nina. "What the hell happened Nina? Who fucking did this?!" Samir shouted with fury.

Nina knew she had to tell him, but she was scared of what he might do. She knew he was fiercely protective and would commit ungodly acts in the name of defending her and Layla. However, she also knew it would be foolish not to tell him. "Somebody tried to kidnap Layla today. This happened in the process," she said softly as she pointed to her badly bruised face.

Samir felt his chest tighten. "What do you mean somebody tried to kidnap Layla?"

Although Nina was the one who took the beating, she sat and comforted Samir as she retold the events of earlier.

Samir's aggressively tapped his foot and exhaled with the force of a raging bull while Nina spoke. When she finished, he looked at her with tears of anger brimming in his eyes. "I'm gonna kill whoever did this," he yelled, but then suddenly his tone softened. "Are you sure nothing happened to her at all? Please don't lie to me." Samir prayed silently that Nina wasn't holding anything back to protect him from the truth. "Do y'all need to go to the hospital, even if it's just to get checked out?"

"Samir I swear, both of us are perfectly fine. I look a lot worse than I feel. I'm good and it ain't a thing wrong with Layla."

Samir' shoulders slumped under the weight of gratitude that they were really okay. He began to speak slowly and deliberately. "Nina, why am I coming home to find this out? Why didn't you call me?" Nina's lips parted to explain, but he cut her off. "You call me for everything else, but for this I get nothing? I have to walk in to see you looking like this and to hear that someone tried to kidnap my child?" In Samir's eyes was a look of anger and sadness.

Again, Nina began to speak, but instead of the reasoning she was going to give earlier she only said, "I'm sorry."

Samir hung his head and whispered, "I'm not gonna rest until I find out who the fuck did this shit. And then I'ma put a bullet in his fucking head! Until then, we gotta keep things tight with you and Layla." He exhaled deeply. "I don't want y'all outta my sight, especially Layla, but if we change up her routine too much, it's gonna spook her. My baby has been through too much in such a short span of time. I just want her to feel like things are normal, so we just gonna work around that. First thing in the morning, I want you to call her school and give them a general overview of our concerns, so they can be on the lookout for anything or anyone suspicious. Let them know because of new safety concerns Layla isn't to be released to anyone except you, my mother or me."

Nina listened intently, but couldn't help but hear everything he wasn't saying. She knew he asked her to take care of contacting Layla's school because he would be busy searching for whoever had attacked them. This worried her more than anything.

"What happened today doesn't leave this room. Don't tell nobody. If they think they got away with this shit, then they definitely gonna slip up and make a mistake. And when they do…" Samir turned his head towards Layla's room.

Nina grabbed his hand but said nothing. Both of them needed the silence. They sat quietly, hand in hand staring at the television without really looking at it until the hum of Nina's vibrating phone broke the spell. She didn't feel like speaking to anyone, but she picked up when she saw GeGe's mother's number. "Hello?"

The voice on the other end was panicked and shrill. "Nina, baby please get over here! Please hurry!"

"What's wrong Mrs. Brown?" In all her years of knowing GeGe, she never heard her mother sound like this.

"It's GeGe! Nina, I don't know what to do!" Mrs. Brown let out a guttural scream. "She's foaming at the mouth! Oh Lord Nina, I don't want my baby to die! Please! You gotta come help me!"

"Mrs. Brown call 911 right now! I'll be right there!" Nina shouted as she grabbed her keys off the coffee table and bolted out of the door in her pajamas. Without a goodbye, Nina hung up the phone and quickly dialed Samir. "Baby, I had to run out like that because I think GeGe is overdosing! I'm heading to her mom's house right now!"

"Wait, what?"

"Samir that phone call was from Mrs. Brown and it sounded like GeGe overdosed, and she might be dying right now." Guilty tears began to flow down Nina's cheeks. "She's been on hard drugs for months, and I didn't do nothing, I didn't tell nobody. I didn't help her at all, and now it might be too late!"

Samir heard the car start in the background. "Hold up Nina. You don't sound like you in any condition to drive. Let me grab Layla and I'ma drive you."

"No, you stay there and let Layla rest." She replied. "I'm good, I promise. I just need to get over there."

"Call or text me as soon as you get there Nina," Samir responded with concern in his voice. "And Nina, it's not your fault. Regardless of who you told or who you didn't tell, it's not your fault. Just know that."

Nina ignored his statement and slowly said, "I'll call you."

While she made the short drive over to Mrs. Brown's, Nina cried and prayed between her sobs that GeGe would be okay. In spite of everything Samir said, guilt ripped through Nina's chest. *I should've told somebody; anyone.* Her breath caught in her throat when she thought about GeGe's little girl growing up without a mother and tears began to pour harder. *Oh Ge, why couldn't you leave that shit alone?* "Come on Ge; you're a fighter. Don't let this beat you," Nina whispered just as her phone rang. The caller ID let her know it was Mrs. Brown calling back. Her stomach knotted in fear. "Hello?"

"Nina baby we're with the paramedics. We're headed to County right now, meet us there."

"I'm on my way." Nina made a U-turn and sped away towards King's County Hospital. She arrived at the hospital in record time. After parking the car, Nina rushed to the elevator and headed up to the Emergency Room. She stood outside of the Emergency Room doors for a few minutes. Nina stood transfixed

196

by the soft whoosh of the motion sensor doors as they opened and closed multiple times. Her feet felt like they were cemented in place. She closed her eyes and willed herself to move. It wasn't until she opened her eyes and allowed them to focus that she saw Mrs. Brown sitting in a chair on the other side of the door. She walked over to her and sat beside her.

"Mrs. Brown, how's she doing? Have they updated you yet?" Nina asked softly.

"Not yet baby." Mrs. Brown replied before noticing Nina's bruised face.

As Mrs. Brown turned to make eye contact with Nina, she was shocked by the condition of her face. Without hesitation, she quickly said, "Baby what happened to your face? Did you get into a fight or something?" Nina calmly responded, "No ma'am I was in a little car accident, but I'm okay though. Just a couple of bruises that's all. The good part is that it wasn't even my fault."

Nina could tell Mrs. Brown was concerned about her face, but at the same time was too overwhelmed with what had happened to her daughter. She knew Mrs. Brown was trying hard to be strong.

Mrs. Brown straightened her posture and rubbed her eyes. "Oh Nina, I'm sorry you got into a car accident. You're hurt, and my baby is laying in there. I just don't know what to do. Please Lord, give me strength."

Nina's stomach sank.

Mrs. Brown took a deep breath then said, "I can't believe she was on drugs right under my nose, living in the same house and I didn't even know it." Her eyes watered and her voice trembled. "I would have gotten her some help. I just feel like I failed my baby."

The hair stood on end at the nape of Nina's neck, and bile began to rise in her throat. She swallowed hard before forcing words out of her mouth. "Mrs. Brown, I…"

As if she could read her mind Mrs. Brown raised her finger to stop Nina. "Don't blame yourself, you hear. This here is a mess of GeGe's own doing. She's been hanging around a lot of no good people lately and going missing for days. I didn't give it much thought. I just assumed she was living out her carefree teenage years she missed when she had the baby so young. I

honestly thought it would all pass; I thought it was just a phase."
Tears began to fall from Mrs. Brown's eyes. She gently wiped
them, but no sooner than she cleaned her face, a new set of tears
fell again. "Oh Nina, since you two been friends, you've always
tried to babysit GeGe. This isn't your fault. You hear me? We all
missed this one." She gently tapped Nina on the knee.

"Please don't cry, Mrs. Brown. You gonna make me start
crying again and we both gon' be up in here looking a hot mess.
We both know Ge ain't gonna let us live it down if we walk up
in there looking tore up."

"You have always been one to make a heavy situation just
that much lighter." Mrs. Brown said as she smiled for the first
time. "Thank you, Nina, and thank you for always being a
positive role model for GeGe."

Nina felt as if she had been punched in the chest. She knew
what she had done and the part she played in the destruction of
GeGe; all for the love of Samir.

"So, we just gonna sit right here and wait for one of them
doctors to come out here and tell us she's gonna be okay." Mrs.
Brown softly nodded her head in agreeance. "That's right; she's
gonna be alright. I can feel it. I prayed on it, and now I'm just
gonna give to the Lord."

"You're right Mrs. Brown, I just never would have imagined
this would be happening to my girl."

Mrs. Brown waited before speaking. "Me either, even with
the history of drugs in our family. Did GeGe ever tell you about
her Aunt Patty?

"Yeah, she told me a lot about her Aunt Patty, but she never
mentioned she was an addict."

Mrs, Brown shared Aunt Patty's story of addiction and
eventual death until they heard someone calling GeGe's name.

"I'm looking for the family of Ms. Gianna Brown," a
distinguished-looking doctor wearing dark blue scrubs asked.

At the sound of her name, both Mrs. Brown and Nina both
ran over to him with pleading eyes and silent prayers.

Mrs. Brown was the first to speak. "I'm Mrs. Brown. Please
tell me that my baby GeGe, excuse me, Gianna, is okay."

"Hello Mrs. Brown, I'm Dr. Stevenson." His eyes drifted to
Nina as he focused on the bruises on her face. "Are you okay

young lady?" "Do I need to take a look at that?" Nina simply replied, "No sir I'm fine. I just had a little fender bender earlier that's all. It's not as bad as it looks. I'm good." Once the doctor was assured Nina was okay, he then turned and asked Mrs. Brown, "do you mind if we step away for a bit of privacy for a moment?"

Out of respect Nina started to step away but was stopped when she felt Mrs. Brown's hand on her shoulder. "Nina is family; she can hear anything that you have to say. Now, is my daughter okay?"

"Your daughter is stable now, and it appears there are no immediate long-term effects of her overdose."

Mrs. Brown's hand flew to her mouth as she whispered, "Thank you, Jesus!" Tears welled in her eyes, and she let go of a breath she had been holding in.

Dr. Stevenson continued to speak. "It was touch and go for a minute, but we were able to stabilize her quickly and stop the seizures. If she weren't brought in when she was, this would be a very different conversation. I'm going to take you back to see her. I have to warn you, at the moment she's sedated and won't be able to speak back to you. After we were able to stop the seizures, Gianna became extremely agitated." Dr. Stevenson stopped outside of a wall of curtains. "Mrs. Brown we will be admitting Gianna for overnight observation. As I said earlier, there doesn't appear to be any lasting effects of the overdose; however, some issues may manifest over time. As soon as a room opens up, someone will be down to move Gianna." With that, he nodded a polite goodbye and pulled the curtain aside revealing a worn looking GeGe.

"Thank you, Dr. Stevenson," Mrs. Brown said, as he walked away. She turned to Nina and smiled. "God is so good Nina. I told you to trust in Him, and He will deliver. Thank you, Jesus. Thank you, Lord."

Nina felt like she was going to cry again at the sight of GeGe. She looked frail, beaten and nothing like her usual vibrant self. Mrs. Brown walked over to her and gently kissed her forehead as one of her tears rolled down her cheek onto GeGe pale face. The rhythmic beeping of the IV machine played in tune with the song Mrs. Brown sang softly in GeGe's ear. The endearing scene compelled Nina to walk over and grab her best friend's hand. "Thank you," she whispered.

Sooner than either of them anticipated, an orderly pulled the curtain of GeGe's makeshift room. "We're moving Ms. Brown to a room now."

Mrs. Brown and Nina watched as the orderly prepped her for transfer. "Nina, you go on home now and get some rest."

Nina didn't realize how exhausted she was until that very moment. "Are you sure?"

"Yes, baby. Don't you worry yourself. I'll be right her with her the entire time. If anything changes, you will be the first call I make. Now go on and get out of here. You have done more than enough, and I thank you for it," Mrs. Brown smiled sweetly despite the weary in her eyes. She reached to Nina for a hug. "You get home safely now. Okay?"

"Okay, Mrs. Brown. Is there anything you need? Do you need me to take care of Madison tonight?"

"I don't need anything, and I squared my grandbaby away before I left the house, but I thank you for offering."

"I'll see you tomorrow."

"Goodnight, baby."

As Nina approached her front door it dawned on her she had forgotten to call Samir. *Damnit!* She walked inside to find Samir waiting for her on the couch. He stood up to greet her.

"How's GeGe?"

"I'm so sorry I forgot to call you. I lost track of time. But to answer your question, GeGe's gonna be okay."

He lead Nina back to the couch. "It's okay baby. I know you had bigger things on your mind." Samir kissed her cheek. "Do you need anything?"

"No, I'm okay. Thanks for understanding."

Samir could see Nina was still worried about GeGe. "Come on, let's go to bed, you look like you could use the rest."

Nina looked around and considered going with Samir in the room. "You know what; I think I want to be alone for a minute to gather my thoughts. I'm just gonna sleep out here tonight. Okay?"

Samir more than understood what she was going through. "I'm here for you if you need to talk."

"I know babe," she replied with sincerity.

Nina laid on the couch staring at the ceiling waiting for sleep to come. The events of the last few months played on repeat in her mind until her eyelids grew heavy. As her eyes closed, she was grateful tomorrow would bring a new day and the worst of today was finally behind her.

CHAPTER TWENTY-FOUR

Nina slept for what felt like minutes before she was awakened by her ringing phone. Through sandpaper eyes, she looked at her phone. She didn't immediately recognize the number but picked it up anyway noticing it was a local number. *Must be important,* she thought. "Hello."

"Nina, it's Mrs. Brown. I'm sorry for calling at such an hour but…"

All signs of sleepiness left Nina immediately, and her heart began to race. "What's wrong? Is everything okay?

"No, No Nina. I didn't mean to scare you, baby." Her voice was light and comforting. "I'm calling with good news. GeGe is up, and she immediately asked to see you."

"Thank goodness!" Her words hung in the air as she took the time to say a silent prayer of thanks. "Mrs. Brown that is excellent news. I'll be over there shortly."

"I'll tell GeGe. See you soon baby."

Nina checked the time and decided there was no point in trying to go back to sleep. She got up, made breakfast and prepared Layla for her day at school. While Layla ate, Nina headed into her bedroom to prep for the shower. "Hey Samir, you up?" she asked as she undressed and wrapped a towel around herself.

"Yeah, wassup?" Samir eye's widened, and he smiled slyly at the sight of Nina in nothing but a towel. "Come here sexy."

"I know what you're thinking, and the answer is no," Nina said good-naturedly. "I gotta hurry up and get dressed. GeGe's up!"

"Word?"

"Yeah, so I wanna get outta here. I gotta drop Layla off at school and make sure I have time to speak to her teachers about our security concerns before heading over to the hospital."

"Yeah definitely make sure you got time to have that conversation with baby girl's school." Samir sat up and stretched. "Aye, tell GeGe I asked about her."

Nina walked into the bathroom but quickly came back into the bedroom with a pensive look on her face. "Hey Samir," she asked, "I've been thinking. If Ge was pulled over and was riding dirty, how is it that she was home?"

Samir face lit with the realization of exactly what Nina was saying.

The two let the wordlessness hang between them afraid to say what they were both thinking. Nina rubbed her eyes and returned to the bathroom silently regretting the day she involved GeGe. While Nina showered, Samir sat on the bed with a million thoughts and possibilities running through his mind. One such thought was he was glad he had Wolf who was a thoroughbred like no other; they just didn't make them like him anymore.

Fresh from the shower, Nina resigned to stop worrying until she got a chance to talk to GeGe. In an effort to distract herself, she asked Samir about his plans for the day.

"Not much. I'ma hit the block to collect. You know, check on the team and shit," he responded.

"Are you going to see Wolf?" she asked warily.

Samir's posture stiffened, and he exhaled, clearly annoyed with her question. "Don't start Nina."

"Just don't get with Wolf and do something stupid. We have too much on the line."

His expression softened. "Look Nina, I know you're only looking out for my best interest, but trust me when I tell you Wolf keeps me out of a lot more than he's ever involved me with. He only calls me when shit calls for someone he can totally trust. Samir walked over to Nina and grabbed her hand. "Does that put you at ease?" he asked with a smile.

She couldn't help but grin. "Mmmm, maybe. Now gimme a kiss. I'm out." With that, Nina rushed into the den meeting a patiently waiting Layla. "Baby girl you ready?" she asked.

"Yup, just waiting on you," Layla answered sweetly.

"Okay. Let's get you to school."

As the two rode to school, Nina turned down the radio. "I'm gonna talk to your teachers today so that they can keep a close eye on you and not let you leave with anyone other than your father or me." Through the rearview mirror, Nina could see that Layla didn't like what she was saying, but her manners stopped her from saying so. "Layla I can tell you have something to say. You know you can say it right?"

Layla took a beat before speaking. "If you talk to my teachers they will treat me like a baby and all the other kids will pick on me." She traced figures into the back of Nina's seat. "I'm not a baby Nina. I'm a big girl. Plus, my daddy taught me how to protect myself." Tears threatened to well in her eyes. "You saw me the other day when that man was trying to pull me out of the car, right?" She paused waiting for Nina to respond. When she didn't, Layla continued. "You saw me right Nina? I didn't let him take me. I fought him just like daddy told me."

Nina was both proud and saddened. "Yes Layla, I saw you, and you did a very good job." Layla's face brightened. Nina made the decision to call Layla's teachers later in the day instead of going inside to protect Layla's feelings. "Okay, Miss Thing you win. I won't go in and speak to your teachers," Nina said making sure not to lie.

"It will be our little secret," Layla smiled and stuck her picky across the front seat for Nina to shake.

"Our little secret," Nina repeated as they pulled in front of the school. "Have a good day. I love you."

"Love you too," Layla yelled over her shoulder as she ran up the walkway.

About an hour later Nina walked into GeGe's room feeling grateful that her friend was alive. Nina stopped just inside the door and smiled. "Miss Gianna Brown! I am so glad that you're okay." For a split second, a strange look crossed GeGe's face. Then, just as fast as it appeared it disappeared. Nina charged it to the fact that she had lied to her about the seriousness of her drug use.

GeGe ran her hands through her hair nervously. "Hey girl, I know I'ma mess right now, so please don't say it," she said with a hint of a smile. "My mom just left a few minutes ago to get some edge cream, a comb and a brush, so I won't be in here looking like I stuck my finger in a socket."

"Ge you are the only person I know that can survive a near death experience and be worried about their appearance." Nina walked over and gave GeGe a hug before sitting on the edge of her bed. "How are you feeling Ge?"

"I'm good. I'm just cold as hell in this thin ass hospital gown. But damn Nina, the real question is, are you good? Your face all beat up. What happened?"

Girl ain't nothing. I got into a little fender bender that's all. But anyway, when the nurse comes I'll see if they can get you an extra blanket."

Nina shifted her position, so she could look GeGe in the face. "Ge don't ever scare me like that again."

GeGe turned her head to look out of the window. She couldn't stand to see the pain in Nina's face.

"Okay I get it, you don't want to talk about it, but that's too bad Ge. You almost died. How do you think I felt or even worst how do you think your mom felt seeing you like that? What if your daughter was the one who found you? Have you thought about any of that?"

GeGe's lips parted, but nothing came out.

"Ge we talked about this, and you said you would stop with the coke bullshit."

"I know Nina and I will. I got this," she said softly still looking out of the window.

"That's what you said last time," GeGe said more to herself than she did Nina.

Although she spoke barely above a whisper, Nina heard GeGe. "I'm for real this time, seriously. Before we get too deep into this conversation, I got some real shit to talk to you about."

When GeGe finally turned to face her, Nina noticed that she wore the same expression she had when Nina initially walked in. Nina now recognized it as guilt, and her stomach dropped. She listened intently as GeGe began to speak.

"So you know I got locked up and shit after the cops pulled me over, right?"

Nina nodded with a yes.

"Yeah so, um, when they stopped me I had some weed and coke in the car." GeGe looked at Nina for a reaction.

Nina sat quietly. Her heart pounded against her chest as she waited for GeGe to finish.

"So when I got down to the station, the cops questioned me for mad long, but it was weird. It was like they weren't too concerned with me, like they really wanted whoever I got the weed and coke from."

Nina felt her breath catch. "What did you tell..."

Ge continued to speak in spite of Nina's interruption. "Nina I've been working for B." The confession rushed out of her, and she once again looked to Nina for a reaction.

"Wait...what?" Nina shook her head as if to clear GeGe's word from her mind. "Are you fucking serious? How long have you been doing that dumb shit?"

"I'm very serious." For the next few minutes, GeGe went into details about her working relationship with B."

"But why?" Nina asked.

"Since I been down with you and Samir, I see all the type of money it is to be made out here and Nina, I ain't going back to no nine to five. And yeah, I got money with y'all too, but it was only when you needed me for a job. So, I found a way to get money on my terms and my timeline. Plus, we both know you weren't ever gonna let me sell anything, so I had to go get it elsewhere."

"But I would've given..."

"Nina, don't you get it? I didn't want your money. I wanted my own. But look that's neither here nor there. The point of me telling you this is because the only reason the cops let me go is so I can be their snitch." GeGe turned her head back toward the window. "Nina I don't wanna be no snitch, but I don't have much of a choice. If I don't give them the information they want, I'ma get like mad years." Tears streamed down GeGe's face. Her mouth moved as she struggled to speak.

Sensing that this was only the beginning of GeGe's story, Nina waited patiently for her to gather herself.

After a few minutes past, GeGe wiped her face, took a deep breath and slowly began to speak again. "So when the cops let me go I had to have an explanation for B for the lost time and product. The only thing that I could think of was that I was robbed. I thought since I had been with him for a while he would trust me enough just to let it fly, but I was so wrong. He was more pissed than I have ever seen him. B told me I have one hour to get his money or his product." The tears returned, and GeGe could no longer look at Nina. "So I came up with a plan."

This cannot be good. The hairs on Nina's neck stood on end. "What was the plan then Ge?"

The tears streamed harder, and GeGe covered her mouth with her hands as if to keep her next words from slipping passed her lips. She slowly moved her hand, and through a barely opened mouth she said, "I told them if they kidnap Layla, Samir would pay any amount of money to get her back."

Nina hopped off of the bed as if it were on fire. "You did what?" She grabbed GeGe by the throat and through clenched teeth in a voice barely above a whisper she said, "You fucking bitch! You lined me and my motherfucking family after everything I did for your coke head ass!"

"He said he wouldn't hurt her. He said he would just take her for the money. I didn't..." The look Nina gave her stopped GeGe cold.

Nina's grip loosened as she heard Samir's voice in her head. For as angry as Nina was she had to remember that GeGe knew too much about their business and had just proven that she had no problem throwing whoever under the bus to save her own ass. *The end justifies the means.* Despite the pure hatred, she felt for her former best friend, Nina stayed and put on the best performance of her life. "I'm sorry GeGe I didn't mean to put my hands on you and call you out of your name, but you know how I feel about Layla." She sat back on the bed. "I can't lie Ge I was pissed, but deep down I know that you would never do anything to hurt Layla. All Nina could say to herself was how she really felt about GeGe. *Fucking fake ass bitch*! You just did what you had to do to get away from B alive." *I promise, you gonna pay for this!*

"I swear Nina, that's all it was. I'm so, so sorry. You know I love Layla, and that's why I OD'ed. I regretted coming up with the plan as soon as I said it. I need you to believe that."

207

GeGe reached for Nina's hand. It took sheer willpower for her not to recoil and slap GeGe. "I know Ge, I know. By any chance do you know the guy who tried to take Layla?"

Delighted with the opportunity to redeem herself GeGe quickly gave Nina what she wanted. "His name is Rob. Nina, he's crazy. Like for real crazy."

Nina made a quick mental note. *Got you, bastard*! Her thoughts on revenge were interrupted by GeGe.

"I know a lot of shit about B and his boys, but I don't wanna tell the cops unless I can get immunity."

Although Nina hated GeGe, she couldn't help but tell her the truth. "Ge, those cops don't give a shit about you. If they did, they would have offered you some protection from jump. Your best bet is to hold out until they offer you something or just shut up. If the time comes when you have to give them something, give them some of B's young, low-level workers. I promise you at least one of them will have no problem snitching. That way you get them to do the dirty work and keep B off you and get the cops off your back. It should work, as long as you stress to the cops that they're young boys and that they've been with B longer and would know more of his moves." A thought suddenly occurred to Nina. "You wearing a wire?"

A look of confused crossed GeGe's face. "Nah, they don't even know I'm here or at least I don't think they do. Besides, if I did have one on I would have let you know. I wouldn't do no shit like that! What the fuck Nina?! I would never tell them anything about you or Samir."

All Nina could do was feel her blood boiling inside. *Is the bitch for real?*

"Besides, they didn't even ask about the bodies we got or the drugs. They only wanted to know about B."

Nina couldn't believe her ears. She shot GeGe a look and pulled out her phone. After quickly typing a note, she showed GeGe the screen which read; don't ever speak on that shit, all while speaking. "Ge are you okay? You might be having some side effects from your overdose. You're talking crazy. Do I need to get the doctor for you?"

GeGe understood and played along. "Nah I'm good, I think I probably just need some rest."

"I'll let you get your rest." Nina began to walk away.

"Nina, you're not mad at me anymore right?"

"Not all, Ge. We good." Nina walked back over to her bed and kissed GeGe on the cheek. *I fucking hate you, you traitorous bitch*! The room was silent except for the light clicking of Nina's shoes as she walked out the room and GeGe's life.

CHAPTER TWENTY-FIVE

While Nina's friendship with GeGe died, Samir and Wolf were across the borough making plans for later on in the evening. Samir's phone rang. The caller ID showed Nina's number. "Hey bae, can I call you back? Me and Wolf need to finish discussing some B I real quick."

Nina wanted to fill him in on everything she learned but understood he was busy. "No problem, but make sure you call me back as soon as you guys are done. I got something very important to talk to you about."

Samir could hear the concern in her voice. "Everything okay, Nina?"

"It will be, just make sure you call me back. Okay?"

"Will do." Samir hung up the phone feeling a little uneasy, but shook it off and continued his conversation with Wolf. "So what's the plan?"

Wolf wore a hardened expression. "Plan is we running up on them niggas and taking everything! I ain't risking going in the crib.

"Aight. When are we doing it?"

"Tonight."

"Cool." Just then Samir spotted Darion and called him over. "What's good boy. How you doing out here?"

Darion exhaled, and his jaw tightened. "Everything's good for now, but it's getting wild out here. Me and the crew been moving shit, but keeping a low profile because them boys are out hard. Like for real son! They just jumped out six deep on a few of B's boys, and it wasn't no talking. They took them straight down to the precinct. Word is, it could be a snitch out here because the way the cops was moving, it was like they knew something. It wasn't nothing random about what they did."

Samir's mind automatically went to Nina's phone call and the unsettled feeling it gave him, but he didn't let concern cross his face. "Damn. Well keep your eyes open and your ears to the streets. We just gonna have to move more carefully, but we ain't shutting shit down. The way I see it, it looks like they're after B and his boys. So, if we lay low and move smart we can avoid them and pick up all of B's customers."

Darion shook his head in agreement and gave Samir dap before heading back out to the block.

"Damn son that's all I need is B's punk-ass making shit hot out here. Even when he's not fucking with us, he's fucking with us," Samir said as he and Wolf drove off. "So cuz, you got anything you wanna do while we wait to make moves tonight?"

Without a second's thought, Wolf replied, "You know what, let's not wait until tonight. Let's just post up and take the opportunity whenever it presents itself. I don't give a shit if it turns out to be in broad daylight, mid-afternoon, or night time it's all the same to me. I'm tired of waiting, let's just do it."

Samir didn't know how he felt about making moves without the cover of night, but he was down. "So what's the plan?"

"Ain't no plan. It's gonna be simple as pulling up and taking their shit. What you scared or something? If so, just say it, you know I won't look at you like you soft."

For a split second Samir almost forgot he was dealing with his cousin and the vein on the side of his neck strained as he fought to check his anger in what he felt was an attack on his street cred. "First and foremost, I ain't ever scared. This shit right here ain't about being scared; it's about being smart. We got one shot a this, ain't no second attempts. I ain't tryna be sloppy out here and mess around and get shot. Shit, I got hit with a .45, five times in fact, and ain't risking getting hit again."

Feeling the heat coming off of Samir, Wolf let it be known that he meant no harm. "Yo cuz, I ain't even mean it like that. I was just looking out for you. I ain't tryna force you to do nothing you don't wanna do, that's all. But if you down, we don't need no detailed plans. As long as I got your back and you got mines, we straight. So let's head on over to the spot and check things out."

"Aight, let's do this."

Samir and Wolf had only been outside of the mark's spot for an hour when a black truck pulled up. The driver went around to the side entrance of the home, returned with several boxes, loaded them into the truck and pulled off. Samir and Wolf knowingly looked at each other.

"Yo that's the shit right there," Wolf said almost giddily as they pursued the truck. They followed closely behind the truck until they were both stopped at the corner by the red light. They kept their eyes on it but were immediately distracted by the barrage of police cars that headed towards them. "Shit, you clean?" Wolf asked Samir.

"Except for the damn guns we both got!" Samir said with an edge to his voice. "Shit!" Samir felt his pulse race as the cars grew closer. *Please don't let it go down like this. Nina is gonna kill me.* He drew in a breath in preparation for what was about to happen, but the cars sped passed them and stopped in front of the house they were just watching. In the rearview Samir saw cops with guns drawn storm the house.

Wolf saw what was going down behind them as well. "Yo, we need to make our move now."

The truck pulled away as the light turned green. As the truck began to move Samir bumped into the back of it. The driver of the truck threw it into park and hopped out to survey the damage. Samir put his acting skills to the test. He walked over to the truck and innocently inspected the damage. "Damn son, my bad. I got a little distracted with all of the commotion going on. You aight?"

The driver shot Samir a dirty look. "I'm good fam. You ain't even gotta worry about it."

Before he could get back into the truck, Wolf crept behind the driver. "Gimme the fucking keys!"

"Ain't giving you shit, muthafucka!" The driver didn't make a move until he felt the cold, hard tip of the gun up against his spine.

"If your ass plan on walking away from this shit, you better have a quick change of heart and gimme the fucking keys."

The driver's eyes darted as the cops positioned down just a few blocks.

Without seeing his face, Wolf knew exactly what the driver was thinking. "You think I give a fuck about them cops? I'll leave your ass leaking right here in front of them. These blocks get mad long when you're laying on payment praying to be saved. Now I'm gonna say this just one last time before I make you tomorrow's headline, gimme the keys." The driver handed the keys over. "Glad to see you're not fucking stupid."

He turned to Samir. "Yo watch his ass."

Wolf used the keys to unlock the truck bed cover and opened the tailgate. Just like he was unloading groceries, he took the boxes one by one and loaded them into the car.

The driver stood fuming. "Yo, you don't know who you fucking with. You better take the shit you got and get the fuck out of the city because I promise you, your ass is dead."

"Tell B to eat a dick," Wolf said with a laugh.

The corner of the driver's mouth rose into a sinister smirk. "You have no fucking clue. I don't know no fucking B, but he's the least of your problems now."

"Whatever, muthafucka. Get your bitch ass back in the car."

The driver begrudgingly did as Wolf instructed. Wolf motioned for Samir to get back into the car. He then threw the driver's keys down the street as hard as he could and hopped in the passenger seat before Samir sped away.

A short time later, Samir and Wolf sat in the stash house arranging and surveying the boxes they just lifted from the unsuspecting driver. Wolf's eyes blazed with mischief and lust as he began counting the strapped bills that filled the boxes.

"Yo boy, we came off! Shorty told me this spot was holding, but damn. There's enough cash and product in here to lock down our spot at the top of the game." Wolf picked up a stack and kissed it. "We back, son. We are muthafuckin back!"

Samir smiled, more than content with their haul. He looked across the room of the woman's home Wolf had converted to the stash house. He had been so preoccupied with the boxes that this was the first time he noticed her sitting there. Samir leaned in close to Wolf and whispered, "You trust this chick? This is a lot of shit to have around somebody we ain't too sure about."

Wolf glanced over his shoulder at the girl. "Nah cuz, she good."

Samir wasn't too sure if he fully believed his cousin, but decided now wasn't the time to debate about it. "Aight." He looked at the girl once more and suddenly remembered that he needed to return Nina's call from earlier. She picked up on the first ring. Without giving him the opportunity to say hello, Nina began immediately speaking.

"Samir, there's so much I need to tell you. I'll get into GeGe's shit in a minute, but we got a big fucking problem!"

Samir's spine stiffened, and he rose from his seat to step out of earshot of Wolf and the girl. "What is it, Nina?" He tried to keep the panic out of his voice, but hearing Nina say that there was a problem did not sit well. With everything that has happened lately she never once told him they had a problem, and that scared him. He could hear the soft rasp of her deep breath before she began speaking.

"We are so screwed. We're not gonna have any product to move for a minute. What we have now is all we're gonna have unless we can find another connect."

He was more confused than ever, so much so that he continued with the conversation even though he knew that it wasn't one for the phone. "What the hell are you talking about Nina?"

"I just got a call from Lazo. Somebody hit his team while they were in transit and got away with mad product!"

Fuck! Samir silently cursed and hoped that this was a coincidence. "Yo, when did all of this happen?"

"Honestly, he was so pissed I didn't even ask. All I know is what he told me."

Samir hand instinctively rubbed the back of his neck to release the building tension. "Nina let me call you back. I gotta get some things straight." He turned to Wolf with the newfound news weighing heavily on his mind. "What we looking like in there? It better be looking right, so this was worthwhile because shit's about to get deep."

CHAPTER TWENTY-SIX

Nina stood on her terrace, her lips tightly pressed together while she fought to keep GeGe from sensing the irritation and rage she was feeling at the mere sound of her voice.

"I'm gonna hook everything up for you. I see how Rob is always looking at me and I figured he would jump to get some of this ass. So I'm gonna call him and tell him to meet me at the Howard Johnson in Brownsville. Once he's there, we can get his ass." GeGe said giddily anticipating Nina's approval of her plan.

Nina rolled her eyes. "Ge, that plan has flaws, you can't just depend on pussy to get this dude. Plus you didn't even take into consideration that he knows you're on B's shit list over you supposedly getting robbed." She couldn't believe that GeGe was naive enough to believe that the drugs hadn't affected her looks. "How about this? You call Rob and tell him that you found a way to get B's money. Let him think that you need him to tie up loose ends and you'll cut him in if he helps. That way, you should have no problem getting him to meet you at the hotel. If there's one thing I know about men like Rob, it's that money always trumps pussy."

"Oh, that sounds good Nina. He will definitely meet me for a chance to make some paper. Hold on, let me call him now." Nina waited on hold while GeGe called and set her plan for revenge on Rob in motion. After about a few minutes she clicked back over. "Nina you there?"

"Yeah, but hang up and call me back to make sure the line is clear. Don't wanna take no chances."

GeGe did as she was asked and the two discussed the details of the plan on the now secure line. Soon Nina was satisfied enough with the solidity of the plan, and she no longer had the desire to continue her conversation with GeGe. "Alright, Ge I'll see you tonight. You know the time and place."

Before hanging up the phone, oblivious to Nina's true feelings, GeGe gushed about how grateful she was that their friendship had survived her screw-ups. "Nina, I'm so glad that I was able to redeem myself with you," she said in a voice barely above a whisper.

The lie tasted at home in Nina's mouth. "Ge you good and we okay."

For a brief, fleeting moment, Nina felt guilty when GeGe softly gave her thanks, but reality soon set in and she remembered the fear she and Layla felt when Rob attacked them. Nina would never trust GeGe again, regardless of how many thank you's and sweet sentiments she spewed. Nina hung up the phone and went inside to busy herself until her meeting with GeGe and Rob.

Almost exactly an hour and a half before Rob was due to arrive at the hotel Nina gathered the needed supplies and walked out the door. While exiting the parking garage, she ran into Samir.

"What's up beautiful?" he asked kindly.

Nina's mouth curved into a sweet smile. Even with the serious business she was about to handle, the sight of him elated her. "Nothing really, I just gotta handle some business real quick. I'll be back soon so we can discuss Lazo and I can tell you about what happened at the hospital. You should probably order something to eat since Layla is with her grandmother."

"Okay. I'll do that," he said returning the smile. "Just don't be too long if you can help it. I really wanna talk to you about earlier and hear what you gotta tell me about GeGe and the hospital."

Nina ran her finger diagonally across her chest and then again in the opposite direction. "Cross my heart." She winked, blew him a kiss and pulled away to execute her revenge on Rob.

Upon arriving at the hotel, Nina circled the parking lot making sure she found the perfect spot to aid her in a quick and clean getaway before heading to GeGe's room. She wasn't there long before there was a knock at the door.

"Shit he's early!" Nina quickly positioned herself, so Rob wouldn't see her when he walked in. "Follow my lead," she whispered before instructing GeGe to open the door.

Rob entered the room hungry to get his hands on the money GeGe tempted him with.

"Wassup Rob?" Nina was surprised how natural GeGe sounded. There wasn't the faintest hint of nerves in her voice.

"Just the paper you told me I could get my hands on," he growled. "Now where is..." He stopped midsentence when he felt the gun rest on the back of his head. His lips drew back into a snarl. "What the fuck is this shit GeGe?" GeGe stood silently. She didn't move until Nina gave the signal for her to frisk Rob and take his weapon. With her gun still pointed squarely at his head, Nina circled Rob until he could have a full view of her face. Recognition dawned on his face and hatred clouded his features.

"Yeah you recognize me bitch," Nina taunted. "Though I'm sure I look a little different with my face not being banged into a steering wheel, huh?"

He went poker-faced. "Look that shit was business, nothing personal. I just did what I was told." His eyebrows rose when a thought occurred to him. "As a matter of fact, if you wanna know the truth, look no further than this trifling bitch right here," he growled as he lifted his finger in GeGe's direction. "It was all her idea."

Nina internally flinched. Even though she already knew of GeGe's betrayal, it still stung. "Get your ass on the bed and shut the fuck up! And just so you know, this shit is just personal!" Nina motioned for GeGe to tie Rob to the bed. "And you better not try no funny shit either," she growled. "Be careful Ge; we don't need to leave any marks."

"You bitches are dead. When I get outta here, I'm gonna put the bullet in the back of your heads myself." Rob suddenly let out a sinister laugh. "Yo, you think you're so fucking smart?! I don't care how loud you turn that TV up, there's no way you gonna pull that trigger and be able to get outta here without someone hearing that shit. So you might as well go on and let me go and maybe, just maybe you'll make it out of all this."

It was now Nina's turn to laugh. Rob had been so preoccupied; he hadn't noticed GeGe's absence from the room nor her subsequent return.

"You got it Ge?"

GeGe nodded and lifted the syringe. Rob's eyes widened and the condescending smirk he wore just seconds earlier slipped from his face. GeGe pounced on him almost instantaneously. He had no time to scream out. With the precision of a surgeon, she grabbed Rob's arm, located a bulging vein courtesy of her precision restraints and pushed the plunger of the syringe until its entire contents coursed through his blood. Rob shouted, "Yo what the fuck did you just do? What the fuck was in that needle", he screamed. Within a few minutes, his eyes rolled back in his head, and his restricted movements slowed until he appeared to be sleep. Nina patiently and quietly sat by the bed until she was satisfied he was no longer breathing. In the time it took for Rob to be no more, Nina pondered upon her relationship with GeGe and how at one point she wouldn't have ever been in this position. Although she could no longer trust her, deep down she still loved her and would miss her. Nina made peace with the fact that by having her do the dirty work in the murder of Rob, the odds were in her favor that GeGe wouldn't be able to blackmail her to B or the cops. Her eyes were glossy, and she fought back the tears. She blinked them away ensuring that they would never betray her true thoughts to GeGe. She cleared her throat to rid it of regret. "Ge you sure no one recognized you when you checked in right?"

GeGe nodded yes.

"And you disguised yourself and used an alias?"

Again GeGe nodded yes. "I gave them a fake name, and they didn't even ask for ID. Plus, I paid with cash."

"Okay good, now let's get rid of any evidence we were ever here."

While GeGe cleaned and wiped the room down, Nina planted the drugs and paraphernalia believably around Rob's body, then untied him. "When they find him, they'll just think he got a bad batch of dope." The ladies walked out of the room under the cover night and went their separate ways.

An hour later, an emotionally spent Nina stood on the other side of her door preparing to tell Samir about the events leading up to the demise of Rob. Her keys jingled in her hand; she grasped them tightly to calm the noise. Her chest rose and fell with a deep breath. Nina plastered a smile on her face and entered her home to find Samir sitting on the couch. "Hey you. I'm surprised you're still here. I just knew you would find a way to sneak out before I got home."

"Look, you crossed your heart on a brotha, so I knew you meant business," Samir said with a smile. "Plus, to be real, I have a few things I wanted to talk to you about too."

Nina raked her fingers through her hair and sat beside him on the couch. "That's cool, but I think I need to go first."

Samir reached over and gently rubbed her shoulder. "Okay, you go first because it seems like you have a lot on your mind."

Again, Nina's hands rose to her hair as she mindlessly twirled one of her ringlets. "So you know I went to see Ge in the hospital."

"Yeah, and?"

Nina sighed softly. *Just say it, Nina.* "Ge knows who attacked me and tried to kidnap Layla."

Samir exploded off of the couch. His body shook in anger. "Who the fuck was it Nina? I'ma kill that mutherfucka!"

Nina reached over and grabbed his arm. He jerked away and paced the room. "I have more to tell you, but I can't if you're gonna act like this." She walked over to him and guided him back to the couch. "Look, I know you're furious right now, but you have to keep a clear head. Nothing good will come out of this if you're judgment is clouded with anger."

He knew she was right. Samir clenched and unclenched his fist until his breathing returned to normal. "Who was it Nina?" he said with restrained anger. "Was it B? Did he have something to do with it?"

Nina's mouth hung open in shock, "Wait, how did you know?"

Samir jaw tightened. "I didn't know for sure until right now. Since I never heard anything else and he's the only one I been beefing with, I figured it was him."

Nina debated if now was the time to share the rest of the information, but thought better of keeping GeGe's part in the kidnapping to herself. "He knew Layla's movements because GeGe's down with him." She dared not tell him that it was her idea. The last remaining loyalty she had to GeGe compelled to offer this fraction of protection.

He closed his eyes, and his nostrils flared. He took several deep breaths before he spoke in a low, menacing tone. "That grimy ass bitch. I'ma choke the shit outta her until she tells me everything." Nina shuttered under the blazing heat of his eyes. "You brought that bitch into the fold, and I bet you she lined you. Both of them gotta go, plus the nigga who did the shit!"

"That's the other thing I gotta tell you. Ge and me killed Rob tonight. Well, I made her do the actual work. He's the one who attacked Layla and me. We set it up to look like he OD'd."

Samir looked at her, his eyebrow raised in confusion. "You still working with that snake bitch? What the hell is wrong with you Nina? What if she tells B or snitches to the cops?!"

Sounding way more confident than what she felt, Nina replied, "That's why I had her do the actual killing. I had to make sure I had something on her. Besides, she wanted to do it as the first step to regaining my trust after the whole working with B shit. I seriously doubt she'll tell the cops she's working with about a murder she committed. Shit, she's trying to stay outta jail." As soon as the words slipped out of her mouth, Nina knew she had fucked up. *Shit!* She had no intention of telling Samir about GeGe's snitching while he was so angry.

Samir's head jerked up. "She's working with the fucking cops?! And you knew this when you murked son? Nina what the fuck is wrong with you? You can't think this shit was smart?!" He calmly stood from the couch and walked to his weapons stash.

Without looking, Nina knew where he was headed and did her best to stop him. She was all for payback, but not if he wasn't clear headed. "Samir wait!" she pleaded.

He ignored her and walked passed her with a bulge in the back of his waistband that could be easily overlooked by anyone, but her.

Dear Lord, I know what he's doing is wrong, but please protect him.

Samir made it to Brownsville in a matter of no time. He was a man on a mission. He took the stairs up to B's apartment two at a time until he finally stood outside of his door. With the side of his closed fist, Samir thunderously banged on B's apartment door until it finally swung open. To Samir's surprise, there B stood in the doorway.

"Well, well, well, if it ain't little Samir."

B barely finished his sentence before Samir, in one fluid motion, cocked his arm back and landed a solid punch to his face. Unprepared, B stumbled backward and fell to the floor.

Through a bloodied and twisted mouth, he gazed up from the floor with hate filled eyes. "You must be crazy!" At that moment, he regretted sending his soldiers out just a little while earlier. "I should..."

Unfazed by the threat that was sure to follow, Samir stood over him with his hand ready to draw his gun. "You come after my family again, and I promise you, my face will be the last thing you ever see in your sorry ass life."

"Yo, what are you..."

"Save it muthafucka; I know everything!" A steady red light in the corner of the room caught Samir's attention. *A camera.* "The only reason I ain't put one in you yet is I know you got mad cameras, but trust me. You say one thing outta line or make another move and I'ma kill your ass. Now, you listen and listen fucking good. Stay away from my fucking family, and I'll stay away from your's." Deep down Samir knew it was only a matter of time before he killed B, but he couldn't do it like this. Not with cameras watching, capturing enough evidence to put him under the jail. He knew Nina was right; he had to handle this when he cooled off. *Shit, I shoulda listened.* He needed to take care of B but needed to remain a free man to raise Layla.

B wiped his mouth and smiled. Nothing more, he only smiled.

Samir turned and left the same way he came in. Without knowing, as soon as he left the room, B slid his phone from his pocket.

"Yo," he coughed clearing blood from his airway. "You still outside? Good." B proceeded to give Samir description and hung up the phone. His smiled returned.

Samir pushed out of the exit and was greeted by two men and a woman. He attempted to walk passed them, but they quickly surrounded him. The smallest of the three reached around his neck and tugged at the silver toned chain he was wearing until a badge slowly appeared from under his shirt. Samir tried to keep his cool. This was New York; it was nothing to be stopped and questioned by a cop. As long as he cooperated, there should be no reason for them to harass him.

"You live here?" one of the other officers asked.

"Nah, I was just looking for somebody, but I think I got the wrong building." Samir knew not to give too many details. He had no intention of backing himself into a corner he couldn't get out of.

"Well, it seems that you fit the description of someone we're looking for. What's your name and birthdate?"

Samir gave his name and birthdate. He knew his name was clean and there were no warrants out for his arrest.

"Step over to the car."

Shit. "I know my rights. I haven't done anything wrong, and I'm not stepping anywhere." Samir stood his ground until he felt a whack on the back of his knee and he began tumbling towards the concrete ground.

"I don't give a fuck about your rights! The sooner you learn that, the sooner this shit will be over with," a gravelly voice said from behind Samir. "Put your arms behind your back before I break them."

"What the fuck?" Samir asked loudly. He knew this was bad.

The cop pulled Samir's arms around his back and tightened the cuffs around one of his wrists, but suddenly paused. Samir knew exactly why. Time stopped. In those seconds he saw Layla and heard Nina's warning not to leave so upset. His heart sank. New York's gun possession laws were notorious, and here he lay, surrounded by three cops with a gun in his waistband.

"Well look what we have here boys," the woman officer said with far more glee than necessary as she pulled the gun from Samir's pants. "Put his black ass in the back of the car."

Nina picked up her phone from the coffee table and dialed Samir's phone number for what seemed like the hundredth time. Just like every other time she called, it went directly to voicemail. *Where are you?* She prayed nothing had happened to him. Her phone vibrated in her hand before she could put it down. *Unknown caller? Who could this be?* Something deep inside of her told her to answer. "Hello?" she said in a low shaking voice.

"Nina, listen it's me."

She relaxed when she heard Samir's voice. "Baby, where the hell have you been? I've been calling you all night!"

"Nina listen; I don't have no time to talk. I need you to do me a favor and call my lawyer."

Nina's heart pounded, and her back stiffened. "Why?"

"Cause I'm in jail."

Nina's heart sank as one of her worst fears was confirmed, but she quickly recovered. Her back stiffened with resolve as she began to speak, "I got you bae don't worry about nothing."

CPSIA information can be obtained
at www.ICGtesting.com
Printed in the USA
BVOW04s0542150317

478540BV00001B/35/P